open minds

Susan Kaye Quinn

Summary: Sixteen-year-old Kira Moore can't read minds in a
telepathic world, but soon discovers she can control them instead and
is slowly dragged into an underworld of dangerous mindjackers.

November, 2011 Edition

Cover and Interior Design by D. Robert Pease
www.WalkingStickBooks.com

Edited by Anne Victory

ISBN: 1466354267
ISBN-13: 978-1466354265

For my mom,
who always believed in me more than I did.
And who never once tried to mind control me.
I think.

praise for OPEN MINDS

"*Open Minds* pushed me to the edge of my imagination and then tossed me over the edge as I screamed for more. Quinn has created an intensely dangerous world both inside the minds of her characters and outside—a world that left me asking myself questions I would never have asked before. When you can literally control the thoughts of others, how far will you go? Quinn takes the reader to this reality with breathtaking control and sparkle. Read this and you'll never look at your thoughts the same again."

— **Michelle Davidson Argyle**, author of *Monarch* and *Cinders*

"*Open Minds* boils with action, adventure, and surprises. I was fully invested in this inventive world and the protagonist. A story that had me imagining *what if*, long after I finished it."

— **Terry Lynn Johnson**, author of *Dogsled Dreams*

chapter ONE

A zero like me shouldn't take public transportation.

The hunched driver wrinkled a frown before I even got on the bus. Her attempt to read my mind would get her nothing but the quiet of the street corner where I stood. I kept my face neutral. Nobody trusted a zero to begin with, but scowling back would only make the driver more suspicious. I gripped my backpack and gym bag tighter and climbed the grime-coated steps. The driver's mental command whooshed the door closed behind me.

Yeah, junior year was off to a fantastic start already.

Students crammed the bus, which stank of too many bodies baking in the early morning heat. I shuffled past the dead-silent rows, avoiding backpacks and black instrument cases. Two years of being the Invisible Girl had taught me a few things. As long as I didn't touch an exposed arm or speak out loud, the blank spot of my mind would go unnoticed in the swirling sea of their thoughts. Which was great, until I needed a seat on a crowded bus.

With a soft hiss of water exhaust, the bus lurched forward. I grabbed a sticky seatback to keep from falling on three girls deep in mental conversation.

Two senior boys leered from the back row. The whole bus was within range, so they knew there were no thought waves beaming from my head. Yet, instead of ignoring me, they stared like hungry sharks. Last year, looks like those would have gotten them pummeled by my six-foot-two brother, Seamus. But Seamus had graduated, and the protective shadow he cast over me was gone.

Whatever sims the boys were thinking, students four rows ahead of them turned to watch. Shark Boy tipped his head to his friend, obviously discussing me as they stared. His friend's lips parted to show a sliver of teeth, and he gestured to the only open seat on the bus.

Right in front of them.

I could complain to the driver, but she wouldn't believe anything a zero told her. Shark Boy's thoughts wouldn't carry over the mental chaos of the bus, and speaking out loud would only get me thrown off.

I turned away from the wide grins on the boys' faces and slowly sank into the seat. My cheeks burned with the expectant stares from the back half of the bus, but I kept my gaze on the suburban houses ambling past the window. The heat of Shark Boy's hand reached me just before he brushed my bare skin, right below my t-shirt sleeve. I jerked away and clutched my gym bag like it was a shield.

Shark Boy and his friend rocked back with noiseless laughter, as if touching a zero was the height of funny. I shivered in spite of the heat and decided to take my chances with the unfriendly driver. By the time my shaking hands found handholds to the front, we had rounded the corner to the school parking lot. I ignored the driver's insistent stare. As soon as the bus stopped, I pounded the button on her dash to manually activate the door and scurried out.

Once inside the main entrance of school, a scuffle of feet warned me to step back as a group of girls sailed past, looking all mesh with their band shirts and synced steps. One—Trina—cut too close and knocked shoulders with me. At first it seemed intentional, but then she acted as though I was something she would never touch on purpose. Heat rose in my face.

Harassment from readers shouldn't get a rise out of me anymore, but I'd fallen out of practice, sticking close to home over the summer. Trina's snub wouldn't have hurt at all if her sweater wasn't still hanging in my closet, a casualty from a time when we traded clothes and secrets. I guess she didn't miss it.

I dug my schedule out of my backpack. At least the administration hadn't put me in Changelings 101 again. As if a class on mindreading etiquette and self-control would help a zero like me. An anger management class would be more useful.

My first-period Latin class beckoned from a dozen yards down the hall, its blue plasma lights gleaming like a lighthouse in a hurricane. I narrowly avoided a pair of students air-kissing and skittered to the classroom door.

The new Latin teacher tried to be mesh with his shiny *nove-*fiber shirt. A circle of admiring students laughed silently at some mental joke. Seamus had warned me that I would need a hearing aid this year so the teachers could whisper their lectures to me while instructing everyone else via mindtalk. I had put it off, waiting for my brain to finally flip a switch and become normal, and hoping to get by in my classes until then. Meanwhile, to the teacher and his fans, I might as well be a dusty trashcan in the corner. I found a spot in the back, and a knot of certainty tied tight inside me.

I will never be like them.

My chair gained gravity and sank me deep into my seat.

Long ago, everyone used to be zeros. When those first reader kids hit puberty and discovered they could read minds, the world didn't know what to make of it. That first wave of Reader Freaks grew up to have more Reader Freaks.

Now the only freaks were the few people who never changed. *Like me.*

I physically shook that thought from my mind. *Don't give up.* Just because most kids changed by the time they were thirteen or fourteen didn't mean *everyone* did. Seamus didn't change until he was fifteen. Mom told me over and over she was a late bloomer. I told myself for the hundredth time that the Moores simply changed late, and that I was the slowest of the bunch.

The change could come any day. In the meantime, I would have to keep up in my classes any way I could. If the teachers were all mindtalking this year, then I'd get that hearing aid and make do. If I gave up now, I would have no chance at college, much less medical school.

Students moved to their creaking metal desks, probably

motivated by a thought instruction from Mr. Amando. Everyone pulled out their e-slates, and I peeked at my neighbor. We were starting with translations of *Aeneid*. Again.

Although my thoughts sounded English in my head, I knew thought-waves weren't a language at all. They could be read by any person over the change age, as well as by mindware interfaces. (Yeah, even the bus was better at reading minds than me.) But until the tech guys created a computer that could mindtalk back, the world would need written words. Latin was quickly becoming mesh, being a root language. All the latest mindware had a Latin option, plus Latin was required for college, so mastering the ancient language wasn't optional.

I scribbled with my stylus, trying to decode Juno's wrath against the city of Troy. Even after two years of Latin, my translations were still a literal jumble. *Tantaene animis caelestibus irae?* It meant Juno was wreaking her goddess anger on the Trojan people, yet the literal translation stuck in my head as *vast minds of heavenly wrath.* If I changed *tantaene* to *deminutus*, it could just as easily describe the small minds of Warren Township High.

I let out a long sigh. At least we weren't working in groups on the first day of class. I redoubled my efforts to force the translations into something better than gibberish.

The bell gave a soft tone that disturbed the utter quiet of the room. I slipped past the other students, wrapped in their mental conversation. The crowds thinned at the back of school, but I kept to the edges until I reached my locker. By the time I had my gym bag stowed away, the metallic sound of my locker door slamming shut echoed down a nearly empty hallway.

At the far end, a group of readers had formed a tight circle, all facing inward. I cringed, knowing some freshman changeling was in the middle, being harassed by the *small minds of heavenly wrath* that populated my school.

I dragged myself toward them, not wanting to get involved, but I couldn't stand to see another kid go demens, driven mad by the change. Some kids fuzzed out on obscura to escape the mental chaos of reading minds. But the three suicides last year were sent spiraling by more than simply the voices in their heads. As a zero, I endured dirty looks and menacing boys. It could get a lot nastier for the changelings.

The girl huddled on the floor inside her ring of tormentors, clutching her head and squeezing her eyes shut, as if that would keep out the sims that surrounded her newly minted reader mind. What they were doing was a misdemeanor thought crime, but I couldn't exactly turn the pravers in. The administrators might get their true memories under questioning, especially if they brought in a truth magistrate, but they wouldn't do that based on the word of a zero.

"Hey!" My voice cut through the quiet. "Go be evil somewhere else!"

Their heads swung in unison, lit with astonishment. Of course they hadn't sensed me. They glanced at each other, then turned as a unit and walked down the hall in the creepy synchronized way that readers sometimes did. Hassling me must not be worth the tardy.

The changeling still sat with her eyes shut, clutching her

knees and slowly rocking. I waited until the others disappeared into the chemistry wing before I edged over to her.

I kept my voice soft so it wouldn't travel. "It's okay. They're gone."

Her eyes snapped open. She scrambled away from me, banging into the locker wall. She braced herself up from the carpet and slowly backed down the hall.

Even the harassed knew who was lowest on the social ladder.

I shook my head. The changeling was on the wrong side of the pravers today, but if she survived the change, she might do something important one day, like heal people or rescue them from burning buildings. *It's still possible*, I told myself. *The change could still come.* But I wasn't sure I believed it anymore.

And no one would trust a doctor whose mind they couldn't read.

chapter TWO

Mr. Amando may be mesh, but Mr. Chance was *the* teacher to have in junior year.

I shuffled past him into second-period English. He was already filling the minds of the students circled around him with the sights, sounds, and smells of exotic sims I would never experience. Mr. Chance looked half-demens with his old-fashioned patched jacket and feathered hat, but his students were clearly entranced.

I had as much chance of passing his class as the chair I was sitting on.

Life wasn't always this bleak. Back in junior high, Trina and I had talked for endless hours about nothing, everything, and boys. Raf tried for a year to convert me to that screechy synchrony music he likes. Then Trina went through the change and Raf wasn't far behind. Nearly everyone had their change parties by the end of freshman year.

The longer I remained a zero, the more likely I would be that one-in-a-thousand who would never change. Zeros didn't attend college—no one trusted them to do real work, so what did they need college for? I'd have to get some low-paying job where I wouldn't have to mindtalk or be trusted. At least I didn't live in a country where they sent zeros to asylums. In Chicago New Metro, I'd just be relegated some job that readers couldn't stand, like guarding the demens ward of a mental hospital.

Raf, in his fitted soccer jersey and oversized shoes, blew into class on the final bell. Female attention swept down the aisle with him, and he glided into the chair next to me. When we won the State Championship last year, Raf became the Portuguese Soccer God, and girls still swarmed around him like bees in a field of clover and honeysuckle. He eased his backpack to the floor and flashed me a grin. I returned it, powerless to resist when he was the only one not treating me like furniture.

"You're going to wreck your image, sitting next to me," I said quietly.

He caught two girls ogling him. "I need something to take the shine off."

I smirked. "I'm just the zero to help you out with that."

A stormy scowl crossed his face. "Don't call yourself that, Kira." His Portuguese accent got stronger when he was riled. I'd missed it while he was away at soccer camp.

I shrugged and traced the non-slip pattern on my desk. The world and I were at a standoff, waiting for me to change, but the world didn't care. If I never changed, it would move on and leave me trying to catch up in a race I would never win. How long would Raf hang around? How long would I keep hoping, not giving up?

Sooner or later, we would both have to face the truth.

My face must have shown the pity party in my head, because the storm on Raf's face gentled into a soft flurry of concern. I concentrated on twisting a strand of my hair. Thankfully, some unspoken thought from Mr. Chance commanded everyone's attention.

He was scribbling on the same wireless board the teachers used last year, when they still taught out loud for the readers who hadn't mastered their skills. If only he had a mindware board, he could focus his thoughts on that and transmit them straight to our e-slates. Instead, students had to mentally focus to hear his thoughts. Great for them, to increase their mindreading skills, but it wasn't making my life any easier.

Mr. Chance's board notes claimed that his grandfather had taught with antique paper books, and he proceeded to walk between the rows and pass some out. I didn't understand why we weren't using regular books. I tried not to break my copy when I cracked the pages open. Bits of paper dust floated up from the yellowed pages and smelled musty, like dried grass. I peeked at Raf's book, and he showed me the pages we were supposed to read. I sped through the opening chapter of *The Scarlet Letter*, careful not to crumble the pages to dust.

When I finished, Rafael was still bent over his book, dark curls hanging off his forehead as he plumbed the depths of Hester's pain. A summer of running drills had tanned his light olive skin, and his lips pursed in concentration. I wondered if his thick eyebrows were soft or bristly. His blinding smile sent me scurrying back to my own book.

It wasn't fair that every other girl in school knew his thoughts better than I did.

If I changed, things might be different. Until then, well, zeroes simply didn't date. Some pravers like Shark Boy might enjoy feeling up a zero girl, but no normal boy would want a mental-reject with a pre-adolescent brain. It was like dating your friend's twelve-year-old sister.

If I didn't change, boyfriends would be like college—an experience other people would have while I figured out my life as a zero. I pushed that thought from my mind.

Students swung their seats around, and I realized we were breaking into groups. I had lucked into having Raf nearby, since no one else would want to pair with me.

"What's up?" I asked.

"We're supposed to discuss the symbol of the rosebush outside Hester's prison door." Raf kept his voice low, but he still gathered annoyed looks from two readers next to us.

"Even the author says he doesn't know what it means."

"Well, I guess we're supposed to be smarter than him." Raf scooted closer so we could whisper. I flipped through the paper book and tried to ignore the nearness of Raf's arm on my chair, but it was hard to focus with him so close.

"So what's your theory, Soccer Cyborg?"

"Hey!" Raf pretended to be affronted. "I'm more than just an athletic machine!"

"Yeah. You have awful taste in music, too."

"As if you don't have *Cantos Syn* on your player."

"Whatever." But I smiled. "So, the rosebush?"

He leaned closer and spoke in a mock grave voice. "I think it means she likes flowers." My strangled laugh didn't distract Mr. Chance from his animated sims up front. When we were done, we spent the rest of class in more reading, with only the flipping of paper pages and rustling of seats to disturb the silence. Raf smiled his goodbye, and a cluster of girls captured him up front. I didn't watch, not needing that particular torture, and slipped out the rear classroom door.

My ex-friend Trina and a dark-haired girl hunched over a shared mindware phone by the girls' bathroom, like it held the answers to the universe's most pressing questions. If I had the ability they took for granted, I wouldn't waste my time conjuring holographic unicorn games.

My snort carried across the hall, but didn't attract their attention. Unfortunately, I did catch the notice of another couple of students. They leaned against the wall five steps down from Trina and smiled at me like I was their next meal.

Shark Boy and his friend, Shark Junior.

chapter THREE

I spun away from Shark Boy and Shark Junior and their leering grins.

Raf and his gaggle of admirers were still working their way down the hall. I scurried up to blend into his group of fans. No one noticed me, not even Raf. Shark Boy's thoughts must not have carried over the mental clamor of the hall. If he touched me out in the open, he would be violating the No Touching Rule, but that hadn't stopped him on the bus. If he tried anything now, at least Raf would help me fend him off.

Seamus had explained the No Touching Rule shortly after he changed—how readers shared feelings when they touched. That was all the information I got before my brother had turned red and bolted from the room, but it explained why everyone became bizarre about their personal space after they changed and why air-kissing was as far as things went in public.

Not that I knew much about what happened in private.

I didn't hazard a look back until our ragtag group had rounded the corner. Shark Boy and his friend seemed to have given up, probably waiting for a time when fewer witnesses would be privy to their nasty thoughts. My heart didn't stop pounding until I was safely in my seat in biology.

I managed to muddle through the rest of my morning classes. The soaring humidity of the Chicago New Metro suburbs was like an extinct rainforest simulation, and my jeans were sticking to my legs.

All right, wearing jeans in August—that was my fault.

After lunch, I had high hopes for Algebra II. I was Mr. Barkley's top student in freshman Algebra I, and I managed to pass Geometry. Being all written work, it leveled the playing field.

I strode into class right before the bell and smiled at Mr. Barkley as I passed his desk. His unexpected smile in return distracted me, and I stumbled over a backpack, left like a land mine halfway down the center aisle. Then three things happened in rapid succession: I fell forward, I grabbed the edge of a desk to catch myself, and I pivoted down into Simon Zagan's lap.

Falling and catching myself: fine. Landing on Simon Zagan: a tragic catastrophe.

Our arms tangled, all sticky from the heat. He jerked back, dumping me off his lap.

"Watch it, zero!"

I scrambled to avoid face-planting on the floor, but my backpack spewed its contents under occupied chairs on either side. I was glad no one could hear the elaborate profanities coursing through my mind. The nearby students stared as though I had gone demens and leaned away as I retrieved the items under their seats.

As if I might jump them next.

When I had finally gathered my scribepads and stylus, my thankfully intact e-slate, and Mr. Chance's battered paper book, I slung my gaping, empty backpack over my free shoulder.

I paused to shoot a daggered glare at Simon.

Under normal circumstances, I wouldn't have been so bold. With his black, arrow-straight hair and dark, intense eyes, Simon seemed slightly dangerous. He never got in any real trouble that I knew of, but he hung out with the kids voted least likely to graduate.

Unfortunately for Simon, I had reached my quota of self-righteous pravers for the day. So I glared at him, and he glared back like he was trying to drill into my head. Then the strangest look came over him, as if he was puzzled by something I said, although I had been successful in biting my tongue and not saying anything at all.

What was his problem?

Sure, I broke the No Touching Rule, but I was a zero. My accidental encounter with Simon shouldn't have affected him at all. Unless he was like Shark Boy and liked to prey on girls who hadn't changed. I turned my glare frosty. Simon slouched in his seat and looked away, which was fortunate for him. I took the seat behind him and hoped he felt the chill of my disgust.

A breathless quiet settled in as we tackled the worksheet Mr. Barkley cast to our scribepads. I straightened out the mess of my stuff and buried myself in sines and cosines.

Mr. Barkley walked between the rows and tapped the tip of his finger to the back of each student's hand. A few of the rich kids were wearing Second Skin, and Mr. Barkley waited patiently while they tugged off the sheer, elbow-high gloves. The touch-check was new, and it seemed to violate the No Touching Rule. I would have to scrit Seamus to get his true thoughts on that.

When Mr. Barkley reached me, I smiled up at him. His blue-gray eyes matched his crisp blue shirt, and the wintery stripe in his black hair had grown wider since freshman year. Of course, he would have to check my answers the old-fashioned way.

He cleared his throat. "It's nice to see you in my class again, Ms. Moore." He spoke softly, but his voice carried over the scratching of styli and creaking of chairs. "How are you doing?"

"Great. Thanks." The silence closed back in, punctuated only by Mr. Barkley's footfalls toward the next student.

After math, my legs twitched with the need to run and escape the *small minds of heavenly wrath*. I had a free period next, so I retrieved my gym bag and changed in the locker room.

The long legs I inherited from my dad flew me down the street, past suburban houses sticking up like skinny fingers and carefully spaced apart to avoid hearing the neighbors' thoughts. I dodged small yippy dogs and sprinklers trying to revive the rings of dead grass that buffered each Gurnee house from the next. The heat lay like a wet blanket on everything, and the late-blooming day lilies bent under its weight. Sweat coated every inch of my skin and seeped a sense of normal into me.

If I had been born ninety years ago, I would have felt this way every day. Back then, it was the first readers who were different and paid the price for it. Grandma O'Donnell's stories about the camps where the government held her dad and the other early readers still gave me the creeps.

Only later did they find the pharmaceutical cocktail that had been brewing in the world's drinking water supply. The mixture of drugs was everywhere, around the world, and by the time anyone understood what was happening, it had already started to activate the part of people's brains that sensed thought waves. And it was too late to stop it.

Even if I never changed, at least I wasn't destined for an internment camp simply for being a zero. The world had become more civilized since the experiments on those first reader kids. I would simply struggle along, one step above the demens on the social ladder. I rounded the corner to school, trying to outrun my fate. Even my shoes pounded it out.

Ze-ro. Ze-ro. Ze-ro.

I seriously needed mental help. Maybe I could join one of those positive-thinking cults that were trying to bring peace to the world by thinking good thoughts. That idea made me laugh so hard, I coughed and gasped for air.

They wouldn't want a zero either.

After a quick shower and an overly long band rehearsal, I hurried out to catch the late bus. Just before I stepped aboard, its darkened windows caught my eye. I couldn't tell who was on board without actually getting on, and the driver wasn't looking any friendlier than the one this morning.

I turned and strode down the sidewalk, opting to walk home in the afternoon heat.

chapter FOUR

My mom didn't have many friends.

Sarah Moore wasn't quite a heremita, those readers who shut themselves away in their bedrooms to hide from other people's thoughts. But she came close. She kept up the appearance of normal by baking cookies for PTA functions she never attended, but mostly she stayed home and cleaned.

The sour smell of silver polish wafted from the sink where she attacked an elaborate tea service. With Seamus off at West Point on scholarship and Grandma O'Donnell passing away over the summer, Mom's cleaning had taken on shades of OCD. She followed me around, scrubbing things and keeping an eye on me, like I was a ticking bomb that would explode at any moment.

I tried to ignore her while I ground through my Latin homework at the kitchen table.

Normally, I encouraged the hands-off approach appropriate for unidentified explosive devices. It was better than the alternative, which might include talking about my dwindling number of friends. But today, her noiseless polishing only echoed the silence at school.

The quiet made my skin itch, and the words tumbled out. "So, today sucked at school."

She gave a start. I couldn't read her mind, but her clenched jaw and the abused silver radiated her disappointment. She set down the tortured sugar spoon and leaned against the counter with crossed arms. Her hair, auburn and gray, flew about in wisps.

"What happened?"

"Nothing." The incidents with Simon Zagan and Shark Boy were better left unsaid. "I just decided I'm going to walk this year. And I'll need that hearing aid after all."

She nodded slowly, as if moving too quickly would set the bomb off.

"I don't suppose the hearing aid comes in the color *invisible*." I meant it as a joke, but her face fell a tiny amount. I was turning out to be a zero, just like her mom.

"I'm sure I can find one that won't be..." She struggled for the right word. "...obtrusive."

"There's no hiding the fact that I need help, Mom." It came out snippier than I meant. "But, yeah, something that isn't neon orange with a giant zero stamped on the side would be good."

She grimaced at the word *zero* and opened her mouth, but the front door creaked open and interrupted her. My dad came up the stairs to the kitchen, all spit and polish in his Navy dress uniform. Coming home this early wasn't a good sign. It usually meant deployment.

He pressed his lips to my forehead. "Hello, baby girl." I grimaced and pushed him away, even less fond of that nickname today. His flash of grin extinguished when he kissed my mom. They must have exchanged feelings, and Dad couldn't hide his disappointment like Mom could.

"So, you're home early," I said, hoping to cut off any Kira-related questions they might be thinking up. "Going on another secret mission?"

My dad worked for the Office of Naval Intelligence. When we were kids, Dad told us he was a spy, which was quite the joke. Politicians exchanged all key information at the annual Trust Conferences, and spying was a hold-over romantic notion that hadn't quite died out. Dad probably coddled some high-ranking officials. Mom knew what he did, and my brother found out once he changed, but I still wasn't sure where the sims ended and the truth began. Whatever he was doing, he would disappear for months at a time.

"Unfortunately, yes. Someone has to stop bad guys." Merriment shone in his eyes, but he held my mom's gaze a little too long. I knew they couldn't help reading each other, but it was not mesh of them to mindtalk in front of me. Especially when I was likely the topic of conversation.

He turned back to me. "I'm leaving in the morning, probably be gone for a month or so."

I searched for an exit strategy. Doing homework in my bedroom suddenly became very attractive. "Okay, well, send us a postcard." I pushed back my chair.

My jab didn't distract him. "So, hard day at school today?" He stared at me in that weird way he often did, as if he could get my brain to change by the force of his will. I only wished that were true. As if my day wasn't bad enough, his stare was giving me a headache.

"Yeah." I scooped up my e-slate and stylus. "Um, I think I'll go study in my room."

Before I reached the stairs, my mom blurted out, "Kira, wait! Would you like to go with me, to look at the options?" She meant the hearing aid.

"No, you go ahead, Mom. You'll find something totally mesh." I managed a weak smile, despite my heart sinking like the Titanic, and sprinted up the two levels to my room.

I dropped onto the pink comforter draped over my bed and willed the world to disappear. It didn't obey, and I laughed out loud. As if I could do anything so dramatic with my mind.

I fished my phone out of my pocket to scrit Seamus. He was probably doing drills or cleaning guns or whatever they do at a military school before dinner.

Can u touch w/o sharing feelings?

He would scrit me back when he got a chance. I studied the afternoon light painting shadows on the walls. Demens plush creatures jammed the shelves on my bookcase, most of them won at carnivals with Raf. Trina gazed at me from a rose-colored glass frame. The picture faded and was replaced by another friend from the past, for whom I was no longer present. My room was a childish palace of pink fluffy dreams, filled with wishful thinking and childhood relics.

A serious overhaul was needed.

Ode to Joy sang from my phone. *Seamus.* The rapid callback wasn't a good sign.

"Hey." I propped myself up. "You didn't have to call. It's not a national emergency."

"My little sister scrit me about *touching*?" His voice rumbled a few notes lower than when he left, only two weeks ago. "Yeah, what did you expect?"

Warmth filled me at hearing his concern. "I just had a question."

"Is someone bothering you?" I imagined him hovering over the phone, ready to take down whoever might mess with his kid sister. But there was nothing Seamus could do from West Point.

I needed to reel him back in. "Cool it, action hero. It was something I saw in my algebra class." He huffed out a breath. "My teacher did a touch-check, only a finger touch. What's that all about? You said it was like sharing feelings."

"Is that all?" He paused. "Touching isn't always like that. Your teacher was only checking to see if they understood the lesson."

"Well, I got that, Sherlock," I said. "But why is it different than, say, lip-locking with the hot girlfriend you're keeping there?"

"*What?*" he asked. "I don't have a girlfriend here!"

"Matter of time."

"Can we stick to talking about you?"

"If we have to. You're much more interesting."

His snort only reminded me how much I missed him. "A quick touch is just a little more... *complete* than reading thoughts. Your teacher would sense if they fully understood the problem."

Open Minds

"So, if you touch for longer, then what happens?"

He paused. "Can't you talk to Mom about this?"

"Did you really ask that?"

"All right." His voice hushed. "I'm only saying this once, so don't ask me to repeat it."

I sat up and pressed the phone hard against my ear. "Okay."

"When you touch for longer, you feel what they feel, like you're joined together into one person. You can explore their emotions. If they like what you're doing, it can be very... intimate. If they don't like it, well, you feel that too."

I waited for more, but it wasn't coming. "Is that it?"

"What? Yes, that's it! You'll understand better when you change."

I gave a short laugh. "Yeah, well, no change, still strange."

"It could still happen."

"Sure." The silence hung on the line and closed in on my throat. "Hey, I don't want to keep you from shooting Bambi, or whatever you're doing for meals there..."

"Kira." I barely heard him. "Some guys like to take advantage of girls, before they change. Before the effect of touching protects them. You know that, right?"

I swallowed and felt the ghost of Shark Boy's hand on my arm. "Yeah, I know."

"So if *anyone* bothers you, call me right away," he said. "I want to make them regret it."

"I can take care of myself, too, you know." But my voice was small.

"I know. Make sure you do."

23

"Yes, sir, Lieutenant Moore." He couldn't see my mock salute, but it still earned a laugh.

"I have to go to mess," he said. "Scrit me tomorrow. Let me know you're all right."

"Okay," I said. "Bye." I clicked off the phone. Seamus wanted to pound anyone who might hurt me, but the truth was I didn't have a big brother lurking the hallways to protect me. And I couldn't count on Raf being there when I happened to need help. I had to take care of myself.

I tossed the phone on my bed and strode over to my shelves. Anything pink or remotely fluffy was coming down. The few pictures of me and Seamus could stay, along with the ones of my mom and dad. One greenish stuffed monster that Raf had won for me this past summer deserved a spot in between the frames, but the rest had to go.

Time to toughen up.

chapter FIVE

I practiced my tough-girl skills at school the next day.

I glared at anyone who crossed my path and refused to cower on the sides of the hallways. If Shark Boy thought he would get a free feel, I was determined to leave marks on him for trying. But he never showed. In fact, no one noticed but Raf. His wrinkled looks of concern hindered my scrappy new attitude, so I ditched the crowded lunchroom to run.

The blistering noontime sun burnt toughness into me. I flew through the side streets, an invisible ninja warrior in training. There was barely enough time for a shower before class, so lunch was a small, scarfed-down apple. I hurried into algebra and remembered just in time to check for land mines in the aisle.

Preoccupied with skirting backpacks, I didn't notice Simon until I got close. His dark eyes locked on me like search beams and he frowned. I scowled right back and cast *Don't mess with me!* body signals. Simon smirked when I passed him, but I was too busy being hostile to care.

Without the hearing aid, I was completely lost in all my

classes, even math. Raf offered to bring his notes to the chem lab during our free period to keep me from getting too far behind. It was a good place to spread out, and people seldom studied there. *Which means no one will see him hanging out with me.* That thought scratched at the edge of my mind, but I pushed it away.

I arrived first and dropped my backpack onto the black stone benchtop. The lab smelled of acid experiments gone wrong, but had the benefit of plenty of room. Raf sauntered in with one of his Pekingese girlfriends on his tail. Her name was Jessica, or possibly Ashley, and she wore her skirt tight and her hair loose. Her Second Skin gloves had sparkle dust on them, and she swung her arm close to his, as if hoping he might suddenly decide to hold her hand.

"Hey, Kira." Raf tossed his backpack on the benchtop next to mine. "You know Taylor?"

Okay, Taylor. Whatever. "Hi." It sounded reasonably polite.

She paused, as if she had forgotten there was a cripple in the room. "Oh, right. Hi."

"So, we're going to study," Raf said to her. "I'll see you after school?" Raf still talked out loud whenever I was around. Which was very nice of him, but didn't help the heat rising in my cheeks.

She must have answered him in her thoughts. Then she added, "Right. After school." She leaned in to air-kiss him, but Raf dipped his head away from her public display of almost affection. At least they didn't actually touch. I didn't want that mental image with me for the rest of the day. When she was gone, Raf pulled out his e-slate and scribepads.

I couldn't hold back. "So the Pekingese are still hot on your trail?"

"You shouldn't call her that." He avoided my gaze, arranging his things on the benchtop.

"Well, you didn't like it when I called your girlfriends Shih-Tzus."

He threw me a grimace. "What is with you and the little dogs?" His accent transformed *little dogs* into *littal dugs*. I had to stop myself from smiling.

"I don't care for the yippy ones, but you seem to like them, Wolf Boy." The Portuguese have an excess of names, and Rafael Amaro Lobos Santos was no exception. Wolf Boy was an old nickname, and Raf didn't seem to appreciate it.

"She's not my girlfriend, anyway." He pulled out his ancient *Scarlet Letter* paper book. "Are we going to study?"

The annoyance in his voice made me soften my tone. "Only if we have to." We settled on the stools. "So, not your girlfriend? And she knows this?"

He tapped his temple twice. "She knows."

Huh. Mindreading must leave less room for misunderstandings in the relationship department. "So, why's she guarding your rear flank?" If a boy wasn't interested in me, I wouldn't go sniffing after him. Not that I had any actual experience in this, just as a matter of principle.

"We have a disagreement about the future of our relationship."

"Sounds complicated."

He set aside his scribepad and searched my plain blue eyes. "You have no idea. Sometimes I think you have it easier. Not knowing what everyone is thinking all the time."

"Easier?" My voice soured. "Really? Maybe we can trade places and you can see what a joy it is to be a zero."

His face softened in a way that made my stomach flutter.

I couldn't stand the sad looks Raf gave me sometimes, his pity about my bleak future written in the lines on his face. But the look of longing he wore now, as though he wanted to touch me or maybe even kiss me, twisted me into knots. Because he and I couldn't be *that,* not while I was still a zero. No decent person would prey upon a mentally impaired freak like me. And Raf was... normal. Perfect. Destined for a life brilliant with possibility.

I ignored Raf's stare and pretended to scroll through my scribepad. Eventually, he gave up and transferred his class notes. "Thanks," I mumbled. Quiet had fallen around us. I studied the notes. He read his paper book. We shifted in our seats as the minutes passed, silent and separate. This wasn't how I wanted to spend the short time I had with Raf. I would rather live vicariously and avoid any actual work, like we normally did. But almost half the period disappeared into a wasteland of studying.

I was absently tapping my stylus against the scribepad when warmth stole over my hand. Raf was *touching* me. I should have pulled my hand away, but I couldn't make it move. There was no surge of intimate emotion sharing, like readers apparently had when they touched. But having Raf's hand on mine was like a drink of cool water after a hundred days in the desert.

My breathing tried to match the pounding of my heart. I searched for something witty or sarcastic to say, but I couldn't unscramble my brain. I dragged my eyes to his dark brown ones.

The longing look was back in force.

A war raged in my mind, a battle between the side that desperately wanted to know what Raf's lips would feel like pressed to mine, and the better side that knew kissing Raf was something I could only keep if I was normal. If I changed. And if I didn't, losing it would only tear me apart.

Please stop, my better side begged. *Please don't make me tell you to stop.*

But he didn't stop. He leaned toward me, and I saw as clear as the half-grin on his face that Raf was going to kiss me. Before I could make my lips move, I thought, *STOP!*

And then my brain exploded. Electric shocks seemed to sizzle through it, and tiny phantom stars flew past my eyes.

Raf crumpled. He folded in on himself like a marionette whose strings had been cut by an evil puppet-master. His head hit the bench, and my arms automatically shot out to catch him as he slid off the high stool. I couldn't stop him, couldn't even slow him down as he headed for the floor. I managed to get under him, to cushion his fall and keep his head from hitting the stone tiles of the chem lab floor. Pain stabbed my ankle as it twisted under Raf's dead weight.

My head swam with dizziness. Had I hit my own head on the way down? Those tiny stars danced in and out of my field of view. I wrestled with Raf's body, trying to move him without dumping him on the floor. I finally wriggled free and rolled him on his back. His wide-open eyes stared unseeing at the ceiling. A chill ran through me like a ghostly wind.

Oh my god. I killed him.

My hands fluttered, useless, over his body. After a terrifying stretch of seconds, it occurred to me to check his breathing. I bent my ear to his mouth, and a warm draft brushed it.

Oh thank god. My hands trembled as I gently shook his shoulders. "Raf! Raf!" He just lay on the floor like a perfectly sculpted mannequin. I pressed the heels of my hands to my eyes and tried to think. *Oh, please, Raf, wake up!* I decided I should check his pulse, so I bent over him again, only to find him blinking back at me.

"Raf?" I gaped.

"What happened?" he asked.

Water pooled in my eyes. "Wh... what happened? You almost scared me to death, that's what happened!" I shook from head to toe. My hands did that fluttering thing again. He struggled to get up, only to press a hand to his head and roll back down again. He made a noise that sounded like "ugh" and closed his eyes.

My panic surged. "Raf! Are you okay?"

"*Merda*... my head." He didn't move.

A rush of relief calmed my hands, and I let out a shaky laugh. If Raf could curse, he would probably live. I gently pried his hand away from his head. The angry red lump on his forehead was turning purple as the blood pooled under his skin.

"You've got a serious bump, Raf." The visible sign of his injury was oddly soothing. He winced when he found the growing bump. "What the... How did I end up on the floor?"

I didn't know what to say. *Sorry, Raf, I nearly killed you with my incredible mind powers?* It was ridiculous. *No. Stick to the facts.* "Well, you took a head-dive into the lab bench." I gestured behind us to the abandoned homework station. "And then you fell off your stool, and I kind of cushioned your fall." My right ankle throbbed, but I ignored it.

"Did you say something, right before..." He struggled up to rest on his elbow. I felt the blood rush out of my face. "I think I heard you, Kira. In my mind. You said something, but I know your lips didn't move, because..." He gave a tiny smile. "Because I was kind of staring at your lips at the time."

"Wh..." My voice faded away. "What did I say?"

"That's just it, I can't remember." He frowned. "Maybe it's the bump on the head."

"Yeah," I agreed quickly. "I mean, you can't hear what I'm thinking now, right?"

He peered at me. "Are you thinking I'm some kind of idiot that faints during homework?"

I laughed but it sounded choked. My hand shook again. "Yes. That's exactly what I was thinking. That, and we need to get you to the hospital. C'mon." I stood, and my twisted ankle screamed its displeasure. A wave of dizziness made me sway.

"Are you okay?" He tried to find the source of my pain.

"Yes, but you might want to lay off Mama Santos's desserts." I groaned dramatically as I pulled him to standing. Cautiously putting weight on my injured foot, I pretended to inspect his strong, lanky form. "I don't know where you put it, but you weigh as much as Seamus."

He lit a brilliant smile, then went serious when he saw me favor my right foot. "Maybe you need to go to the hospital with me."

"Oh, I'm going with you. Someone needs to keep you from taking another header into the pavement." I limped to the bench and hastily stuffed our things into the backpacks. He took both packs from me and slung them over his shoulder. I slid my hand around his offered elbow to support my treacherous ankle, glad to feel him warm and alive. Everyone was still in class, so our conspicuous bare-armed grip went unnoticed as we hobbled to the nurse's office.

I clenched my free hand the whole way to keep it from shaking.

chapter SIX

I think Raf's mom caused him more pain than the lump.

Ana Amaro Santos clicked into the office on her high heels only minutes after the school nurse called. Mrs. Santos hovered over Raf, petting his hair with her manicured hands and mind-talking to him in a way that made the nurse grin and Raf's face flush deep red.

I couldn't hear any of their thoughts, like always. I hugged the edges of the cramped nurse's office, keeping my distance. I tried to think about good things in case my thoughts came to life again, like a nightmarish wish come true. Maybe it was only a coincidence. Maybe Raf happened to faint at the same time that my mind ordered him to stop trying to kiss me. But a quiver had taken hold of my stomach, and I knew it wasn't simply chance. That electric storm in my brain had done something to Raf. Everyone said that when they changed, they felt *different* inside their brains. I knew something had shifted inside me, but it wasn't the change I had been waiting for all these years. I had turned into something dangerous instead.

I was afraid everyone could see the guilt on my face. But no one did.

Mama Santos took Raf to the hospital to make sure the bump was all show and no concussion. His mom would have the doctors run tests until she was satisfied he didn't have a brain tumor, but I was pretty sure Raf would recover from his encounter with the benchtop. The nurse insisted on bandaging my ankle until I could barely shove on my shoe.

I limped through the heat on the walk home, taking my chances with the ankle rather than risking a ride on the bus. Mom was out, probably dropping Dad off at the base, although he could have taken the autocab. I was thankful she was safely away from whatever was wrong with my brain. I ditched the bandage as soon as I got home, hoping to avoid any questions. It jammed up the kitchen trash bowl, and I had to punch the button three times to flush it away.

My hands still shook from the trauma with Raf, and my stomach grumbled from the lack of lunch. I craved something warm and glared at the mindware interface for the flash oven, wondering why I had never bothered to learn the manual controls. Navigating the touch pad instructions was like translating Latin. After a minute, I gave up and slammed my hand down on the stone counter. The satisfyingly loud smack felt like it would leave a bruise.

"Kira?" My mom's voice startled me so badly that I nearly tumbled over my weak ankle. I hadn't heard her come up the stairs, but she hovered in the kitchen doorway, her white shirt rumpled and her face harried, as though she had rushed back to make sure I wasn't home alone.

Except that it was safer for everyone if I *was* alone.

"You're home early." She had that bomb-squad look again, like she thought I might blow with the slightest jostle. Only this time, it made me shiver. *Think good thoughts.* I couldn't let my brain malfunction again.

"Yeah. I skipped band practice." I edged along the counter away from her. Just in case.

She held still, poised in the doorway. "Why?"

I grabbed a box of cheese crackers to keep my hands from shaking. "Well, um, Raf fell and hit his head and had to go to the hospital."

A strange mixture of relief and concern warred on her face. "That's awful." She seemed to decide it was safe to enter the room. The refrigerator panel sprung open at her mental command.

"Is he okay?" She pulled out a container of milk.

"I think so. His mom came to school and got him. I asked him to scrit me when he gets done with all the tests."

"Good." She poured the milk into a glass. "I dropped your father off at the base. He said to say goodbye, and that you could call him if you needed anything."

A nervous giggle threatened to escape me, and I clamped my teeth tight. Normally, my dad was incommunicado during his deployments. If he was giving me phone privileges, he must really be worried about me starting school as a confirmed zero. If he only knew. Being a zero was the least of my problems now.

My mom stared, still holding the glass of milk. It was probably meant for me, but I didn't want her coming any closer. I stuffed a handful of stale crackers in my mouth.

"I'm going to the doctor's office later to look at the hearing aids." She eyed me, then took a sip of the milk.

"Great," I said too quickly, glad I had already told her yesterday to go without me. The last thing I needed was a doctor prodding me. I swallowed the dry crackers and scooted along the periphery of the room.

I escaped the kitchen and scurried up the stairs before Mom could question my bizarre behavior. My room looked as though an angry fairy princess had ransacked it to reclaim her things. I curled under the rosy comforter, the only spot of girly left behind. It was only last night that I had decided to be tough, a warrior that no one would mess with. Now it seemed like I was a weapon that might go off at any moment.

It creeped me out.

Returning to school tomorrow seemed like a tragically bad idea. Who knew what might happen? What if Shark Boy found me alone in the hall? Would I strike him down in flash of fear? Mom was running out to get the hearing aid tonight. What if the *small minds of heavenly wrath* decided to hassle me about it, and I slew the whole lot of them in a fit of anger?

A picture sprung up in my mind—students slumped over their desks in Mr. Chance's class, staring but unseeing. I squeezed my eyes shut and tried to think of something else, anything else. I had to believe I wasn't going to kill everyone simply by going to school. After all, I hadn't mowed down the nurse or

Mama Santos or my mom. It had taken the near epic event of Raf almost kissing me to bring on this brain catastrophe, so an ordinary day at school couldn't be too hazardous.

Could it?

The trembling of my hand wasn't very reassuring.

chapter SEVEN

It was after lunch, and no one had died yet, so I took that as a good sign.

Raf was absent from Mr. Chance's class, but he would be back soon. With Mama Santos clucking over him, he wouldn't stay home any longer than necessary. His scrit from the hospital verified he would live: *Head as thick as it seems. Doing ok.*

It was just as well he wasn't in school. I didn't need to worry about him while I was concentrating on not knocking out people with my scary mind powers.

My teachers whispered through the new mini-mics that came with my hearing aid, which eased the ringing silence of school. Some could barely whisper and think at the same time, but Mr. Barkley was completely mesh about it in math. He took the mic patch and stuck it smoothly on the back of his ear in one quick motion. Maybe he had another zero in a previous class.

We tried it out as the other students drifted in and took their seats.

"Testing... testing...," he whispered as he stood by the board a dozen feet away. I smiled to show that it worked fine. "I'm glad you got this, Kira." His lips barely moved, and I only heard him through the mic. "I expect you to do even better on the exams this year." The other students were all in range to hear his thoughts, even if they couldn't hear his whisper. My cheeks ran hot, but if Mr. Barkley whispered everything he was thinking during class, I *would* finally have an equal footing and might actually pass his class.

The glow of Mr. Barkley's praise carried me down the aisle. The class had filled, and the only open seat was directly in front of Simon Zagan. His brooding eyes captured me in their tractor beams again. *Think good thoughts.* Simon didn't deserve to be the next victim of my uncontrollable brain surges, even if he and Shark Boy could start a Creep Club together.

As I willed my legs to move toward him, his face pinched in. He probably wondered why I wasn't returning his glare. When I dropped into my seat, his stare burned a hot spot on the back of my head.

Mr. Barkley's voice whispered in my ear, and once the class got under way, I forgot about the looming force of antagonism behind me. I had missed a lot the past two days and gave silent thanks for Mom and her eagerness. The tiny bud was barely visible once tucked in my ear, although the entire class had to know the zero had a new crutch. Those concerns were buried under my preoccupation with catching up and keeping everyone safe from my thoughts.

Near the end of class, the tap of a warm fingertip seeped through my t-shirt. It had to come from Simon. I seriously debated ignoring him, but then his breath fell on my ear. "I have something to show you." A shiver ran down my back. Before I thought of something not-hostile to say, he was out of his seat and halfway to the door.

A piece of paper had appeared on my desk. As I unfolded the note, the chill settled into my stomach. In messy handprinting it said: *Meet me in the chem lab next period.*

I didn't know what Simon was thinking, but there was *no way* I was meeting him in the empty chem lab. How did he know I had a free period anyway? Maybe he was stalking me. Maybe he was like Shark Boy and wanted to get me alone in a dark, empty classroom. Well, I might be coming unhinged in thinking I had strange mind powers, but I wasn't stupid. Simon could find someone else to play with.

I spent my free period in the library, studying the copious notes I had taken through the day. When the workpod with the manual interface was free, I pulled down some research articles for a paper in history. The silence didn't bother me nearly as much when I had work to do. How could I be a week behind when school had only been in session for three days?

When the final bell sounded, students flowed through the hallway toward the school entrance and their release for the day. I clung to the edges, fighting the current to reach my locker. At least I had survived the day and hadn't injured anyone. And I had a real chance of doing well this year.

I dug around in my locker and decided to leave my running gear behind, since I needed to bring home my e-slate and all my scribepads. Satisfied I had everything, I slammed the locker door closed. My heart lurched when I saw Simon only a foot away, leaning against the wall of grated metal doors.

I let out an awkward sound.

"Did I scare you?" He seemed to be struggling to keep his face straight.

"No." It sounded unconvincing, even to me. "You just startled me." There were no sounds around us, no hints of anyone nearby. The other students must have cleared out while I had been fussing with my locker.

He dipped his head and peered at me through his lashes, which were deep black like his hair. "I was hoping you'd come to the chem lab." A smile curled up one side of his face.

Spasms roiled through my stomach. "I... I need to get home, so I'll just be on my way, all right?" I turned slowly, determined not to run. I would simply walk at a measured pace along the shortest possible route to somewhere safe. Somewhere he wouldn't terrify me into doing something awful. Before I took a step, he grabbed my elbow.

"Let go!" I twisted out of his grasp and restrained the urge to smack him.

He threw up his hands. "Okay!" That he would openly touch my bare arm confirmed my worst thoughts. Maybe I could outrun him, at least to the office. But a strange look of concern on his face overrode any common-sense thoughts I had of running fast and hard.

"I understand why you're nervous." He dropped his voice. "Why you're afraid."

"I... I'm not a-afraid." I cursed inwardly and wished I had

said nothing at all. I wasn't sure if I was more afraid of Simon or of what my brain might do to him.

"I know you are." He leaned closer and whispered. "Because I'm the same as you, Kira. And I remember how it felt."

His words shocked me out of my trance of terror.

"What are you saying?" I glared up and down at his *Cantos Syn* t-shirt and *nove*-fiber jeans. He was toying with me. "Did you suddenly turn into a zero?" The acid in my voice was enough to give him third-degree burns.

His lips drew into a thin line that was not quite a grimace. "I've always been one."

I blinked and took a step back. The words fell out of my mouth, "You can't be. Why would you say that?" Simon wasn't popular like Raf, but he had a crew of friends and plenty of girls who liked his brand of gritty. It wasn't possible for him to be a zero.

He searched my face, for what I didn't know. When he found it, the taut lines of his face softened. "Come with me." He tilted his head toward the back door of the school. "I'll show you what I mean." He clasped his hands behind his back and waited for my answer.

If I ran, I could see he wouldn't grab me again. Somehow that made a difference. I had to be demens to go anywhere with Simon Zagan, but curiosity burned in me, and the choice dangled like an elixir sparkling in his dark, intense eyes.

"Okay."

chapter EIGHT

Simon held the door as I slipped out into the soul-crushing heat.

We crossed the parking lot in silence and crunched across the dead, scraggly grass toward the bleachers. Simon kept casting glances at me, as if we were on a secret mission. His mischievous looks made him seem younger, not a nearly eighteen-year-old senior, just a boy about to break the rules and confident he could get away with it.

My sandals and shorts left my skin exposed to the waves of scorching, metallic heat coming from the bleachers. Clusters of students either watched the soccer players practice in the blazing dampness or mindtalked amongst themselves. I quickly scanned the field for Raf, but couldn't find him in the blur of jerseys skillfully dashing in and out of range of each other.

Of course, no one on the bleachers noticed me. But Simon usually had the same vacuum effect as Raf, sucking in all the female attention in reading range. Yet today we were both invisible as we snuck up the bleachers. Did Simon's zero status flip on and off? How did that work?

When we reached the top, he motioned for me to sit to his right. Two students sat several rows below us, within thought range, but ignoring us. The girl was reading one of Mr. Chance's ancient paper books, and the boy pretended to watch the soccer scrimmage, while stealing peeks at her.

Simon scooted close, his lean, bare legs nearly touching mine. He rested his arm on the railing behind us and whispered, "Do you see that couple down there?" I nodded my assent, eyes glued to them, because Simon was entirely too close.

"He likes her, but she's not very interested. She's thinking about someone else, although she's trying not to. She knows it annoys him."

I leaned away, giving him a skeptical look. "So you *are* reading their minds." I kept my accusation low so it wouldn't carry over the whistles and muscular grunts coming from the field below.

"No." His mischievous smile had returned. "Now watch. I'm going to tell him to take her book." The couple seemed too far to hear his whispered voice, but the boy immediately snatched the book and held it aloft out of her reach. She smacked him on his t-shirt-covered shoulder.

I shrugged. "Big deal, so he read your mind. Just proves you're not a zero." I wondered why we were playing this stupid game.

"He didn't read my mind," he said. "I *jacked* into his." My body froze at the word *jacked*. When I told Raf to stop in his tracks and fall to the ground like a stricken puppet, it had felt like he was obeying my command.

Simon leaned close and whispered in my ear. "Try it. You know you can."

There was no way I could do that again. I clenched the fire-hot bleacher with my hands to force myself to stay in my seat while crackles of alarm sang through my body.

"It's not that bad," he said. "It's even kind of fun..."

Fun? Simon's idea of fun made my pulse pound like I had sprinted up the bleachers. What if I hurt them? It was insane.

As if reading *my* thoughts, he whispered, "It's okay. You won't hurt them, not if you go slowly. Reach toward them with your mind." My head twitched back and forth. The girl below retrieved her book and gave the boy a dirty look. I couldn't hear her thoughts, like every other day of my life as a zero.

But I wanted to.

I leaned forward, as if I could project my mind by pitching toward them.

Simon encouraged me. "Go on. Tell the girl to give him the book."

My mind sizzled, like a short circuit pulsing through my brain, only less powerful than before, with Raf. No phantom stars swam before my eyes, but the space between me and the girl narrowed, as if a vacuum had formed and sucked the air out between us. As I got closer, the sizzle strengthened and then I was touching her, pushing through a barrier into her mind.

I heard her thoughts. *Think you're so funny. You're just making my life difficult, Jeremy.* I thought: give him the book. *Give him the book*, she instantly echoed. Her hand shot out and shoved the book into his chest. He recoiled from her, and I heard his thoughts of surprise only as a faint echo in the thought waves she picked up from his brain. Because I wasn't in *his* mind, I was in *hers*. Her thoughts continued to echo, repeating like a cavern lined with endless tunnels, each a different length. *Give him the book, him the book, the book, book.*

A smell, rich and flowery, filled the back of my throat and caused me to choke. I drew in a sharp breath and yanked back to my own head. My whole body shook in one violent pulse.

I *mindjacked* her. And no one got hurt.

The couple was now arguing further about the book. Simon's smile was a mile wide, but he waited for me to speak.

"All this time... you've been doing *this*?" His grin was his only answer. "Does she know? That I—"

"Shhh!" he said. "She doesn't know. I've been doing this for years, and no one's known. Until you."

The idea that Simon had been mindjacking people for *years* made my stomach turn sideways. The bleachers started to tip, and the heat painted sweat all over my face. Simon caught me right before I fell over.

His dark eyebrows pulled together into a straight line of concern. "Are you okay? I think maybe the heat is too much..."

I nodded. I couldn't form coherent words if I tried. Maybe I had electrocuted my brain. Maybe I jacked the girl and somehow zapped myself at the same time. A crooked smile broke out on my face, but I tried to stop it, afraid of looking like an idiot. Simon's frown pulled tighter. He slid his arm under mine, pulled me to standing, and half carried me down the bleachers.

My head floated above like a tethered balloon that Simon kept pulling down, jerk by jerk, to the bottom of the steps.

We hobbled across the grass and the parking lot because my legs weren't working right. They kept getting tangled with the ground. Simon moved faster and when he pulled open the door to the building, a wash of frigid air swept over us. The air-conditioned hall was like a freezer, and my full-body shiver snapped my head back onto my shoulders. I stumbled, then managed to stand upright, bracing my hands against Simon's chest.

"Are you okay?" He held me as though I were a child that might fall down.

"Y-Yeah." My jaw chattered with the cold. "Thanks."

He smiled, and it stole my breath. It wasn't that annoying smirky thing, but a blaze of happiness. And he was gorgeous when he smiled, his long lashes fighting their way outward from his sparkling black eyes.

I gulped and looked away, needing to sit down. He helped me find a spot, leaned up against the cold, metal lockers. My mind was a complete blank, like I was a computer coming back from a hard reboot.

"I need some time," I finally said, "to think about this."

He didn't say anything, but there was a glint in his eyes.

"How did you know?" I asked. "That I could jack into people's heads?"

A smile flitted across his face. "I didn't," he said. "But you're the only person that I *couldn't* jack, so I figured there was something special about you. Your mind barrier is like nothing I've felt before."

I shrunk away from him. *Of course* he had tried to jack into my mind. Like he did to that boy on the bleachers. Like he had done to everyone else. *For years.*

A surge of adrenaline made my hand twitch. I scrambled up from the dingy industrial carpeting, and a shadow crossed Simon's face as he climbed to his feet.

"Aren't you afraid," I said slowly, contemplating how I could escape if I had to, "that I'll tell someone?"

Simon loomed over me, his dark look solidifying into an icy mask. "No one would believe you, Kira."

I swallowed. He was right; no one would believe a sim like that, especially from a zero. I hardly believed it myself, and I had just jacked into another girl's head.

"I won't, you know," I said. "Tell anyone."

My words seemed to erase Simon's cold look as quickly as it had appeared. "I know." He touched my hair, smoothing it back from my face. "We're the same, Kira. Now that we've found each other, we're in this together. Just you and me." He gently swept his thumb across my forehead. We weren't readers, so there was no surge of emotions between us when he touched my bare skin. But it still sent a shiver through my body.

When he stepped back, I teetered, not sure if I should run or stay. "Take some time to think," he said. "I'll see you tomorrow."

Without another word, he turned and strode down the hall.

chapter NINE

I stumbled through the walk home, my skin slick with sweat.

I told myself it was only the heat, not the traumatic after-school events with Simon, but I was so distracted thinking about my newfound mindjacking ability that I nearly ran into the garage door. I slid in the passkey, and it opened to reveal our red hydro car. Mom was already home, and I searched my brain for a plausible reason to be late.

As I hiked up the stairs from the ground level, the cool air of the house prickled my skin. Mom shuttled back and forth between the kitchen and the living room in a flurry of activity, and the acrid smell of glass-cleaning solution followed her. She had hauled out Grandma O'Donnell's crystal plates, the ones Gram claimed were hand-cut by our distant relatives in County Kerry during the potato famine. She also said Big Foot crashed her eighteenth birthday party.

Gram could make up stories like that, and no one could tell if they were true memories or sims because she was a zero, and zeros were liars. Even a truth magistrate couldn't read her thoughts, in spite of their skin-to-skin questioning.

I wished Gram were still rambling around the house. Given what she had been through—being a zero, having her dad in the camps—she might have understood what I was going through. But my mom... she was always trying to be like everyone else, even with her semi-heremita lifestyle.

And I was about as far from fitting in as possible.

Mom shuffled back from the living room and carefully set another sparkling crystal plate with the others on the kitchen table. "How was school?"

"Um, okay," I said, stalling. "The, uh, hearing aid worked great." Her face broke into a picture of relief. She must have expected a heinous story related to the tiny ear bud that still sat in my ear. I popped it out. "See, I forgot to take it out. Hardly noticed it." That earned me a smile. I edged toward the stairs. "I've got a ton of homework to catch up on. I should get started."

"Why don't you work here in the kitchen?" she asked. "I made a snack for you." Snickerdoodles beckoned from one of Gram's crystal plates on the table. My mom always cooked up a storm whenever my dad was on deployment, as though she could fill the emptiness with baked goods. I longed to eat cookies and spill out the contents of my day so my mom could help me make sense of my life. But I couldn't tell her that I had mind controlled a girl at school. That I had become a freak even worse than a zero. I wrenched my eyes away from the solace my mom had laid out for me.

"I'm totally beat," I said. "I'll just study in my room." I hitched my backpack on my shoulder and slunk toward the stairs. I cast a parting look at the cookies.

It worked.

"Well, go ahead and take one," she said. "You can eat it upstairs." I snagged two cookies and gave her a smile before I trudged up the stairs.

I slung my backpack on the bed. A jitter started in my stomach, and my appetite for the cookies disappeared. After dropping them on the nightstand, I sought refuge from the day under my bedspread. Eventually, the shaking calmed to a quiver.

I jacked into a girl's head today and told her what to do. *And she did it.*

My battered silver phone, tucked in the pocket of my backpack, beckoned to me. I could call Seamus, but then he would want to know: why are you asking about mind control, Kira? And I would have to lie, because I couldn't tell him what happened on the bleachers. Or in the chem lab.

Besides, he would insist that I tell Mom, and she might take me to another doctor, like the one that had wanted to image my brain when I was fourteen. Mom had insisted he use the standard thought-wave cap, but the *Cerebrus* 3D imager had loomed in the corner like a giant bullet, threatening to illustrate in bold, color images precisely what was wrong with me.

I shivered under the covers, sending a wave of pink sheen down the length of it. If anyone found out I could control thoughts, they'd lock me away in a laboratory. Do experiments. Dissect my brain. I understood why Simon insisted that this had to be a secret. Simon, with his dark eyes and smirky grin. He had passed as a reader for years, and no one knew the truth.

Because he mindjacked everyone to believe the lie.

The image of Raf crumpling like a lifeless doll sprang up, and I pulled the blanket tighter under my chin. I was a dangerous, possibly lethal, weapon. Waves of horror at that thought crashed into an upswelling of hope: maybe I wasn't doomed to life as a zero. Maybe I could control this thing and pass for a reader like Simon. The feel of Simon's thumb lingered on my forehead. He knew how it all worked.

Tomorrow I would ask him to teach me.

chapter TEN

I left the house early, hoping to catch Simon before school.

Last night's condensation steamed up from the streets, leaving my shirt damp by the time I reached the school. Students walked in synchronized groups through the hall, breezing past me and unaware of the danger standing next to them.

I watched them, drawn by the new connection between us. All I had to do was reach out and touch them with my mind.... I pressed closer to the lockers, putting more distance between myself and the bustling crowd. Just to be safe.

There was only one person I wanted to talk to, but he wasn't in hallways. I sat in the back of first period, as far away from the other students as I could. Between classes, I peered through the crowds, searching for Simon. I fumbled through the things in my locker and grabbed my paper book for English. My hand stopped mid-reach. Raf should be back in class today, and he had an uncanny ability to know what I was thinking, even if he couldn't read my mind. Would he see the change that was invisible to everyone else?

I realized that the bell had already rung and whirled to join the stragglers hurrying to class. I stopped dead when I saw Raf had saved me a seat. He smiled, but all I saw was the ugly purple bruise on his forehead, which had spread and turned a sickening yellow. The physical reminder of my freakish new power wrenched my stomach. I took the seat in front of him and busied my hands with my backpack.

"Are you okay?" I asked.

"I'll live." I involuntarily shot him a glance and then quickly faced forward so Raf wouldn't see the guilt in my eyes. Mr. Chance had remembered to wear his mini-mic, but it played like a bad phone connection as he only mumbled about half his thoughts.

Raf tapped me on the shoulder. "Are *you* okay?"

I was the furthest thing from okay, but I couldn't have Raf asking questions and piecing it together. *That I almost killed him.* I gave him a short nod and pretended to be fascinated by Mr. Chance's crackling monologue. Raf didn't speak again until it was time to break into groups. Of course, no one wanted to be in a discussion group with the zero. Except Raf.

His irresistible smile was back. I considered feigning illness to avoid sitting face-to-face with him, where he might see the difference inside me. The way my stomach was twisting, claiming sickness wouldn't have been far from the truth. We turned our desks and he searched my face. I focused on my paper book and tried to interpret Mr. Chance's halting instructions.

"Kira." Raf's voice was heavy with patience.

I wondered how long I could avoid looking at him. "Yeah?"

"Kira, what is it?"

"Nothing. I just…" I tried to muster the smile I usually had for him. "What are we supposed to discuss again? Because I'm pretty sure I know nothing about Hester Prynne's life."

Raf scowled to show he didn't appreciate my dodge.

Mr. Chance's voice was a staccato message, "…*Hester …the women…*" Raf glanced up front. "We're supposed to discuss what punishments the women of Hester's time would have given her."

A fitting topic. What was the right punishment for almost killing your best friend? The scraping sounds of turning desks faded as the other students silently engaged in their literary discussions via mindtalk.

"Wait." Raf's eyes refocused on me. "Didn't you get the hearing aid?"

"How did you know?"

"Word gets around."

Of course, the speed-of-thought rumor mill at Warren Township High would be buzzing about my new hearing aid. "Well, yeah, I have it." I glanced over my shoulder at our hapless English teacher. "But Mr. Chance doesn't know how to use it."

"Good thing you still have me to translate." His eyes captured mine.

"Good thing." I broke the stare and pretended to concentrate on the book. "So, what do you think would be a proper punishment for Hester?"

"I don't think Hester deserves any punishment," he said.

I resisted the urge to glance at him. "I don't think Mr. Chance will take that for an answer."

He sighed and I nervously thumbed through the pages of the book. Then he reached across our desks to lay his hand on mine. I flushed at the sideways snickers we were garnering and flashed back to the chem lab. I jerked my hand back. He slowly dragged his away.

"Is this about what happened... before?" he asked. My heart nearly leaped out of my chest and fell dead on the floor. *Does he know?* I peeked at him, but his face only held frustration.

"N-nothing happened before." I forced a grin. "People faint all the time during homework. Just thinking about my homework makes me wish I could pass out."

He had that stubborn look that I knew too well, the one he wore when he insisted I taste Mama Santo's *arroz doce* or listen to his new favorite synchrony band. He would press on until he got what he was after. "I'm not talking about that. I'm talking about *before*..." Then I finally understood: the near-kiss.

Which was why my brain had exploded in the first place.

Why couldn't he have left things alone? Waited until I changed? Then maybe none of this would have happened. And why was he bringing it up now, in the middle of English, where everyone could overhear his thoughts? Everyone except me.

I stared at Raf, unable to speak.

"Please, Kira. Say something."

I gripped my paper book harder. "Nothing happened, okay?" I said. "Just... nothing happened, and I think we need to do our work now."

Raf's face fell.

I was tempted to jack into his head and erase the look that was shredding my heart. But I banished that idea in an instant. There was no way I would ever mindjack Raf again. Even if I could do it without hurting him, the idea of forcing Raf to do something against his will creeped me out. It was wrong. And sick.

We concentrated on our work and concocted some lame answer. By the end of class, Raf's face had transformed into a mask of carved stone, a poor imitation of the true Rafael.

My heart shrank as Raf left English without saying goodbye.

chapter ELEVEN

I skipped lunch again and went for a run in the August heat.

I told myself I needed to get away from the curious eyes and lightning-fast rumors, but I was really avoiding Raf and his stony looks. By the eighth time around the track, sweat drenched me. I headed for the showers, eager for a chance to talk to Simon in math.

I arrived early to find Simon standing two classrooms down the hall, having a pointed silent conversation with a balding, portly man that I vaguely recognized as Mr. Gerek, the shop teacher. I leaned against a wall scarred from rubbed-out graffiti and waited for Simon. Mr. Gerek caught sight of me and Simon turned around. He wore his mesh *nove*-fiber jeans like the day before, but today he sported a band t-shirt for the *Melders*. It sounded like something Raf would like.

Simon left Mr. Gerek and quickly strode down the hall. "Hey," he whispered when he got close.

"Hi," I said. "I didn't know you took shop."

He seemed puzzled. "I don't."

I raised my eyebrows, but Mr. Gerek had already disappeared. Then I tried to remember my burning questions, but Simon beat me to it.

"Have you been practicing?" He brushed a lock of hair from my face, and his fingertips swept across the top of my ear. That simple touch seemed to light my ear on fire. I pulled away from him and glanced around to see if anyone saw us. The students down the hall seemed to be averting their eyes.

How did he do that?

Simon's head-turning trick brought all my questions back in a rush that tangled up in my throat and made my voice disappear into a squeak. "Practicing?"

"Don't be afraid, Kira." His hand lingered by my face. "I'll help you. We're in this together, remember? We'll practice in class. I want to see what you can do."

"I don't know what I can do," I protested. He was supposed to help me.

"Time to find out," he said. "Don't worry. If anything happens, I'll fix it."

My eyes went wide. *If anything happens?* He only smirked and stepped back. A couple of students walked past us into Mr. Barkley's class. Simon tilted his head toward the door. I gritted my teeth and filed into class with the others.

Mr. Barkley checked in with me on the mini-mic, because he's mesh that way. "Good afternoon, Ms. Moore." I smiled my acknowledgement. I tried to focus on his introduction of tangents, but I was hyperaware of Simon in the seat behind me.

A few minutes later Simon whispered, "I'm waiting."

The boy sitting in front of me was as tall as a basketball player and had to hunch over his scribepad. Ignoring the soft-spoken math instructions in my ear, I leaned forward and stretched my mind toward him. The distance between us shrunk until I pushed into his mind.

It was like Jell-O that was not quite set—solid, but gooey and on the verge of turning liquid with a few good stirs. I shuddered. His thoughts and an echo of Mr. Barkley's played at the same time, like a harmony. *The tangent is the ratio of the cosine to the sine...*

Nathan—his name popped up like a nametag on the back of his head—translated Mr. Barkley's lessons into magnetic ink on his scribepad. The scent of freshly mowed grass tickled the back of my throat, and I remembered the overpowering flowery mind-scent of the girl on the bleachers. I wondered if every person had their own flavor.

For no reason at all, I decided to have Nathan draw a smiley face. Before I could form the words in my head, a crooked face smiled from the middle of his notes like a sinister hiccup in his writing. I pulled back out of his mind, which cut off his thoughts like a switch.

Simon laughed quietly. "Is that all you've got?" His words were soft, so they wouldn't carry over the shuffling sounds of the room. I gave him a dirty look and twisted forward, jacking back into Nathan's mind. After a moment, the first three verses of *Mary Had a Little Lamb* scrolled by on his scribepad. While still in his mind, I reached to the student ahead of him. *Janice.* Soon she was writing nursery rhymes as well. Then I noticed something in both of their minds, a hard presence, like a marble. I pushed at the marble but invisible forces held it firmly embedded in their gelatin brains.

Simon.

I looked back and his face had gone deadly serious. I held Simon's gaze while I gave the marble another nudge. It didn't move. The barest smile parted Simon's lips. I lost my focus, causing Nathan and Janice to return to copying the lesson.

Simon grinned, and my face grew hot.

I turned my back on him and reached into mind after mind. Students twenty feet in every direction had the cold, hard spot of Simon infiltrating them.

He must be jacking *all of them. At the same time.*

I finally found a girl up front who didn't have a hard marble suspended in her head. She only half listened to Mr. Barkley and the echoes of the other students, with the rest of her thoughts occupied by a dark-haired boy. Her mind lingered on his curly hair and how she'd like to run her fingers through it. I was about to leave, feeling like a voyeur, when I recognized the boy... *Raf!*

Taylor. Raf's Pekingese fangirl. I clenched my teeth and wanted to jack those thoughts out of her head, but her next ones froze me. *I wish he'd stop hanging around that pathetic zero. He should just do whatever he wants with that little charity case and get over it...*

My fingernails dug into my palms. A tornado swept all thoughts out of my mind and drove them toward the soft jelly of Taylor's brain. Her head flopped forward and a sudden force shoved me out of her mind. Her head popped up and shook, as though she had nodded off and snapped back awake.

At the same time, Simon launched out of his chair, grabbed me by the arm, and hauled me out of my seat. I sputtered, but couldn't get any words out as he dragged me past Mr. Barkley's desk toward the door. Before we left the classroom, Mr. Barkley whispered in my ear bud, "I hope you feel better soon, Ms. Moore."

In the hallway, I finally had enough wits to resist. I pulled against Simon's iron grip on my upper arm, but I didn't even slow him down as he dragged me down the hall. Once we were around the corner, he let me loose. I backed against the lockers, a surge of horror washing over me. I had nearly knocked Taylor out. It was like Raf all over again, only this time Simon was there to save her before I sent her crashing to the floor.

"I... I..." I couldn't breathe. "I didn't mean to..." But it was a lie. I did mean to. I wanted to shut her up; I just didn't mean to hurt her.

Simon leaned on the locker next to me, his arms folded. "Well, it's a good thing I was there to stop you. Next time we'll have to be a little more careful."

No. This was crazy. I was dangerous. I couldn't do this anymore...

Simon unfolded his arms at the look on my face. "Hey, it's okay. It's fine now." He leaned close. "I took care of it."

"How..." I stopped to clear the quavering in my voice. "How did you stop me?"

"I pushed you out of her mind." He ran a finger down my cheek. "You felt it, didn't you?"

There was no one in the hall, and even if there had been, Simon would have jacked them to avert their eyes. His touch calmed my pounding heart a little.

"But what if next time..."

"Next time I'll be there," he said. "We can practice some more before we try the math class again. You just need to work on your self-control."

A shiver ran up and down my arms. I was definitely not in control. Not like Simon, who seemed unfazed by the whole event. He was right—I had to stick close to him until I figured out this jacking thing.

My shaky nod brought a gentle smile to his face.

"Come on. I'd better take you to the nurse, since you felt so horribly sick in Algebra that you had to leave." He took my hand and pulled me away from the lockers. "Stick with me, Kira, and everything will be fine."

I wasn't so sure.

chapter TWELVE

Simon jacked the nurse into believing I had a math anxiety attack, and she let me go with some instructions on how to meditate.

By the time we reached the library, my shakiness had diminished to a nervous jerkiness. Simon seemed to think the library was the perfect spot to practice my nascent mind control skills. Of course he wanted to know what Taylor had done to bring out my fury—he hadn't been in her mind when she took the head dive. I only told him that she didn't think much of zeros. He touched my cheek and said my days as a zero would soon be over. That settled the last of my nerves.

I wanted this to work.

We huddled on the hard, tiled floor by the library door while students filled the hallways between classes. Simon said he regularly skipped his last-period biology class and that he jacked the teacher to believe he had chemo treatments in the afternoon.

I wasn't sure if he was kidding or not.

I kept my legs tucked out of the flow of students filing by

while Simon jacked them to ignore us. He made it look so easy, having everyone do as he wished, all the while thinking he was a reader like them. By the time the next period started, I was ready to dive into practicing.

My exuberance pulled a grin out of him. "Easy there, changeling. Don't want you killing off the library patrons."

I made a face and reached past the peeling paint of the library wall, searching for the nearest mind. Not seeing my target was tricky, like fumbling in the dark until my hand sunk into a plate full of goo. Kind of gross, but not too bad once I knew to expect it. Of course the hard lump of Simon was already firmly in place.

"That's, um," I fished for the name, and it popped into my head. "Anthony. Soccer player, sophomore." Anthony's thoughts were focused on summoning historical research from the mindware interface of his workpod. His mind-scent hinted of freshly shaven wood chips.

"And what would you like Anthony to do?" Simon asked.

"I suppose the Chicken Dance would be too disruptive?"

My eyes were closed to make it easier to concentrate, but I heard the smile in Simon's voice. "A little showy."

"Maybe have him move books around in the stacks?"

"Subtle, yet subversive. I like it."

Anthony leapt to his feet, determined to carry out the directive I had implanted in his mind. He strode past the multimedia pod and Literature Lab to the librarian's desk. She gave him the passkey to the climate-controlled paper book pod tucked in the back. Once he was on his way, I searched for another Jell-O to mold. Naturally Simon was already there.

"Okay, she's, uh…" Names were integral and came unbidden, but with some probing I could call up a lot more. Name? Rank? Serial number? They popped up like displays on a console. "Sheila, junior, has a strange affinity for grape-flavored gum. What should Sheila do?"

"Anthony's in the stacks, right?"

"Yup. He's undoing the Dewey Decimal system. Mixing the goldfish with the geraniums."

"Maybe he and Sheila can be subversive together."

My eyes popped open at his lowered tone. "What are you saying, Simon Zagan?"

"I'm saying no one will notice them kissing in the paper book pod."

I leaned away. "You're not serious." Jacking two strangers into lip-locking in the library didn't have much appeal to me.

"I am." His eyes glinted like obsidian, and I narrowed mine.

"Come on," Simon said. "Jacking two people to write the same nursery rhyme isn't much of a stretch. Handling a true interaction between two minds takes more control. I want to see if you can do it."

"Can't they just hold hands?" Considering how intimate touching was for readers, even that seemed a bit much.

Simon huffed. "Fine."

I jacked Sheila to go check out the paper book pod. After getting another passkey and a furrowed look from the librarian, Sheila stepped into the tiny room. She hesitated as the door sealed behind her. I jacked her to make eye contact with Anthony. He flushed, having been caught rearranging the ancient books, and he wondered what possessed him to do such a thing.

Jacking both at once was like seeing double. Plus the commands were reverberating through their minds. With some difficulty, I twisted Anthony's embarrassment into attraction, while at the same time jacking Sheila to admire Anthony's soccer physique. Once their mutual appeal took hold, they found their way to each other. It took some additional jacking to get them to breach their personal space and hold hands. As soon as they touched, their thoughts twined together, which helped with the double vision.

"See. Nothing to it." Then I realized the emotions resonating between Anthony and Sheila were getting out of hand. There would be kissing, if I didn't stop it. I ordered them to return to their workpods.

"Yes. Just like a pro." Simon barely kept his laughter from carrying through the open library door. When I resumed my mind control experiments, I stuck to less intrusive things like dropping styli or making unnecessary visits to a different learning pod.

After a while, Simon's voice interrupted my focused efforts. "Kira." His touch on my shoulder made my eyes fly open again. "It's not only about making them do what you want. You need to link your thoughts to theirs."

"Huh?"

He ran the back of his fingers down my cheek, which completely distracted me. "The only way you can escape being a zero is by convincing them they can read your mind."

"But, they can't, right?"

"No."

"So, how do you...?" This was the one thing I didn't understand. I knew that Simon could control other people's thoughts. But the people around him weren't all puppets on strings. *Were they?* How did he convince them he was a reader?

"Instead of jacking in to control them, just link in and tell them your thoughts," he said. "It's a small difference. You can do it, you just have to practice."

"But how?" The students in the library were packing up to leave.

"Practice," he said, standing and moving away. I scrambled to my feet and wondered why he was leaving. "I'll see you tomorrow," he said quietly. He leaned casually against the locker wall and gazed down the hall as if we hadn't spent the last hour hunkered on the floor together.

The final bell rang, and students flowed into the hallway, a silent stream of faces glad for the end of the day. I pressed flat to the wall, trying not to let my heart contract simply because Simon was acting like I didn't exist. A dark-haired boy greeted him with a head nod, and Simon turned to walk with him. Two steps later, a pretty blonde sidled up to Simon. Close, but not touching, like Raf's Pekingese fangirl. Simon left me standing outside the library without another glance.

Tears pricked my eyes, and I told myself not to be an idiot. Of course Simon couldn't admit we had been together. As far as anyone knew, I was a zero and he was a senior reader, too mesh to hang out with the likes of me. I stumbled upstream through the human river, heading toward the band room for practice. *Practice.* That was what I needed to leave my zero status behind.

I rounded a corner and ran smack into Shark Boy.

He looked as surprised as I was to find himself entangled with me in the hall. That didn't stop him from running his hands over my bare arms.

"What have we here?"

His fingers curled into my flesh and he dragged me up flush against his chest. I tried to pull out of his grasp, but he just dug in more painfully. I jacked hard into his mind. *Let me go!*

He dropped my arms like they were red-hot pokers and took a step back. He teetered, uncertain, and his hateful thoughts filled my throat with a burning sensation.

Go to the principal's office! I ordered him. *Turn yourself in and confess to...* my mind spun, trying to think of something that would pay back Shark Boy but leave me out of it. *Confess to harassing a changeling on the first day of school!*

Shark Boy spun and strode purposely toward the principal's office, my command echoing through his mind. As I pulled back, I caught his name. *David.* Sickness churned in my stomach. Maybe he would come to his senses before he reached the principal's office. Maybe my command would fade. If not, he deserved whatever he got there.

I couldn't bring myself to regret what I'd done.

My shaky legs carried me down the hall, and I made it to band rehearsal before the bell rang. The rich sound of our instruments vibrated through me, soothing out the tension. My fingers found the notes on my saxophone while other students tapped their feet or swayed to the music filling our ears.

Here, I was still a zero. Everyone ignored me, like usual.

Practice. Simon's instructions rang in my head. The first chair saxophonist trained her eyes on the bandmaster and fluttered her fingers with perfect timing. She was Janice from math, the one that I had jacked to write nursery rhymes. I reached toward her with my mind. I could jack her, make her miss her perfect notes. Make her blow every song for the rest of practice.

I shrank back inside myself. What kind of person does that?

I focused my eyes on the sheet music swimming in front of me and pretended to be a zero, instead of a dangerous freak lurking in the third-chair saxophonist seat.

chapter THIRTEEN

I dragged myself into the house and my insides squirmed, sourness from the day's events eating me from the inside out. I trudged up the stairs to find Mom in the kitchen. She was digging around a low cabinet and had pots, pans, and strange kitchen gadgets evicted and strewn all over the floor. She backed out of the long-neglected cabinet, her hair spotted with furry dust worms.

A strangled laugh erupted from me.

"Hey," she said. "Good day at school?"

"Um, yeah." Part of me wanted to tell her everything—Shark Boy, jacking, Simon. *Simon.* He would want me to jack into my mom's mind and control her like the students in the library, but jacking my mom summoned the same internal cringing I felt about controlling Raf.

"How is Raf doing?" she asked, as if she had read *my* mind.

"Raf?" I repeated. "Uh, yeah, Raf's fine. Great."

She smiled and brushed back a strand of dusty hair that had fallen over her face. I could practice like Simon wanted, link in and mindtalk and make her think I had finally changed. But I would have to do it all the time or she would know something was wrong, and I wasn't sure I could pull it off.

Or wanted to.

I couldn't decide which was the worse lie—that I was still a zero, or that I could read minds like everyone else. Either one was better than the truth—that I was a mindjacking freak.

"I need to study," I said and fled to my room before she could ask me anything else. A vision of Raf, with his stony looks, chased me up the stairs.

~*~

The next morning I escaped the house before Mom could grill me, using mouthfuls of breakfast and a manufactured scowl to keep her questions at bay. The empty halls of school smelled of overnight cleaning. I rounded a corner and found Simon leaning against my locker, wearing a *Tactus Dura* t-shirt. I was starting to think he had a collection.

"Good morning," I said carefully, opening my locker.

He rained a brilliant smile on me. "Good morning. How's your practice going? Did you link your thoughts to anyone?"

I bit my lip, pretty sure I didn't want to tell him about Shark Boy. "Well, no."

He leaned against the lockers again and studied me. "What about your parents?"

"I don't know. It just doesn't feel right. You know, jacking into my mom's head."

He let loose an exaggerated sigh. "Kira, you'll have to jack into *everyone's* head."

"I... I'm not sure I want to." I looked away from his disappointment.

"Hey." His hand tucked under my chin. "I know it's hard. But you're going to have to make a choice, Kira. Do you want to be a zero your whole life?" I shook my head, my chin rubbing gently against his fingers. "Then you have to learn how to jack everyone. Even your mom. You'll make her happy when she thinks you can read minds like everyone else. I promise."

I nodded, but the uncertainty must have shown in my face. Simon dropped his hand away. "It's all or nothing, Kira. Because if you pick and choose, someone's going to figure it out. And you're not the only one with a secret here." I nodded more vigorously. What would Simon do if someone found out our secret? I didn't like the tight feeling that came with that thought.

His voice flipped back to soft and tender. "We're in this together, right?"

"Right." It sounded weak, so I backed it up with a tentative smile. I wanted Simon to trust me, and not only because his mood swings set my nerves on edge. I needed his help.

He brushed his fingers against my hair. "I'll see you at lunch, okay?"

As students began to trickle in, he turned away—before anyone saw us together. I ignored the twinge in my chest and headed to Latin with renewed purpose.

Once there, I realized the difficulty of what I was facing. I had only mindjacked two people at the same time before. How could

I juggle thirty minds at once? Instead, I stuck in my hearing aid and listened to Mr. Amando conjugate the verb to teach: *doceō, docēre, docuī, doctus*. I needed Simon to *doce* me how to jack an entire class before I attempted it on my own.

Latin flew past, which meant English with Raf was next. The class was half full, with no Raf, which gave me a disturbing sense of relief. I took an empty seat between two students, leaving no room for him.

A moment later Raf appeared at the door and paused to say goodbye to someone. The set of Raf's shoulders told me he was already mad, but his jaw clenched when he saw I hadn't saved him a seat. He passed by without a word and sat near the back of the class.

I rubbed my face and stared ahead at Mr. Chance. His ineptitude with the mini-mic caused an annoying crackle in my ear. I crept into his mind, slow and gentle. I didn't want to jack him accidentally, so I lingered at the edge, listening to the ear bud play a halting echo of his thoughts. I took it out, shoved it into my pocket, and focused on my essay about Hester's thoughts on the scaffold. At the end of class, I was packing my stuff and didn't notice Raf until he stepped into my view with the oversized sneakers that were fashionable for Portuguese Soccer Gods.

Emotions warred across his face. "Why aren't you wearing your hearing aid?" he asked. Raf was dangerously observant. Had he seen me take notes without the aid?

I stood and fished the tiny bud out of my pocket to show him. "The battery died." I wondered how many lies I would have to tell today. And every day.

"Oh." His face brightened. "Well, you can copy my notes during free period."

I didn't need the notes, but now I had to pretend that I did. "Um, that's okay. I'll figure it out."

"At least meet me for lunch. I only want to talk."

Lunch? I was supposed to meet Simon for lunch. "I, um, was going to go for a run at lunch."

"Kira." He said my name like he was scolding me. "You can't keep avoiding me."

I recognized his Stubborn Portuguese voice, and I felt the same tug as I had with my mom. I longed to tell Raf everything, spill all my secrets. Let him help me figure this crazy thing out before it got any worse.

"Okay. I'll see you at lunch."

How I would manage this, I had no idea. Maybe I could catch Simon and change our plans. I shuffled out of English and glimpsed Simon at the far end of the hall, hanging out with two boys and the blond girl from yesterday. As I approached, he studiously ignored me.

An argument raged in my head. If I jacked into his *friends'* heads, he couldn't pretend that I didn't exist. But there were three of them, and I'd have to jack all of them at once. I stared at Simon. The weight of my zero status hung on me as he refused to look my way.

I spun and stalked off the other direction.

The morning flew by on anxiety-hyped wings. I lingered at the edge of the cafeteria, scanning the room and hoping to flag down Simon before Raf found me. Simon was missing in action, but Raf waved from his seat in the middle of the cafeteria. I would have to explain to Simon later why I ditched him, but he wouldn't want to be seen with me in the lunch room anyway.

The wide circular lunch table seated ten, with chairs still sticky from last period's lunch. Two students on the opposite side pretended not to watch as I slid into the seat next to Raf. I did a final check of the cafeteria for Simon and wondered what I could possibly say to Raf that would make any sense. *Guess what, Raf? I can control minds!*

My fingers drummed the table top. Maybe I should let him go first. "You wanted to talk?" His tortured face only made me jumpier. "What?"

He gripped his knees. "Kira, I'm sorry."

"Huh?" I said. "Sorry for what?"

He dropped his voice so it wouldn't carry over the quiet rustlings of the cafeteria. "I'm sorry I tried to kiss you in the chem lab. I thought that maybe... well, I couldn't tell. I guess you didn't want me to." He was biting his lip and his pain was tearing into my heart.

"Raf, it's not that I didn't..." His ink-pool eyes filled with hope. I traced the non-slip pattern on the table. "It's not that I wouldn't want you to..." This was impossible to say. He leaned closer, so I rushed to get the words out. "If things were different, I mean."

"Different?" He tipped back, his dark eyebrows knitting a frown. "Different how?"

I looked away from Raf, and caught sight of Simon leaning against the Blue Devil mascot painted on the far wall of the cafeteria. His crossed arms and angry stare brought back his icy words. *You're not the only one with a secret.*

All thoughts of telling Raf the truth flew away like birds scattering before an approaching cat. What would Simon do? I couldn't chance finding out. I fisted my hand on the table and then flattened it, debating which lie to tell Raf. The one where I was a zero? Or the one where I read minds? The truth wasn't an option, and the lies were all I had. I looked Raf in the eyes and told him the only truth I could. "If *I* was different, Raf."

His nose wrinkled in disgust. "Is that what this is all about? Because you haven't changed? I don't *care* about that, Kira!"

His incredulous tone attracted the attention of students two tables away, and his thoughts must have been rippling through their minds as well. I kept my voice quiet, but I couldn't help being harsh. "Well you should! I'm not like you." His mouth hung open. I balled my fists and was tempted to pummel the truth into him. Because that *was* the truth and he had to know it, as much as he wanted to pretend otherwise. Instead, I ground my hands into the tops of my legs. "You're going to go to college and meet the future Mrs. Lobos Santos and live happily ever after. And I'm not. I'm not normal like you. I'm never going to be." The bare truth of that burned a hole through my chest and tears stung my eyes.

I tried to blink them back. Simon now stood at attention, his hands clenched at his side. Panic climbed up my back.

"You could still change, Kira," Raf was saying. "And it doesn't matter anyway!" A sudden urge to move gripped me. Before Simon could do something worse than glare at us, I had to get away from Raf. I rose so quickly, I stumbled across the chair.

Raf got up to stop me from leaving. He moved close, hovering over me, as if he could impress me with his height or sincerity, but all I saw were the puppet strings that Simon could cut in an instant.

Raf's voice trembled. "You're my best friend, Kira."

I edged away from him. "You've always been my best friend, Raf." Fear made my voice sharp. "But that's all we can be." The broken look on Raf's face was more than I could stand.

I left him standing in the middle of the cafeteria.

chapter FOURTEEN

I tore through the cafeteria door and blindly stumbled down the hallway.

I tried not run past the few loitering students, but my legs were so strung with tension I could have sprinted all the way home without stopping. I turned a corner, but Simon caught up to me. A sudden tug at my elbow spun me to face him.

"Well." The glare still chiseled his features. "I understand things a little better now."

"Understand what?" I jutted my chin out and refused to be intimidated.

"Why you're so afraid to jack into your boyfriend's head."

My stomach did backflips. "He's not my boyfriend."

"Not for lack of trying." His words were biting, his smile cruel. "But you almost killed him when you jacked him. Didn't you?"

A tremble ran up my arms. *How did he know?* "You were in Raf's head." The accusation hung between us like a poisoned dagger.

"Of course." He didn't quite sneer, but it felt like a slap anyway.

I stifled my anger. *He was in Raf's head. From across the cafeteria.* No one read minds that far. "You didn't... did you jack him?" My mind rewound over Raf's words. It didn't make sense for Simon to force Raf to say those things.

"No." Simon's dark look was back. "I was waiting for *you* to do it."

My shoulders sagged and the fight drained out of me. "I couldn't."

The hardness on his face dissolved, and he heaved a heavy sigh. "You're not *like* him, Kira. You're never going to be like him. We're *different*. Eventually you'll have to jack into his head and control him like everyone else. That's who we are."

I clamped my eyes shut. What good were crazy mind powers when they forced me to control or lie to the people I loved?

Simon touched my cheek. "I know it's tough," he said. "But you need to accept it." His fingers were warm under my chin. "You're a mindjacker and that's not going to change. Jacking is what you're meant to do."

I drew in a deep breath. I could feel the rightness of Simon's words, even if it twisted my insides. All those years of wishing hadn't changed me into a reader. And Raf would never change into a jacker either. We were stuck with who we were.

Students trickled out of the cafeteria and headed for class. They had normal lives and bright futures like Raf. Simple problems like who to date and how to pass their classes.

I will never be like them. My breath leaked out as I

contemplated jacking all of them. Every day.

Simon glanced down the hall. "It's time for class. Promise me you'll try. With *everyone*."

I hesitated. The last time in math class hadn't exactly ended well. "What about Taylor?"

"If she starts thinking trash about you again, I'll knock her out myself."

I gave a short laugh. "All right. I'll try."

"That's my girl." He beamed a smile that seemed to lift me. We walked to class, and Simon lingered close this time. We took seats in the back of class, and I knew what he expected.

Mr. Barkley stood at the board in his starched, white shirt. I crept into his mind, just enough to hear his thoughts. *Linking in*, was what Simon had called it. Mr. Barkley's mind-scent was like crisp apples on a fall day, and his whispering voice in my ear bud spoke a perfect echo of his thoughts.

I always knew he was treating me right.

I wasn't sure what to do next. *You can hear my thoughts*, I told him. *I'm saying hello.* I made the command soft, closer to a suggestion. Mr. Barkley gazed across the rows of chairs and searched for my face. When he found it, I smiled. *Good afternoon, Mr. Barkley.*

His eyes flew wide and he almost spoke aloud. Then a smile lit his face and filled his thoughts. *Good afternoon, Ms. Moore.* He continued the lesson without the whispering commentary. I slipped the hearing aid out and stuffed it in my pocket.

I had more important things to do today than review tangents. I slowly linked into every mind in the class, first the ones nearby, then the rest, but still avoiding Taylor. I linked a mild echo of Mr. Barkley, so that each student believed they heard my thoughts. No longer a mental blank spot, I was part of the chorus of background voices that filled the classroom with mental noise.

It became clear why the silence that made my skin itch was so essential. The cacophony of voices was almost too much to bear. Any audible sound would have been a cymbal crashing on top of the discordant symphony reverberating in my head. How much had I missed, how much life had passed me by while I was an unknowing zero?

I garnered a few brief stares. A thought wave rippled through the class, pulsing my name as everyone became aware that I had changed. *They think I'm a reader.* A rush thrilled my body, a high that made me float in my seat.

I had become visible.

Simon smiled his approval, but then tipped his head toward Taylor. She peered around the other students to find the source of the chatter. I drew in a deep breath and linked into her mind. She thought I was some strange enigma. If she only had any idea. I nudged her mind to let her hear the whisper of my mind's presence.

I thought you were... she thought.

I changed.

Thoughts of Raf and me flitted through her brain. Then she started mentally humming a song. This earned her frowns and irritated thoughts from her neighbors, who were closer to her and heard it louder. I shot a quizzical look at Simon.

He whispered, "She can't keep you out if you jack all the way in."

I had no desire to go deeper into Taylor's mind. I shook my head, and he just shrugged.

Mr. Barkley finally noticed Taylor's humming. Without turning around, he had a thought that riveted the class. *Is there a problem, Ms. Sampson?*

She immediately stopped the noise. *No, sir.*

Mr. Barkley's lecture echoed in every mind, but stray thoughts flitted by as well. Random ideas about lunch or homework, and a surprising number of fantasies like Taylor's, starring the thinker's most recent crush. Everyone's thoughts were open to me, with the exception of Simon. His linked thoughts echoed in the other minds, but they were simple repeats of Mr. Barkley.

The mind-scents of the class blended like a wild country potpourri.

I spent the rest of class pretending to take notes, while trying to juggle a classroom full of minds. When the bell finally rang, my body ached from the tension of maintaining the illusion that I was a reader. I stretched out the kinks as we gathered our backpacks.

Simon walked me out into the hallway. I withdrew from the minds of the math students as they drifted away into the swarm of people. Simon stopped and tugged me to the side. My eyes flew wide that he would touch me openly. He dropped his hand.

"That was perfect." He moved toward me, eyes intense, and walked me two steps back to the lockers. "Time to come out and play, Kira."

I started to ask him what he meant, but his hands were on my cheeks, and he crashed his lips onto mine. My entire body stilled, every sense focused on the contact between us. I wondered if this was how Raf's lips would have felt if our near-kiss in the chem lab hadn't ended in catastrophe. I dropped the backpack that had been dangling off one arm as Simon welded my body to the cold, riveted lockers. When he pulled back, I was amazed that one kiss could make it so difficult to breathe.

I knew nothing about first kisses—they belonged with boyfriends and college in the category of things I wouldn't have as long as I was a zero. But Simon's kiss made my face burn, and that didn't seem right.

I sucked in a ragged breath. The hall had gone still, everyone facing us.

"They're staring," I whispered. My lips were still singed from our blatant display.

"That's because I told them you were a changeling," he whispered back.

"You did *what*?" As I spoke, the students turned away in unison, as if suddenly moving on cue. Which must be exactly what Simon told them to do. The normal ebb and flow in the hall resumed as though it had never stopped. I sputtered, not knowing what to say, or even what to think. The crowd thinned as students hurried to their final period of the day.

"Welcome to real life, Kira," Simon said. "Come on, I have some friends for you to meet."

chapter FIFTEEN

A storm of emotions raged through me, like a changeling being driven demens.

Anger that Simon had outed me as a changeling. Humiliation that he had wantonly kissed me in public. A feeling I didn't want to name had my body still on fire from that kiss.

Simon led me by the hand toward the bleachers. A few students clustered at the top, the supposed friends he wanted me to meet, but everyone else was in class.

I settled on indignant outrage. "You had no right to do that!" I yanked my hand out of his and stopped in my tracks.

He threw me a playful look. "Worked well, though."

"What do you mean by *that*?" Heat radiated from the gravelly surface of the parking lot, but that wasn't what burned my ears. He could at least admit he shouldn't have broadcast my supposed *change* to the entire school, much less kissed me in front of everyone.

"I mean, you can't come out as a changeling one person at a time, or even a class at a time. If you really were a changeling, everyone would know, Kira." His patronizing tone made my fists curl. For the second time today, I was tempted to physically strike a large, stupid boy looming over me. Instead, I turned on my heel and strode back to the school building. That he was right only fueled the raging storm inside me.

"Kira, wait!" He was quickly by my side, but I wasn't slowing down. "I'm sorry?"

"You had no right." I kept my eyes trained on the back door. Simon tugged at my elbow, and I faced him with clenched fists.

"You're right, I didn't," he said. "But it was the only way. If you'd jacked thirty kids, and no one else, someone would get suspicious. Like your boyfriend."

"He's not my boyfriend." The fire inside me blazed anew, having to say those words again.

"So you keep saying."

I glared at him and then the door, debating my options. I could leave him here in the parking lot, show him what little I thought of him and his stupid comments. But I would have to face the other students inside, and word would have spread like wildfire about my status. Or I could go with Simon and meet his friends. Whoever *they* were.

Or I could go home and crawl under the covers and never come out.

Simon brushed away a strand of hair that was whipping around my face in the heated breeze. "I'm kind of hoping you mean it."

I leaned away from his touch. "Mean what?"

"That he's not your boyfriend." He stepped closer. "I was

hoping that position was open."

My mouth flopped open but nothing came out, like a fish out of water and drowning in air. Simon smiled, and he seemed to enjoy making me flustered. Before I could muster a scathing retort, he said, "Don't worry about that now." He bit his lip in a way that made me want to both kiss him and smack that grin off his face. "Will you come meet my crew?"

I glanced at the students hanging out at the top of the risers.

"No thanks." I spun and marched away from his waiting friends. My anger slowly seeped out with every hot-soled step across the pavement, but the embarrassment was still hot in my cheeks. I weaved in between faculty cars and headed for the front of school.

Simon caught up to me near a teacher's sporty black hydro car. "Kira, wait."

I stopped to give him a withering look.

He held up his hands. "At least let me give you a ride home."

I stared, uncomprehending for a second, then my eyes flew wide. "That belongs to *you*?"

He stepped closer to the car and gave me a sheepish smile when it beeped the unlock tone. I didn't know any students that drove to school, much less had their own car. My family shared the hydro car, but my dad would laugh himself silly if I asked to drive it to school.

I circled slowly around the car. "Is your family made of money?"

He gave a short laugh. "No."

He held the passenger side door open, beckoning me. I

decided that giving me a ride home was the least Simon could do. I climbed into the low seat, which shifted to hug me in a soft embrace. A frosty wind from the vents blasted away the hot outside air, and Simon ran around to slide into the driver's seat.

"How can you afford this?" I asked.

He shrugged. "I got a great deal."

I pictured Simon jacking a dealer to sell him this luxury car for a pittance. Simon nudged the joystick, and his too-fast car spun out of the parking lot like a silent black cat.

An empty feeling hollowed out my chest.

I gave Simon directions, and he parked his suspiciously expensive sports car in front of my house. The second floor windows were dimmed against the afternoon light. The drive had me home early, so my mom shouldn't expect me yet. I hoped like crazy she wouldn't decide to clean the windows today.

"Give me your phone," Simon said. I hesitated, then fished it out of my backpack and traded with him. His phone was shiny black, with a mindware interface image floating above the surface. I stared at it while he fussed with mine.

He looked up. "It's got mindware. Just jack in and program your number." My eyebrows hiked high on my forehead. I could jack into mindware? I reached forward and a sour metallic taste tinged the back of my tongue, but the holographic matrix display hovering above the phone shifted with my mental touch. I quickly navigated the software and entered my number.

My smile snuck out as we exchanged phones again.

"I'll scrit you later?" He seemed to be asking permission. I gave him a shrug, not wanting him to think I'd entirely forgiven him yet.

Simon's outrageous, and probably felonious, car sped away before I reached the front door. I expected to find my mom in the kitchen, but it was empty, so I snagged a banana off the counter and headed to my room.

I had the banana half peeled and was about to take a bite when I swung into my room and stopped short. Mom stood next to my shelves and whirled around when she heard me. My bed was neatly made, which was different than the way I left it, and the sweet stench of furniture polish lingered in the air. My track trophies from junior high were glossier than before, and the flotilla of tiny souvenir sailboats from my dad's overseas travels had a new shine. I couldn't imagine what she could find snooping in my room, but I scowled at her anyway.

"I was only... cleaning up," she said, guilt written on her face. "You're home early." She said this like it was some kind of excuse for being in my room. Which it wasn't.

I slowly dropped my backpack on the bed. I could jack into her head and find out what she was up to, but my stomach still clenched at the idea. I mostly wanted her out so I could retreat under the covers and try to forget the day.

"Did you find anything interesting in my room?" I let my sarcasm drip.

She ignored the bait and pulled down a picture from the shelf. An image of me and my brother mugging in front of a snowman flashed by. "Have you talked to Seamus lately?" she asked.

I blinked at the change in conversation. "Um, no. Did he call?"

"No. I just miss him, you know? Will you tell him, the next time you talk to him?"

Ah. This was mom-speak for *whatever is bothering you, call Seamus and he'll help you work it out.* Mom could be pretty tricky when she wanted.

"Yeah, okay."

She put the picture back on the stripped-down shelf, with only a couple other frames and Raf's green stuffed monster. I wondered if she noticed the difference. She gave me wide berth on her way out and called back from the hall. "There are snacks if you want them."

Once she was gone, I flopped down on my bed.

My phone vibrated in my backpack and I dug it out. Maybe Simon had finally decided to come up with a real apology.

It was Raf.

Oh no. I dropped the phone like it might bite me.

Raf must have heard about Simon outing me in the hallway. Like the rest of school, he would think I was a changeling now, right after telling him that I was different and would never change.

The phone buzzed in its crater on my pink comforter. When it stopped, I gingerly picked it up. Raf hadn't left a message.

I wished I could call Seamus, like Mom hinted in her sneakiness, and tell him all about what had happened. But I knew that would only make things a bigger disaster than they already were.

I scrit Seamus instead. *Mom misses you. Tell her we talked and all's good.* Hopefully Seamus would call Mom and have my back, rather than freaking out and calling me. A minute later, he scrit back, *U ok?*

Just need backup.

Got your six, sis.

Seamus was as mesh as big brothers came, but I was glad he was a thousand miles away at West Point. If he was here, he might try to pound on Simon.

And that wouldn't be good for anyone.

chapter SIXTEEN

Raf waited until Saturday afternoon to seek me out.

I was lounging on my bed, coincidentally trying to finish my English reading, when I heard Mom answer the door. I knew it was Raf when I heard his footfalls slowly climbing the stairs.

I had hoped he had forgotten, but I should have known that simmering Portuguese temper of his wouldn't let him stay away. Back in seventh grade, Lenny Johnson had suffered Raf's wrath when he flung a spitball into my hair. It had taken Raf three days to find someone with the combination to Lenny's locker, but only a day after that to cover everything in it with purple ooze he had cooked up in chemistry. I only hoped that Raf's anger wouldn't result in locker full of something disgusting. Although I probably deserved it.

Raf's soccer-trained footfalls pounded a tempo on the last flight of steps. He slowed his pace halfway up, which gave me a few more seconds to get twitchy about what he would say. *Kira, why didn't you tell me you're a changeling? Kira, why did you lie to me?*

I could link into his head and get a preview of his questions. Or I could simply jack in and command him to go away. My shoulders quivered at that thought. I was a liar by necessity. But I didn't have to be a cheat, too. Besides, I didn't trust myself in Raf's head.

He filled my doorway with his broad shoulders. His chest rose and fell underneath his Blue Devil soccer jersey, like he was breathing in the courage to speak.

"Why?" he asked.

I tried to look innocent and failed miserably. "Why what?"

"Why *him*?"

Oh. My eyes widened a bit. He hadn't just heard about my coming out as a changeling. Raf had somehow seen the kissing episode with Simon. Of course. Like every other reader in Warren Township High, he had seen it the minds of the rumor-swirling population.

My heart crumpled under Raf's look of betrayal. I had told him we couldn't be more than friends because I was *different*, and now Simon had let everyone know I was the *same*. And kissing Simon had made the insult a hundred times worse than the injury.

Raf wanted an explanation, but this time I had trapped myself in a box of lies. From Raf's perspective, nothing could justify my bizarre behavior. I couldn't explain what Raf couldn't ever know—that Simon and I were both mindjacking freaks. If Raf discovered our secret, there was no telling what Simon would do.

Keeping Raf in the dark was keeping him safe, but it was

tearing my heart into tiny pieces. As I struggled for something to say, Raf's face shed anger like the tears that were falling off my cheeks. He seemed to want to step into the room, then changed his mind at the last second. He crossed his arms and remained in the doorway, not caving in to my pathetic display.

"Why didn't you tell me?" he asked. "About changing," he clarified.

"I... I..." There was no way out of this hole. "I wasn't sure it was real. I didn't expect Simon to tell everyone." That, at least, was the truth. I wiped away the tears I had no right to have.

Raf drew his thick black eyebrows together and threw his arms out in frustration. "Everyone is uncertain when it happens, Kira. If you had talked to me, I could have told you that."

"I... I..." Stuttering was worse than not talking at all. "I wanted to wait until I was sure."

Raf's face darkened. "Wait. How come I can't read you?"

I sucked in a quick breath. "Um, it, ah... still doesn't work all the time. I can't hear your thoughts either right now." I bolted off the bed because the agitation in my legs couldn't be contained any longer. I pressed my fists into my desk while I pretended to look out the window at the thin slices of grass between houses. Should I jack him to stop asking questions? Link in? Could I keep my secret, if I did?

I didn't realize Raf had crossed the room until he covered one of my hands with his. I closed my eyes. I couldn't bear the softness of his hand on mine when I had nothing but lies for him.

"That's how it is, sometimes," he said, softly. "Changeling

abilities flip on and off for a while. It's nothing to be ashamed of." He tugged my hand, wanting me to turn. It was bad enough to lie from far away. I opened my eyes and stepped back, pulling my hand from his.

He gritted his teeth. "Why won't you let me help you?" he asked. "I'm your friend, but you turn to this guy Simon, when you're going through the change? Why?"

There was nothing I could say without hurting Raf even more.

He stepped closer, and I backed away in equal measure. He fisted his hands at his side. "I don't care if you've changed or not," he said. "If you don't want to be—whatever—more than friends, then fine. At least let me help you with this. And stay away from Simon."

My lies and frustration were fueling a fire inside me. "I can hang out with whoever I want!"

"Kira, I promised Seamus I'd look out for you. Guys like Simon are nothing but trouble."

"*What?*" I demanded. "You and Seamus don't get to decide who I date!"

"You're *dating* him now?"

"So what if I am?"

Raf's Portuguese accent tortured his words. "So he is taking advantage of you!"

"How is that any different than *you*?"

His face blotched red and his jaw worked, but no sounds came out. He unclenched his fists and stalked toward the door. Pausing at the doorway, he gripped the frame and swayed slightly. He turned his head to the side. "I'll leave you alone, Kira. Since that's what you want."

And then he was gone.

I sank to the floor. When the front door banged shut, I wrapped my arms around my chest to keep the sobs from shaking me apart. My mom appeared and her arms lifted me like I was a child. She nearly carried me to the bed, where we huddled and I cried until there were no tears left. Then I only shook. Mom held me and asked no questions, which was just as well.

I had no more lies in me.

chapter SEVENTEEN

Eventually night came.

I was the worst friend that had ever lived. All Raf got from me was lies and insults to his face. I resembled that sludge, the green stuff that forms a slimy coating on the outside of cheese that was so old it had become hazardous waste.

That was me: toxic green ooze.

There was nothing to do with cheese like that but throw it out. And Raf had done exactly that. Good for him. He deserved much better than I gave him today.

Maybe he would find a decent girl now, like Taylor. Sure, she was a yippy dog, but at least dogs were loyal. You could count on them. They didn't lie, and they licked your face because they were so happy to see you.

I pressed my face into the pillow. I felt like throwing up.

Raf should find someone better than Taylor. Maybe now that I had pushed him away, he would find a girl who wouldn't lie and wouldn't yip. One who would stick by him and not insult him to his face. The tears came back and rolled down my nose and off the tip, adding to the growing stain on the pillow.

Eventually, the well of my ridiculous self-pity ran dry. I burrowed under the covers, still dressed in my clothes. Sometime later, Mom switched off the light. I wished I could call Seamus, but I'd have to tell more lies, and I couldn't stomach the idea.

A jittery buzzing sound started and then ceased. I wondered if a fly had somehow been trapped in my room. My head cleared enough to realize it was my phone. I dragged myself out of bed and retrieved the dancing phone from my backpack. Its blue glow lit the room. *Simon.*

Look out your window.

My head whipped around to the darkened window above my desk. I stumbled across the room and dialed the window up to clear. Simon stood in the grassy space between our house and the neighbor behind us.

What are you doing? I scrit him.

Come down and find out.

I was debating a nice retort, when the floorboards creaked upstairs, giving me a great excuse. *My mom's still awake.*

So jack her to look the other way.

It was a dare. I glared at the dark form below, his face lit up by the blue glow of his phone. I didn't want Simon to know I still wasn't jacking my mom. He seemed like a wild thing I should keep as far away from my family as possible.

I could probably sneak out without my mom hearing. I had never done that before, but this week was full of firsts. Besides, sitting in my room and crying over Raf wasn't making my life any better.

I tiptoed past the stairs to my parents' bedroom level and stole down the two flights to the ground level. Picking up my shoes on the way, I crept out the front door. Simon's black panther car waited at the curb. The interior light came on, and I dropped into the passenger seat without a word. As the light faded, Simon's eyebrows pulled together.

"What's wrong?" he asked. My eyes must have still been red from the crying.

"I don't want to talk about it." He didn't press, just pulled up the mindware interface for the car and set an autopath. We slid noiselessly away from the curb. A block from my house, Simon mentally commanded on the headlights.

"Where are we going?" I asked.

"We're meeting my crew, but I have a stop to make first."

We drove a while in silence, streetlights pulsing by. I suspected that we had left Gurnee. It was hard to tell in Chicago New Metro. One town was the same as the next, a seamless flow of spindly houses as closely packed as range ordinances would allow. We passed the Great Lakes Naval Station where my dad worked and pulled up to a convenience store. It was just this side of dangerous and definitely shady.

Simon climbed out of the car, forcing me to follow or be left behind. It seemed safer to go with him. Plasma lights harshly lit the inside of the store. As we stepped through the door, I linked into the head of the attendant. Even though we were out past curfew on the praver side of town, he barely noticed us, instead watching a late night tru-cast whispering from his hand-held screen.

Simon draped his arm over my shoulder and steered us through aisles of ancient snacks and dusty bags of diapers. The only things not coated in dust were emergency boost canisters of hydrogen for hydro cars on empty and an impressive display of beef jerky. We stopped at a refrigerated case. Simon used a mental command to open it and pulled out a four-pack case of green beer bottles.

"What are you doing?" I hissed under my breath and checked the attendant's thoughts. He was watching Magnum Magistrate interrogate two neighbors in a range infringement dispute.

"Don't worry, there aren't any security cameras here," said Simon.

"You've got to be kidding," I said. The frosted glass door swung closed. Simon steered us back toward the front and set the beers down with a clinking of glass on glass. The attendant still clutched his screen in his gnarled hands. He let out an elaborate sigh, muted the screen, and set it aside as Magnum Magistrate took a break to consider his judgment.

Simon's command echoed through the attendant's mind. *We're going to buy this.*

Well, sure you're going to buy that. But you need some money, friend.

From the tired sound of his thoughts, this wasn't the first time Simon had jacked him to illegally sell beer. I nervously checked the parking lot. With my luck, one of my dad's Navy buddies would stroll in to find his friend's daughter buying alcohol.

Simon handed the man two pieces of white plastic, both small and square. The attendant took the cards and held one up, examining it as if it wasn't completely blank. In his mind, the card appeared to be a driver's license with Simon's picture. He handed that one back to Simon and scanned the other one—which appeared to be a tally card—through the register. It beeped its complaint about swiping a useless bit of plastic, but in the attendant's mind, a dozen unos were deducted from Simon's account. He returned the fake tally card to Simon.

Do you want a bag? the attendant thought.

No, thanks. Simon grinned as he picked up the beers and walked me out of the store.

When we were back in the car, I crossed my arms. "I am not drinking that." If Simon's grand plan was to take me out for a night of drinking, he was sadly mistaken.

"Neither am I," he said. "I'm not interested in fuzzing up my mind with beer."

Sometimes the boy was simply demens. "You committed a misdemeanor to buy beer you're not going to drink?"

"The beer's for Martin. We're just going for the fun."

I was sure Simon's idea of fun and mine were not the same.

chapter EIGHTEEN

I held my complaints as we wove though a ramshackle suburb that resembled downtown Chicago. People wandered outside ancient apartments that hadn't been rehabbed to range codes, fuzzed out on obscura or beer, trying to escape their crowded living conditions with distance or intoxication. I breathed a little easier when we left the slums and drove past a forest preserve turned black by the night. It was closed after dark, but keeping with our law-breaking activities for the evening, Simon pulled into the entrance. The car's beams sliced white blades through the ash trees lining the forest drive.

"Are you going to tell me what's going on?" Suffering in my room would be better than getting arrested tonight.

"Kira, relax. We're just meeting some friends to do some dipping."

"Dipping?"

He didn't answer and pulled to the side of the main road. About fifty feet from the road, pinpricks of light danced in the meadow. Simon shut off the car, and the moonlight painted his face silver.

"Dipping is something readers do," he said. "One person does the drinking while the rest dip into their fuzz by touching them somewhere on their bare skin." He demonstrated by tapping my cheek with his fingertips. "They feel all the effects without the actual intoxication or hangover. Except for the drinker. They're pretty messed up the next day."

"I thought... you couldn't, you know, touch without..."

His smile folded into a smirk. "Without getting a little too close for comfort?"

This entire situation was making me uncomfortable.

"That's why they only dip for a second," he said. "Only long enough for the effects to be felt, without all the uncomfortable closeness. Believe me, nobody wants to get that close to Martin."

Now that my eyes had adjusted to the moonlight, I could see figures attached to the flashlights in the dancing light show. "I don't know about this."

"Don't worry." He stroked my cheek where he had tapped. "You won't feel it. You're not a reader, remember?"

Like I could forget that.

"That's why you have to fake it."

I looked askance at him. "Right. Why are we doing this, again?"

He leaned back. "You're a changeling now. Time to be part of the crowd. Blending in makes you seem less suspicious." His voice grew serious. "The worst thing is for people to know what we are, Kira. You have to keep the code of silence."

My eyebrows flew up. "Code of silence?"

"That's just what I call it. The vow of perpetual silence," he intoned with mock solemnity. "Trust me; you don't want people to know what you can do."

I didn't trust Simon, but I knew he was right about that. If people knew we could control them, life would be a whole lot worse. In ways I didn't even want to think about.

The lights in the field had settled low to the ground. Pretending to party with Simon's friends wouldn't be my worst lie of the day. Simon retrieved the case of beer, and we tromped through the grassy field, chirping insects falling silent as we invaded their territory. Simon's merry band huddled on a blanket thrown over the weeds.

I hesitantly linked to them once we were within range. Their chatter roared to life, clamoring in my mind, and I stumbled over a rock hidden in the grass. Their thoughts and mind-scents blended together. Bald curiosity rippled through their minds.

The mental volume stepped down as Simon introduced me. *This is Kira.* His thoughts echoed in their minds.

The girl put a flashlight under her chin and made a face. *Hi Kira, I'm Katie.* Her dark wiry hair was pulled into a ponytail, which exploded into a puff.

Hi, I linked the thought to her. She looked me up and down and pictured a girl that wouldn't be happy about how pretty I was. Before I had a chance to respond, the muscle-bound blond who sat next to her rumbled in with, *Hey, Kira.* His name was Zach and his shirt sleeve was rolled up to reveal pale skin darkened by tattoos. A third boy, Miguel, lounged at the very edge of the blanket, a blade of grass hanging from his mouth. He chimed in with a subdued, *Hey*. I probed and found he was the artist behind Zach's tattoos.

In the dead center sat a boy that must be Martin, the designated drinker. His gangly arms seemed too long for his body, and his legs were folded up like a floppy doll.

His eyes were on Simon. *Did you get it?*

Simon handed him the pack of beers, and Martin tore the paper binding apart. The glass bottles spilled out and clanked together on the blanket. He opened a beer and chugged the entire thing in a long series of gulps. Simon gestured for me to sit near Martin, then sat next to me. He shifted close, nearly touching my leg and earning a raised eyebrow from Katie. An image of Simon pinning me against the lockers flashed through Katie's mind, and my tangle of emotions flared again. She must have seen the whole thing or caught it in the thought-speed rumor mill. The image of a blond girl stomping off pulsed through her mind. I put two and two together. Simon avoided my gaze.

So, Kira, what are you, a freshman? Zach asked. He thought he was very funny.

I linked my thoughts to all of them at once. *No. What are you, a second-year senior?*

Then I heard the most amazing thing. Mental laughter. It sounded like tinkling bells and soft sizzling and little breathy snorts. I was pretty sure the last one came from Miguel. None of them laughed out loud.

I see why you like her, Katie thought. Then Simon's voice rang loud through all their minds, *She's all right.* They all echoed it back. *She's all right. All right. Right.*

Simon finally met my gaze and gave me a crooked smile.

Martin pitched the empty beer bottle into the darkness, and it landed with a soft swish of prairie grass. He cracked open another and flung the bottle cap after the first.

The five of us mindtalked about nothing: the bugs; the blessed event that was the weekend; the lack of true art in tattooing today. I struggled to keep up with the four simultaneous conversations. Their thoughts were lightning fast and played over each other, like strings on a guitar, harmonizing yet separate. Simon's linked thoughts played along, subdued in the harmony and not echoing through their minds, unlike his jacked in command before. It was difficult to keep up, and I wondered how readers managed it all day, every day.

As Martin finished the second beer, Katie and Zach shuffled nearer to him, and even Miguel sidled closer. Martin sent the second bottle sailing and cracked open a third, giving a tremendous belch that sent twitters of mental laughter ringing around the blanket. As he chugged the third one, I leaned away from him. If Martin's stomach rebelled against the onslaught of alcohol, I didn't want to be in spewing distance. No one else was concerned, so I tried to relax.

Martin burst out singing in his head, some bawdy song I didn't recognize.

Jesus, Mary and Joseph, Miguel thought. *If you're going to sing, man, I'm leaving.*

No one's making you stay. Martin sent the third empty flying. With a crash of glass, the bottle met its mates in the weeds. A mental grumble went around the blanket, but no one moved to leave. In fact, they edged closer to Martin, who let his hands fall by his sides. His head flopped forward and his lips moved slightly, as if he'd forgotten that he didn't need to use them.

Good beer, Simon.

Miguel tapped his finger on Martin's bare foot, exposed as he sat cross-legged on the blanket. Martin flinched at his touch and then stilled. Katie and Zach rhythmically touched the outstretched fingers of one hand. Simon gestured to Martin's other hand, a pale silver fish flopped on the blanket. Simon and I each took a different finger. Martin's skin was as clammy as it looked. As for faking the effect of the beer, I wasn't sure what to do. Martin was breathing heavily, and Miguel's eyes were closed. Their thoughts were jumbled.

I glanced at Katie and Zach and was shocked to see them holding tight to each other and kissing. Katie's dark skin mashed against Zach's pale face mesmerized me until the brush of Simon's lips near my ear made me jump.

"This is the fun part." His whisper sent a shudder down to the spot where his hand pressed the small of my back. I jerked away. He gave me a measured look, then pulled me up from the blanket and led me across the meadow, away from his heavily fuzzed friends.

Halfway to the car, he veered to a glistening boulder sitting lonely in the meadow. He leaned against it and laced his fingers with mine. The moon glazed half his face with light, and his hair fell loose in a frame of darkness.

"Still mad at me?" he asked.

"Yes." I pulled my hand away and rubbed my eyes, even more

tired than when I juggled thirty minds in math. At least in class they weren't all talking to me at the same time.

"Is it always this hard?" I asked. "This jacking thing is wiping me out."

"You'll get used to it."

I wondered how long it would take for me to pass for a reader easily, like Simon. I gazed at the partiers who were still linked and kissing and drinking. "Did I do okay?"

"You did great."

I peered up into his dark eyes. "When did you know? That you could mindjack?"

He studied the weeds in the distance. "When I put my sister in a coma over a fight about... something. I can't really remember what it was. I was twelve."

I held my breath, not sure what to say. "Simon, I'm sorry..."

He shrugged and leaned back on the rock. "It took me three weeks to figure out I could wake her up again."

"You were just a kid." I remembered my panic that first day, when I had knocked Raf out and thought I might slay the whole school if I went to class. What if I hadn't inadvertently woken Raf up? I placed a hand on Simon's shoulder, but his face stayed blank.

"You didn't have anyone to help you," I said. "You couldn't have known."

He ducked his head, examining the prairie grass at our feet. His hair fell forward, masking his face in shadow. I wanted to brush it back.

"Well, she's off to college now," he said. "So I guess there was no permanent damage."

I swallowed. "I'm lucky to have you to help me." He looked up, and a smile ghosted across his face. He smoothed down some tendrils of my hair floating in the breeze and stopped with his hand behind my head.

He pulled me closer and his kiss was gentle, but the hot liquid feel of it still made my body sing.

When he broke the kiss, he whispered, "What are you thinking?"

I was thinking that I would rather be kissing than talking, but those words were not going to come out of my mouth, if I could help it. I just shook my head.

"Well, that's new for me," he added. I didn't understand. "Usually, I know what a girl thinks about when I kiss her."

Oh. His smirk drove me to look back to the partiers. Simon had probably kissed a lot of girls before me. Girls that knew what they were doing in the kissing department. I ordered the blood out of my cheeks. Somehow my mind powers didn't extend to controlling my own bodily reactions.

"Hey. What?" He tipped his head to try to catch my eye.

"I don't think I blend very well."

"You're not like them." He touched my cheek to bring me back. "You're much better."

Considering we lied to everyone about who we were, I didn't feel much in the way of superiority. "How do you do it?" I asked. "Lying all the time?"

His face hardened into a mask that sent a shiver through me. "You get used to it." He glanced at his crew, still silently dipping to get their fuzz. "We'll never be like them, Kira. Besides, we're just marking time here. We're meant to do greater things."

"What do you mean, greater things?" I was only hoping for *normal*, but somehow *normal* always escaped me.

He lifted his gaze to the trees in the distance. "My birthday's in two weeks," he said with great solemnity, as if that were some fabulous pronouncement. The boy was definitely demens.

"Um, happy birthday?"

"I'll be eighteen," he elaborated. I was just as lost. "Then I'm going to walk into the principal's office and get my diploma. I'm not going to sit around wasting my time in high school."

Could he really graduate as soon as he had reached the age? Of course. I had yet to hear Simon boast. It made me wonder if there was anything he couldn't do.

"What will you do? Get a job?"

"I've been doing some small jobs. If things work out, I'll have something lined up by then."

My suspicions came running out. "Like what?"

"Something better than hanging out here, pretending to be like everyone else."

"Like what?" I repeated, disentangling from his embrace and stepping away. "More petty larceny at the local convenience store?"

He snorted and rolled his eyes. "I've been doing that since I was fourteen, Kira. That's kid stuff. I want to do something more serious."

"What, serious like grand theft auto?"

He crossed his arms. "I can see you don't think much of me."

"Just leave me out of whatever criminal master plan you have." I threw my hands on my hips and matched his rigid stance.

A two-foot gulf opened between us. "After all I've done to help you, this is what I get?" he asked. "Criminal mastermind?" His stare became an ice dagger that plunged into my chest. Echoes of Raf's departing words rang through my head. *I'll leave you alone, Kira. Since that's what you want.* Simon was the only one that understood the bizarre power unleashed in my brain. And I was insulting him to his face. Driving him away. *Just like Raf.*

I let my hands drop to my side, and my gaze sank to the prairie weeds surrounding us. I shifted from one foot to the other. "I'm sorry...," I mumbled. "I just... the whole beer thing kind of threw me." It sounded lame, even to me.

"I was only trying to help you fit in."

The sound of breaking glass reminded me that Martin was still pitching beer bottles. "Hmm," I said. "I'm hoping we *are* better than that bunch."

Simon blazed a smile. "You, at least, are better looking."

"Yeah, well, you're not too bad yourself."

His face went serious, his jaw cutting a sharp line in the moonlight.

"I *am* sorry," I said. "You know, about calling you a criminal."

He studied my face. "Do you trust me?"

I didn't trust Simon, but I knew I needed him, a thought that made my face burn.

I whispered, "I'm not sure what I'd do without you," and

pulled his face down to mine. He gripped my waist and pulled me up so that my toes just kissed the prairie grass. His lips branded mine, and by the time he set me down, I wasn't sure I could stand straight.

My head rested on his chest. I couldn't read his mind, or feel his emotions when we touched, but the way his heart pounded, it seemed like our kiss affected him too.

"So, I was wondering..." His words rumbled under my ear.

I lifted my head. "Yes?"

"...if that boyfriend position was still open?"

"I think it's just been filled."

chapter NINETEEN

The next week was an endless blur of too many minds.

The first few days, I gripped Simon's arm to combat the dizziness of the hallways, brought on by having to constantly shift focus and link with dozens of minds. Simon wore Second Skin gloves for a while so we wouldn't be conspicuous.

The cafeteria was worse.

Ground zero for thought-wave-rumors, people buzzed about the zero-turned-changeling, and why I was dating Simon and not Raf. Our drama was better than the latest big screen sim-cast.

I caught whispers of Raf's thoughts passed from mind to mind. It was like our childhood game of mindtalk, where we pretended to read minds by whispering messages around a circle. The message had been distorted beyond reason by the time it circled back, which had caused us fits of giggles. Only Raf's messages of anger and pain were far from making me laugh.

Raf kept his promise and kept his distance. He couldn't hear my thoughts, unless I jacked other people's minds and sent my thoughts ringing through the room for everyone to hear.

I kept the mindjacking to a minimum in the cafeteria.

Besides, knowing I was a jacker wouldn't hurt Raf any less. It would only put him in danger. If he knew my secret, so would the other reader minds. It wasn't impossible for readers to keep a secret—just very, very difficult. Like trying to not think of pink elephants. The bigger the secret, the harder it was to keep your thoughts away from it.

And Simon and I had a mastodon-sized secret.

Somehow, the thought-rumors hadn't reached my mom. She must be even more isolated than I knew.

My mom still thought I was a zero, Raf thought I was a changeling, and Simon thought I was jacking them both. It was official: I was lying to everyone I knew.

I didn't have much choice about being a liar, but I didn't have to cheat too. In class I could easily pluck the virtual answer key from our teachers' minds for our take-home tests, but I resisted. Cheating wouldn't help me catch up in that race for normal that suddenly seemed within reach.

But to Simon, it wasn't enough for me to pass for a reader. He wanted me to hone my jacking abilities too. Which I did, until I finally was in control—not of other people, but of myself.

Except when Simon kissed me.

There, control eluded me in a fierce way that found me brazenly kissing him at every opportunity, which wasn't often. Readers did their lip-locking in private or at dipping parties where everyone was doing it. Even kissing in front of the crew would have caught us grief unless we jacked them to look the other way. Which Simon occasionally did, leaving a grin on my face that lasted long after the warmth from his lips had faded.

It was all mesh, but by Friday I was exhausted.

Simon and I waited for the crew to ditch class and join us on the bleachers. All my free periods and after school time had been spent with Simon or his crew or practicing my skills. I wanted to catch up on schoolwork over the weekend. Passing for a reader wouldn't count for much if I failed my classes.

Simon caught me off guard by asking me out on a date.

"I have a ton of homework." I whispered so the couple students at the bottom of the bleachers wouldn't overhear. Simon put his hand over his heart and feigned heartbreak.

"You're turning me down for *homework*?"

"And how would I explain being gone on a Saturday night?"

He shifted to serious. "You haven't told your mom about me?"

I squirmed in my seat. "Well, no."

"But you *are* jacking her?"

"Yes." The lies were getting easier every day.

"So, tell her you have a date." His eyes sparkled. "Besides, I'd love to meet your mom."

A warning siren blared in my head. "No, uh, that's not a good idea."

"Why not?"

He wasn't buying this nonsense. It was time to go big and lie large.

"Because my family is very strict. We're Catholic, and my dad's a Navy man, through and through. He always said I could date when I'm, like, thirty."

"Well, let me meet your dad. I'm sure I can convince him otherwise."

The gleam in Simon's eyes made my stomach clench. "My dad's on deployment right now. If he found out I went on my first date while he was gone, he would skin me alive."

Simon threw his hands up. "*You're* the one in control here. Just jack in and tell them it's okay. You don't have to do what they say."

"I can't jack my dad over the phone 7,000 miles away! Unless you have some super-secret power you're holding out on me?"

He narrowed his eyes. "Sneak out." He was challenging me now. I could probably sneak out of the house, but I had to focus on school or all of the lying would be for nothing. And his order didn't sit well with me.

"Maybe I'll tell my mom I'm going out to meet Raf. She'd probably be fine with that."

"*What?*" His eyes went wide. "I thought you were staying away from him." Zach and Katie started hiking up the steps. Simon followed my gaze, but snapped back to stare me down. "Well?"

I dropped my voice. "I'm just saying it would be one way to get out of the house."

He exhaled a long, low breath, and I was glad I couldn't read his mind at that moment.

As they came into thought range, Katie frowned at Simon. *Trouble in paradise?*

Everything's fine. Simon's thoughts boomed in her head.

Oh, everything's fine, she and Zach echoed, serene smiles

relaxing their faces. Jacking feelings was the same as jacking thoughts, but my stomach twisted every time Simon made me do it. I nudged the hard presence of Simon in Katie's mind, a warning. As my skills had improved over the week, I found I could push that marble after all. And I'd push him right out if he kept manipulating Katie.

Simon's eyes flashed, and he nudged back, but the creepy smiles disappeared.

Tell Simon I need to study this weekend. My command rang loud and clear through Katie's mind.

Tell Kira she better not sneak out to see someone besides me. As Katie echoed Simon's words, I threw my hands out in frustration.

Katie, let them fight their own battles, Zach interrupted. *You're killing my fuzz, here.*

Simon pulled out his black mindware phone and bent over it. He must have sent a scrit, but when I gave him a questioning look, he pocketed the phone and ignored me.

The four of us chatted idly, pretending the tenseness didn't exist. Right before the final bell Simon's phone buzzed and he checked and re-pocketed it. He ignored my questioning look again. When the crew got up to leave, Simon shook his head, indicating I should stay. I seriously debated marching off with Katie, but decided I had already angered Simon enough for one day.

When they were out of mind range, he glared at the bleachers for a moment before speaking. "People like us don't follow the rules, Kira," he said. "People like us make them up."

I had spent an entire week passing for a reader. I was finally getting a taste of *normal*, and I liked it. *A lot.* I didn't want to think about the freaks that we really were.

When I didn't respond, Simon asked, "What are you thinking?"

"That I'd rather not be a mutant?" I tried to say it with a smile, but it came out sour.

"We're not, Kira." He pulled me up from the bleacher seat. "Come on, there's someone I want you to meet. If I can't get you out of the house, then we'll have to meet him at school."

"Who is it?" I followed him down the steps.

"Mr. Gerek."

"The shop teacher?" I vaguely remembered him talking to Mr. Gerek in the hall. But why would Simon want me to sneak out to meet his buddy, the shop teacher?

Simon gave a short laugh. "I wasn't sure if you'd recognize the name." His voice had lost its seriousness. "You never took shop, did you?"

"No." Mr. Gerek's class was famously popular, second only to Mr. Chance and his animated sims of the past. But I was seriously disinclined toward tools of any kind. I had taken Advanced Topics Biology instead, which was more useful to a doctor anyway.

"I wondered how you had escaped his notice." The grass crunched under our feet as Simon led me toward the building for our strange after-school meeting with the shop teacher.

"Wait, what?" I said. "What are you talking about?"

"Just come see him?" His voice softened. "He wants to talk to you. It won't take long."

I sighed, but kept following him into the building and out of the heat. The shop class was near the back of the school, crammed with tool chests and instruments that seemed designed to torture wood. Mr. Gerek teetered on a stool next to a giant laser saw and swept a thick-fingered hand over his prematurely balding head. He seemed too large for his seat. Everything, including Mr. Gerek, was covered by a thin film of sawdust.

I reached toward his mind, hoping to get a heads up about this bizarre meeting, but I was shoved away before I could even link in. I whirled to Simon, wondering why he was trying to keep me out of Mr. Gerek's head, but he was busy pulling over a tall stool. I tentatively climbed up, my feet not quite reaching the floor.

"Mr. Gerek, this is Kira Moore," Simon said with great ceremony. Why was he speaking out loud, when everyone at school thought I had gone through the change?

"It's a pleasure to finally meet you, Ms. Moore," Mr. Gerek said. A polite smile graced his face, but his stare was intense and kind of creepy, like he was trying to drill a hole into my head.

"Hello," I said carefully. Something was wrong with this entire situation.

"Simon has some very flattering things to say about you." I shot a look to Simon. He had already retreated to the shop entrance, like he wasn't planning on being a part of the conversation.

"Um, okay," I said. "He hasn't told me anything about you."

Mr. Gerek broke his stare to give Simon a short nod. "Well, if he had, I would have been disappointed in him."

It seemed like I should be asking questions. "What is this is all about?"

"I'm a jacker, Kira," he said. "Like Simon. There are more of us than you probably realize."

My jaw dropped. Simon's face was blank. He had known Mr. Gerek was a jacker all along, but he had let me believe we were the only ones. "Who else?"

"I can't tell you that."

My hands clenched the stool. "Why not?" Mr. Gerek appeared about thirty-five, and if he was a jacker, anyone could be. There could be hundreds, maybe thousands of them. "Are there more at our school?"

"No. At least," he glanced at Simon, "not that I'm aware of. We're rare. But there are many of us in the New Metro area. I can't tell you any more until you've joined the Clan."

Clan? Alarm bells started ringing in my head. "What is that, like, your secret club?"

"The Clan is like a family, Kira," Mr. Gerek said. "We know what it's like to be different." He spread his hands wide. "We only want to extend our welcome. You don't have to be alone anymore."

The alarm in my head cranked to full alert. Simon had lied to me. Mr. Gerek was a jacker, which meant he was a liar too. I didn't know what this Clan was all about, but I doubted they were only concerned about my loneliness. I slid off the high stool and put it between me and Mr. Gerek. I didn't know if either of them intended to let me go, but it was definitely time to leave.

"Okay." I edged away from the chair. "That's a very nice invitation, and I appreciate it, but I should be going now." A quaver had found its way into my voice.

Mr. Gerek remained in his seat, which eased my panic a little. I backed into something solid and let out a yelp.

"Kira, it's okay," Simon said, his face unreadable. "There's nothing to be worried about."

His words didn't reassure me at all. "I'm leaving!"

"It was nice to meet you, Kira," Mr. Gerek called from his seat. "That invitation is open, whenever you're ready for it."

I slipped around Simon and shoved open the shop door. Simon shuffled behind me.

"Kira, stop." He tugged at my elbow.

I wheeled on him and pounded my fists into his chest. "You lied to me!" He shrank back from my blow, which certainly didn't injure him. But he still seemed wounded.

"I didn't lie," he said harshly. "I just didn't tell you everything."

"What's the difference?" I held my fists at my side and resisted the urge to hit him again. Of course he lied to me. Simon was an expert liar.

"You know the difference." His face hardened. "Besides, I couldn't tell you about the Clan. The code of silence is real, and the Clan takes it very seriously. They don't let just anyone in. They have to be careful." He looked me up and down. "I told Mr. Gerek that we could trust you. That you wouldn't tell anyone."

I swallowed. What would the Clan do if I said *no* to their offer? What had Simon gotten me into? "What do they want with me?"

Simon studied the floor for a moment, and then looked into my eyes. "It's like Mr. Gerek said. It's a family. We take care of each other. It's a place where everyone understands what you are."

What I am? I was just a girl who wanted to be a reader like everyone else. I would take being a zero any day over these layers upon layers of lies. The tears started to tickle my throat, and I clenched my teeth against them. They spilled out anyway.

Simon reached to wipe away a tear that had run down my cheek, but I leaned away before he could touch me. "Are you okay?" he asked.

"I don't want to be like this." I couldn't keep the words in. "Why are we like this?"

"I don't know." His voice was soft, almost kind. "I know you don't like it. But in time, you'll see. We have to stick together. And you know you can't tell anyone about the Clan, right?"

"Code of silence?" My voice was bitter.

His smile was grim. "Yeah."

I left him standing in the hallway, unsure if I ever wanted to see him again.

chapter **TWENTY**

I ignored about a dozen scrits from Simon.

As the weekend lurched along, my anger about his secret society of mindjackers fizzled. Of course Simon and I weren't the only two jackers in the world. If I hadn't been adjusting to everything and trying to pass for a reader, I would have figured that out. According to Mr. Gerek, there were jackers all over the Chicago New Metro area, which included half of Illinois and millions of people. Were there hundreds of jackers among those millions? Thousands? Our high school had almost 4,000 students, yet Simon and I were the only jackers. Were we a one-in-two-thousand mutation? Or was it a fluke that we were in the same school? I tried to do the math, but it seemed impossible to know how many jackers were hiding in plain sight, like Mr. Gerek and Simon—and me.

And what was up with this mysterious Clan anyway? Simon claimed they were a family, like some kind of support group for freaks. Did they recruit jackers for their cause, like a band of super-heroes? Shop teacher and secret jacker Mr. Gerek didn't exactly fit the super-hero stereotype, but he didn't seem like a super-villain either.

I didn't know what or who to believe any more.

If I could pass for a reader, college and med school were possible, even if I had to lie to get there. I didn't see how joining a gang of jackers would help with that.

But I didn't want them angry at me either.

On Monday, Simon found me before school and pulled me into an empty hallway where we could talk. "You haven't answered my scrits." He seemed tense, like he thought I would announce the existence of the Clan over the student council's morning tru-cast.

"I've been thinking about what a fantastic liar you are." So maybe I hadn't completely gotten over my annoyance with him.

He set his jaw. "Look, I'm sorry about that, okay? I couldn't tell you anything until I got clearance from Mr. Gerek."

"So, he's the boss of you?" My smile seemed to irritate Simon further.

"No." He let out a frustrated huff. "But he is my contact with the Clan, and I'd rather not mess that up."

I couldn't help being curious. "So what's this business with Mr. Gerek? I mean, if I was a thirty-five-year-old jacker, I'm not sure I'd be a shop teacher."

Simon shook his head and leaned against a paint-chipped locker wall. "He's a great guy. He's been a recruiter for a long time, and he's taught me a lot." He pulled a half-grin. "It still grates on him that I found you first."

"He recruits jackers for the Clan?"

"Yeah. He watches for changeling jackers as they come through the school." He gestured at the empty hall. "Most kids pass through his class around the time they change. He would have found you, but you hadn't changed yet. And you didn't take shop."

"But he found you?"

"Actually, I found him. I changed early, before I got to high school. By the time I went through his class, I was already jacking everyone."

"Show off." I nudged his chest. Maybe I could forgive him. All of Simon's lies were somewhat mitigated by my own half truths—about my mom, about Raf. "So, what does the Clan do?"

He glanced at the still-empty hall. "Well, you could join us and find out." I scowled and he dropped his voice. "It's a place where you can belong. Where you don't have to lie about who you are."

His words pulled at me. I didn't want to admit how much the lies were wearing on me.

"Who all is in the Clan? Besides shop teachers and their students." Maybe my dream of being a doctor didn't have to mean staying away from the Clan. Maybe I could do both.

"There are all kinds of people." He cracked a grin. "Depends on how good your skills are."

I arched an eyebrow. "You mean jacking skills. I suppose your skills rock."

"I'm not bad," he said with false modesty. "Molloy has a soft spot for the younger jackers and wants the recruits to finish high school, or they would have taken me sooner." It was the first time I had seen Simon boast about anything.

"Who's Molloy?" I wrinkled my nose. That name sounded very familiar. "There's that big building, off the T-41 Metra line, with Molloy Enterprises written on it. Is he related to that?"

His mouth dropped open, but he quickly shut it. "You can't say anything about that. Look, you've got to promise me you'll keep the code of silence. They're really serious about that."

"Who am I going to tell?" My skeptical look made him relax.

"Good." He shuffled closer to whisper. "Kira, you belong in the Clan. You'll see, if you just come join us. It's a place where you can do what you're meant to do."

"What exactly does that mean?" If the Clan was all about using their jacking skills, that couldn't add up to anything good. I doubted they were running around solving crimes or aiding the poor. All the secrecy probably meant they were shady, like Simon's too-fancy car and stolen beers.

"Just come and see," he said.

"Thanks, but no thanks." His face fell.

I walked away.

I avoided Simon at lunch and chewed on the idea of the Clan. I couldn't blame him for wanting to be part of them. Not having to lie, being with people who understood you. If Simon hadn't been around to help me, I'm not sure what I would have done. Probably gone a bit demens.

But I was just getting used to passing for a reader and having a normal life.

By the time math rolled around, I was ready for a truce. I didn't say anything, just sat next to him in class. During free period, we tamped down the swirling rumors about our impending breakup by hanging out in the library. Afterward, I air-kissed Simon in the hall and insisted I needed to go to band. He looked uncertain, but didn't try to stop me.

At the end of band practice, Trina stood at the door. She was out of range, so I ignored her, but by the time I finished packing my instrument, she was still there.

Trina and I used to be in band together, a zillion years ago, until she quit when it wasn't mesh anymore. When hanging out with me wasn't mesh anymore. We hadn't mindtalked directly since I changed. As I walked into range, I tentatively linked into her mind. Her thoughts were jumbled, like she wasn't sure what to say. I wasn't sure what I wanted her to say either. Maybe *Sorry for ditching you when you needed a friend most?* It would be a start. It was tempting to force an apology, but it wouldn't mean much if I had to make her say it.

Hey, Trina, I linked to her as coolly as I could.

Her thoughts crystallized as soon as she heard mine. *Message,* she thought. *Give Kira the message.* Her thoughts had that hollow, repetitive sound of jacked mind. I scanned the hall for Simon, but found Mr. Gerek instead, staring me down, just out of range.

An icy fear trickled through me. My eyes locked with Mr. Gerek's as I linked a thought to her. *What's the message, Trina?*

We can make your life better, better, or much worse, worse, Trina thought earnestly, like a parrot repeating a phrase it had memorized.

My mouth went dry. Mr. Gerek tipped his head and walked away.

Hey, Trina thought. *You're still here. Still in band, I mean.*

It took me a moment to realize that she wasn't under his control anymore.

I coughed to clear the dryness from my throat. *Yeah, well, some things don't change.*

Some of us are going to the Fuse after school, she thought. *Would you like to come?*

Still tense from the encounter with Gerek, I almost laughed out loud. Being invited to hang out at the gameplex was probably the last thing I expected her to think.

I laughed mentally instead, which wasn't easy with lots of people shifting by. *I don't exactly have much practice with mindware games. Like none.*

She gave me a bright smile. *It's time we got you up to speed then. What's the point of changing if you can't waste your skills on mindless games?*

She sounded like the old Trina. Only I wasn't the old me, not even close. But this was what I had wanted all along, right? The way it used to be?

I arrived home late from school. The mindware games' metallic aftertaste lingered on the back of my tongue. It had been a challenge to run the games while linking my thoughts to the crowded gameplex, but our synchronized Blue Devils team trounced the rival Stevenson High players. It was fun. Really great.

Except for the dread left behind by Gerek's threat.

He'd obviously controlled Trina to deliver his not-so-subtle message. But did he jack her into inviting me to the Fuse too?

She didn't seem controlled, but maybe he only messed with her emotions. Was that what he meant by making my life better?

It gave me the chills.

Of course Gerek controlled people. He was a *jacker*. But did he make the threat because he thought I would blow the Clan's cover? Or did he really want me to join the Clan that badly? Either way, like Simon, it was better to be on Gerek's good side.

The next day, my gaming at the Fuse had finally killed my changeling status in the thought-rumor mill. I now routinely linked into everyone's minds, passing for a reader without thinking. This caused a problem at the tail end of Tuesday, when I almost reached into Raf's mind by accident. He was waiting for me at the school entrance. Simon had already left with Martin, to do something he vaguely explained as *business*.

Raf's sudden appearance in Simon's absence couldn't be a coincidence.

I slowed my pace as I came into range. Part of me wanted to treat him like everyone else. Simon was right—it would be less suspicious if Raf thought I was a reader. But once I was inside his head, I didn't know if I could keep from spilling my secrets. I'd had a hard enough time lying to him when he simply held my hand.

Then Gerek came out of the administration office, two doors down from the entrance. Whatever Raf was thinking caught his attention, and he swung his head toward us, narrowing his eyes. I stumbled to a stop, but it was too late—I was in range of Raf, and he was already frowning because he couldn't read me.

I quickly jacked into Raf's head.

Just want to talk, Kira, just want to talk. Why can't I hear her yet? Raf's thoughts burst into my head.

I put on a big smile, trying not to be obviously weird. *Raf! There you are! Come on, let's go!* I breezed past him out the door, praying he would follow without having to jack him.

Hey, Kira, I just wanted to talk, he thought.

I know! I know! My sandals clattered on the stone steps as I hurried down.

You know?

When I reached the bottom, I glanced back. Gerek wasn't following us, so I slowed and tried to step down my panic. The humidity had finally released its hold on Gurnee, but I was still breaking out in a cold sweat.

I pulled out of Raf's head before I was tempted to tell him too much.

He matched my pace as I headed away from the school. "I can't..."

"Still a changeling, I guess." I gave a jerky laugh. The school had emptied out, so there was no danger of being seen talking out loud. And it was unreasonably good to hear his voice.

"Can I walk you home?" He whispered in that conspiratorial tone we used when I was a zero. I let him stay by me, not knowing what to say. Before, I would have shared anything with Raf. Now that my life was an intricate maze of lies, it seemed there was *nothing* I could share.

We walked in silence for a while.

"You seem to be doing well. With the change, I mean," he said. "Well, except for now." I smothered the part of me that cared that he noticed.

"Yeah, it's good."

"Maybe sometime, when you're able to read, we could hang out. Just mindtalk for a while."

Well, that wasn't going to work. At all. "You said you were going to stay away from me." A lump in my throat cut off anything else I might have said.

"Yeah." He dropped his eyes to his oversized sneakers. I picked up my pace, to outrun the heartache that loomed ahead. "I've messed this whole thing up," he said. "I don't want to be that guy that was yelling at you in your room."

Water pooled in my eyes and blurred the sun-burnt grass and the white concrete together. Raf was killing me with guilt by trying to take the blame for a mess that was completely mine.

When I didn't say anything, he kept going. "I want to be a better friend than that. And you're right. You can date whoever you want." He was making an effort to keep the anger out of his voice, but I still heard it. Raf was trying to be the friend he thought I needed. He couldn't have found a more lethal way to break my heart. The tears pooling in my eyes crested the dam.

"You *are* my friend, Raf." I choked on the words. "You're a great friend. The best. Ever." I bit my lip, hard, because the secrets were welling up inside me, threatening to spill out like the tears. *I'm a mutant jacker, Raf. Everything is a lie.* I bit even harder, welcoming the sharp pain that held the words in. *Gerek,* I reminded myself. My secret was even more dangerous for Raf now. I stabbed the urge to tell Raf anything, hoping it would die quickly.

"Hey, are you..." He peered at me. "Why are you...?" I was walking so fast I was nearly running. I needed to get to my house before my resolve faltered. Raf kept pace by my side. Within a minute, we had reached my front door.

"Kira." He stopped me before I could bolt to safety inside. "If you want to talk about anything..." I threw my arms around his broad shoulders and marked his soccer jersey with my tears. Then I dashed in the house and closed the door on him. Leaning against it, I slowly sank to the floor.

"Kira?" my mom called. She peered down the stairs, holding a long silver ladle and a soft cloth. Seeing me slumped against the door, she hurried down. I stared at the floor, unable to get up or muster a lie.

"Raf," was all I said. She pulled me close with the hand that still clutched the ladle and let me spill my tears on her shoulder.

chapter TWENTY-ONE

The next morning, I complained to Simon about Gerek's threat.

We were in our daily hushed, early-morning meeting at my locker. I didn't mention the fact that Gerek nearly caught me not jacking into Raf's head.

"Gerek was only trying to convince you to join us," Simon said, but he looked troubled.

"I said I'd keep the Clan's secret," I said. "Didn't you tell him? Why is he harassing me?"

"He's just worried," he said. "It would be easier if you joined us, Kira. Then they wouldn't be concerned about you blowing everyone's cover."

"Yeah, well, I'm not interested." Although I was rethinking that now. If I joined the Clan, maybe they wouldn't stalk after me and my friends. Or maybe I could convince them I wasn't worth the trouble. "Besides, my skills aren't rockin' like yours. Why do they even want me?"

His eyes grew a little wider. "I told you. Molloy has a soft spot for the younger jackers."

My occasional glimpses of Gerek made him seem less concerned about young jackers than making sure I didn't get out of line.

For the rest of the week Gerek kept his distance and didn't send me any more cryptic messages via friends from the past. Raf kept his distance as well, but I saw him everywhere.

He lingered in the hall or sat nearby at lunch—within sight, but out of thought range. It was reassuring, in a strange way, except for the permanent scowl etched in his forehead. I hoped his dark looks were only for Simon at my side.

The crew gathered at our usual Friday meeting spot on the bleachers, conspiring for the weekend. The next day was Simon's 18th birthday, so Katie teased him, saying she'd turn him in for touching a minor. Simon declared all activities remotely considered kissing would cease.

I hoped he wasn't serious. Sometimes it was hard to tell, with him being a consummate liar and me not far behind.

I scoured my brain for a gift for Simon. What do you get a boy who can mindjack to get anything he wants? Then I realized *I* was the one thing that Simon couldn't have just by using his wily powers. He couldn't force me to be with him or his Clan of fellow jackers. He couldn't jack his way into my heart.

Maybe I could start acting like a real girlfriend.

When Simon asked me out before, it was only an excuse to meet with Gerek. But I could tell the hurt and anger when I brought up Raf was real. A genuine date might make the perfect gift. It was true that I didn't date, and my dad probably *would* skin me alive if he found out. Then again, he would have a heart attack if he knew half of the things I'd done in the last three weeks. As I was devising a way to sneak out for a birthday date with Simon, Katie and the boys rose up from the bleachers.

Leaving so soon? I asked Katie.

Leave us. Simon's voice boomed through their minds, and I flinched. What was the hurry? School hadn't even let out. He draped his arm across my shoulder, careful not to touch my bare arm.

Leave, Katie echoed. *Ok, we're going, love birds.*

I waited until they were out of range before whispering, "What was that all about?"

"Sorry." He didn't look sorry at all. "I couldn't wait any longer to show you." He pulled a rolled sheet of parchment out of his backpack. The official holo-stamp of the high school hovered above a bunch of writing testifying that he had received his diploma.

"Get out!" I said. "But your birthday isn't until tomorrow."

He bit his lip. "I'm impatient."

I rolled my eyes. "How many people did you have to jack?"

"It was easy after I convinced Martin to hack into the school system and change all my classes to *complete*. He has his uses."

"Wait." The idea of completed classes sank in. "Aren't you coming back on Monday?"

He stuffed the diploma into his pack, then captured me with that intense stare of his. "No."

The word hung in the air. I wouldn't see him in class or the hallways. No more jacking practice in the library or sneaking up to the bleachers to hang out and sometimes kiss. My stomach looped into a knot. "What are you going to do?"

"You know," he said. "I'm working for the Clan full time now. I'm giving Molloy my vow tomorrow."

"Vow?" I said. "Sounds more like a cult than a job."

He scowled. "It's my chance to get out of here."

"But... you're not leaving Gurnee, are you?" My voice hiked up. Would his work with the Clan take him out of town? Would I not see him again, even outside of school? I didn't like the panic climbing up my throat.

He searched my eyes. "Come with me, Kira."

I swallowed down the fear. "Come with you where?"

"Just come to the ceremony. Check it out. There's a big Clan meeting tomorrow and I'm going to make my vow then." He lightly brushed my hair back. "I want you to be there."

My birthday present to Simon crystallized before me. Simon was jacking his way out of high school, and I could help celebrate his acceptance into his Clan of fellow mindjackers. And if I came to the ceremony, maybe pretended to consider joining, Gerek wouldn't be so suspicious. The Clan might let me hang out until I graduated like Simon, and they'd leave my friends alone.

"Okay," I said. "I'll come see what this Clan of yours is all about."

He pulled me close and pressed his lips to mine. "Thank you," he whispered between kisses. "Thank you."

"Okay, okay." I laughed lightly, basking in the warmth of his lips.

I seriously hoped the kisses wouldn't end tomorrow.

chapter TWENTY-TWO

Mom had some demens idea about a Mom-and-Kira night. The smell of popcorn wafted from a bowl on the couch while she flicked through the sim-cast choices on the screen. My breakdown over Raf on Tuesday had convinced her I needed a girl's night intervention, and it couldn't have come at a worse time. The Clan ceremony loomed barely an hour away, and my options for escape were disappearing.

"One of these is a romantic comedy," she said. The scrolling sim-cast list halted for a moment, then continued on. "It has that actor you like, the cute one."

"They're all cute, Mom."

She grinned, as if I was playing along. "Here it is." She directed the mindware display to start the download. "*Seventeen Days*. Have you heard of it?"

"No, but I'm sure someone falls in love and lives happily ever after." I crossed my arms and hovered at the edge of the living room, refusing to come in. "I don't think a romantic comedy is good for my state of mind right now." I hoped she would buy my pathetic gambit. It wasn't too far from the truth, with my worries about Simon leaving school.

"Oh." She stopped the sim-cast mid-download. "Well, we can watch whatever you like. Come take a look." She gestured me over to the couch. I stood my ground and contemplated jacking her to watch while I went out. My insides squirmed at the idea, but I couldn't sneak out, and I had no plausible excuses to leave. Her shoulders dropped and she flicked a glance at the time display on the screen.

I narrowed my eyes. "Are you expecting someone?"

"Well, um, Rafael called earlier."

My mouth fell open. Mom wasn't usually this underhanded.

"I only told him we were watching a sim-cast tonight." She stared at the popcorn bowl, like she might find forgiveness there. "He said he might stop by," she said quietly.

The blood rushed to my face. Through the haze, I realized that Mom had inadvertently given me a way out. "I can't believe you invited Raf!" I shouted more forcefully than necessary. "I'm so out of here." My shoes were lying near the stairs. I tugged them on with exaggerated passion and surreptitiously checked my pocket for my phone. I would scrit Simon once I was free of the house.

"Kira, wait!" She spilled popcorn in her haste to rise up from the couch, but I didn't want to give her a chance to apologize.

"I'll be back when you're done having Raf over!" I pounded down the stairs and slammed the front door on my way out, hoping my display was sufficiently violent to keep her from coming after me. I knew she would worry and resolved to scrit her later.

But she should have known better than to invite Raf.

I pulled out my phone to scrit Simon. My running shoes whispered down the street, and the late afternoon air seeped heat through my shorts and t-shirt. I didn't have a chance to dress up for Simon's big ceremony, but I was lucky to get out of the house at all. It would have to do.

Simon's black hydro car was waiting when I arrived at the school parking lot. My fortuitous exit plan gave us a little extra time, which we spent making out in the car. His starched white shirt crinkled under my hands, leaving him rumpled for his big event. To be fair, it wasn't entirely my fault. Simon's kisses were more enthusiastic than normal.

"Where does your Mom think you'll go?" he asked between nibbles on my ear.

"I don't know. Probably figures I'll walk it off and come home." I remembered my earlier plan. "Maybe I'll scrit her and say I'm going to a friend's."

"Good idea. Then she won't call the police when you don't show up an hour from now."

I sent her a vague scrit about an unidentified friend, giving me room to conjure a good lie before I came home, and went back to kissing Simon until we had to leave.

Once Simon had programmed an autopath and we glided out of the parking lot, I belatedly asked, "Where's the Clan meeting?"

He glanced sideways at me. "Molloy owns a warehouse in Glenview, and the Clan holds their big meetings there."

I shifted in my seat, remembering a Glenview stop along the T-94 line on a rare trip south into the city. My dad had taken us to visit Navy Pier, one of the few museums left when the city de-populated under the range ordinances. The towering downtown skyscrapers filled with commuting workers during the day, but Dad insisted we take the train out before dark.

"Are we taking the Metra?" I checked the sun sinking in the sky, hoping Glenview wasn't too close to the city.

"It's only about forty minutes by car."

It was easier and faster to take the train and an autocab rather than weave through endless suburban streets. Maybe Simon wanted to show off his sporty car to the Clan. Or maybe he didn't want to leave a record of our trip.

"Does everyone drive?" I asked.

"I don't really know. The Clan doesn't usually all gather in the same spot, but this is a special occasion. I think most of the Clan will be there. Only Molloy has met all the members. It's safer if we don't all know each other."

"Safer from what?" What could a band of mindjackers be afraid of? Sure, they didn't want their cover blown. But was there more than that? "Are there other Clans?"

He paused for a moment. "Not in Chicago New Metro. Clan Molloy is the only one here." I arched an eyebrow at him, but he ignored me.

We broke out of the forest of housing tracts and wove through a run-down industrial park that reminded me of the area where Simon found the only convenience store in North America without security cameras. Gray metal warehouses lined up like ammo cases and caught the red glow of the setting sun. Jagged shadows made the ramshackle buildings seem ready to collapse. Simon pulled up to a side door and parked between a scattering of cars.

"Are you ready?" he asked.

I eyed him. He was the one who should worry about being ready. I was only checking out the Clan and supporting him on his big day. But I nodded anyway.

"All right, once we're inside, just stick by me and follow my lead."

"Sounds simple enough."

His soft gaze turned into a softer kiss, then he stepped out of the car and opened my door. I hadn't expected him to be a gentleman, so I was already halfway out. He held my hand and shut the car door. The sound echoed off the metal canyon of warehouses.

He paused at the door of the warehouse and took one last look at me before pulling down the handle. About two dozen people milled around the cavernous warehouse. Pallets of goods lined the walls, and giant chains hung by a garage door on the far side. Clutching my hand a little harder, Simon steered us toward the loose crowd gathered in the middle. They orbited a tall, beefy man standing next to a gray metal table and chair. His long red hair flared out from his head, tamed only by a band in back, and he greeted each Clan member as they drifted his way.

Simon whispered, "That's Molloy," which I had already figured out. He appeared about thirty-five and stood like a man used to giving orders. Scanning the other jackers, I recognized a couple of faces. A dark-haired Hispanic woman lingered at the periphery of the crowd and looked very much like the reference desk librarian at the Gurnee Public Library. A gangly man with a hook nose stood next to her and appeared to be the ticket guy from the old Marcus Theatre that Raf and I liked to visit. There seemed to be more young jackers than old, with Molloy the oldest, but the Clan members were like anyone you would see at the grocery store or a soccer game.

All jackers hiding in plain sight.

Was this it for the New Metro area—a couple dozen jackers that occasionally met in a rickety warehouse? But Simon said the Clan was careful and didn't let in just anyone. There had to be more, like me, who would rather simply pass for readers and have a normal life.

A thin, pasty man shadowed Molloy, his face impassive. He was plain in every way except for the steel gray eyes that were trained on me. I glared back at him and wondered what his problem was. His stare was like a force on my head, like he was trying to push on my mind, which didn't make any sense. Simon had told me he couldn't get into my head, and I was pretty sure it was simple bad manners to try to jack me as if I were a reader he could control. Pasty Man's eyes widened slightly and the corner of his mouth turned up as the pressure got worse.

I pushed him hard, away from my head and all the way back to his.

I gasped when I sank deep into the gel of his mind. He was a visitor, not part of Molloy's regular Clan, and he had special plans for me, if my head was as hard as they thought. Before I could think about what that meant, he pushed me back out. It had all taken less than a moment, but I realized a crucial thing in that tiny slice of time.

I could jack into another jacker's head, but he couldn't get into mine.

There's something different about me.

Simon had missed the entire exchange, intent on working our way toward Molloy. Simon had let me think I couldn't jack into his mind or even link in.

And I had never questioned it.

My stomach clenched hard. That Simon would lie was no shock, but this was different. Danger seemed to radiate from the crowd circulating around Molloy.

I tried to link into Simon's mind and slipped in no problem. *He better hold up his end of the bargain....* Simon shot me a look. *What is she...?* He pushed me out his mind and yanked me close to his side with our clasped hands.

"Don't do that!" Then his head snapped to Molloy, who had locked his emerald-green eyes on us. He resembled an oversized, maniacal leprechaun, and the Clan members parted before his determined stride to meet us. Simon dropped my hand like it was on fire and stepped away as Molloy neared.

Molloy bared his teeth in a simulated smile and loomed over me. Seamus, with his wild red hair and imposing linebacker build, would have disappeared in the shadow of Molloy. He grasped my hand and held it with surprising gentleness, like a giant cradling a kitten. I didn't dare link into his mind. My voice had fled, and my legs wished they could follow.

"Welcome, Kira. We are so glad you could come." His teeth glinted in the blue plasma lights of the warehouse, and he stared at me too long. Pressure built on my mind, an echo of the mental force from his pasty minion. I slowly extricated my hand from his grasp.

Molloy arched an eyebrow as I took a small step back so that he wasn't crushing me with his presence. The pressure on my mind ceased, and Molloy checked with his spook over his shoulder. His nod caused Molloy to break into wide smile.

He showered his approval on Simon and grasped his hand. Molloy must have linked into Simon's mind and exchanged words mentally, because Simon's look of horror was replaced by a tentative grin.

Molloy took a step back, dropping Simon's hand and raising both of his.

"Friends!" he said to the crowd. "We have a new member to welcome to our Clan!" He swept a hand out, encompassing Simon and me. "You all know Simon, Alec Gerek's young recruit. He wishes to make his vow tonight." There was a patter of applause and Simon flushed.

I clasped my hands together, trying to stop the quivering and summon my inner ninja.

Molloy was still talking to the crowd. "Simon brings us a new friend, today. Someone to welcome into our Clan as well." He smiled a row of shark teeth. The eyes of the entire Clan turned to me. I was a minnow in a pool of sharks. Simon sent me reassuring looks, as though he hadn't just betrayed and abandoned me.

It didn't seem wise to tell them I planned to run as soon as I could. I took a deep breath so my voice wouldn't quaver. "Um, yeah. I'm still thinking about that."

Molloy's predatory smile grew, but Simon's grin evaporated with my words. A twitter went around the room. Pasty Man started toward us with silent footfalls.

"I see you and Andre have already met," Molloy said, ignoring my words.

Andre arrived at his elbow, steely eyes still trained on me. A faint smile turned his plain face menacing. "Hello, Kira." His voice was bland, his words gone almost before they were spoken. "I think we have much to talk about."

Talking to Pasty Man was the last thing I planned to do. Top priority was finding a way out of the shark pit that the warehouse had become. I couldn't possibly outrun them. And besides, I was somewhere in Glenview with only Simon for transportation home. Simon's face had gone blank.

In one enormous stride, Molloy cut the distance between us and hovered over me again. I tried not to shrink away, although the gesture was no doubt useless. My eyes went wide as he ran his large, rough thumb over my forehead, the way Simon had ages ago when we first met. A chill ran from that touch to my clenched stomach.

"Your mind is indeed a wonder," he said. "Even my friend Andre says so."

I didn't understand exactly what was happening, but one thing had become clear: Simon had not brought me here to watch his ceremony or learn about the Clan, but to sell me out to the Red Giant and Andre the Spook. They wanted something from me that had to do with my hard head. My impenetrable mind.

Which was apparently different from everyone else.

My breath hitched as I realized the depth of my trouble. Simon stood several feet behind Molloy. I was tempted to link into his head and tell him what I thought of his betrayal, but I had to focus on a way out.

Molloy seemed amused. "Kira, my dear, don't be angry with Simon." His massive hands clasped around mine. My pounding pulse beat a tempo in my wrists. "He only wants what we all want. For you to join us, your family. Your *true* family. Whether you realize it or not, Kira, you belong in Clan Molloy."

I yanked my hands out of his grip. "You're not my family."

He shook his head. "I very much hope you change your mind about that. You don't want your mother or father, or that delightful brother of yours, to be involved in this, do you?"

My lower lip started to tremble. How did he know so much about me? "Leave my family out of it!" The words jerked out of me in gasps.

He stepped back. "Well, now, that's up to you." Another Clan member slipped behind him, and they seemed to exchange thoughts. Molloy arched his eyebrows and announced to the crowd, "It appears we have an opportunity for young Simon to prove his loyalty today." Simon's impassive face cracked into a frown. "I'm sure he won't mind," Molloy continued, staring down Simon.

Molloy swept his hand to the back door as two figures walked in, one blond haired and head held high, the other with dark curls and head hanging as if examining the floor where every foot fell. His hands hung slack at his sides.

My body tensed. Maybe this was the distraction that I needed. I made ready to run and stole another glance at Simon. His face had drained of color. The blond Clan member seemed to be mentally steering the black-haired man to the chair in the center of the room. As he sat down, his arms fell limp down the sides of the chair. He raised his head and gazed unseeing at the table.

No! My heart seized up. *Raf.* His eyes were glazed, a puppet under the control of the Clan minion, but clearly Raf.

"It seems we have a spy amongst us." Molloy laughed as though that was some kind of private joke. The Clan's chuckles echoed around the warehouse, bouncing off the concrete floor and the metallic walls.

The urge to run drained out of my body. What was Raf doing here? And what were they going to do to him? As the laughter died away, Molloy turned to me. "It seems we aren't the only ones who admire you, lovely Kira," he said. "Yet we can't have readers stumbling into our meetings. You understand, I'm sure." He glanced at Simon and consulted silently with his spooky sidekick. Simon's face had turned ashen and his jaw worked.

I linked into his head. *This is not how I had...* He threw me a sharp look.

Simon, what is happening? What're they going to do to Raf?

Kira, I have to... I don't have any choice...

Have to what? What?? He ignored me and jacked fast into Raf's mind. Raf's head slowly bent down until it rested on his chest. I jacked into Raf's head, too, and found Simon's presence had tunneled deep, going past the thoughts that were jacked by

Molloy's guard and into the part that controlled breathing. And heart rate.

No! I reached for the solid marble of Simon's mind and pushed *hard*. Simon flew back out of Raf's head. I kept pushing until Simon was back in his own mind.

And then I jacked hard into Simon's mind, until he dropped like a stone to the warehouse floor. Back in Raf's mind, I found the guard and flung him out as well, pounding him back into his own head until he collapsed like Simon into a heap.

A gasp went around the room, and I knew I couldn't stop.

I slammed into Molloy and Pasty Man with all the force that I could. *Stop!* I commanded and they fell, collapsing onto a Clan member that had been hovering nearby. I closed my eyes, and one by one, I sought them out and cut them down, a chorus of cries and gasps rising and then falling as they hit the floor with sickening thuds. The last one was trapped under Molloy's body, but he reached out to me with his mind. I slammed him back into his own head and commanded, *Stop.*

He was still.

chapter TWENTY-THREE

I opened my eyes.

The warehouse looked like a battlefield littered with jackers as still as corpses. They lay motionless, one on top of another, with limbs bent at odd angles. My feet were riveted to the floor. The jackers weren't dead, but I had erased their conscious thoughts, like words wiped from a scribepad. I was pretty sure they wouldn't move again unless I told them to wake up.

Something banged against my knees, and the floor rushed at me. My hands flew in front of my face to keep it from smacking into the concrete. I stared at the floor, and air wheezed in and out of my lungs. The fallen bodies haunted the edge of my field of view.

Suddenly hands grabbed my shoulders and lifted me. Raf's face swam into view. "Kira, are you okay?"

His thick black brows drew together. I reached up and touched them. Soft like feathers. They moved under my hand when he frowned deeper.

"I'm getting you out of here," he said. He reached his arm

around my back and hoisted me from the floor. My legs didn't work right. I tried to walk, but my toes kept catching on the concrete floor.

Or maybe the bodies.

Raf hauled me across the endless cavern of the warehouse until we reached the door he had come through. He kicked it open, and we stepped out into the clammy night air. The ground disappeared as Raf hooked his arm under my legs and carried me across the street. He set me down by the passenger side of his car and opened the door. The car light spilled out onto the grass and jump-started my brain. I felt sick and bent over, sucking in gulps of night air to stop the queasiness.

"Oh god, Kira, are you okay?" Raf rubbed my back. The sickness climbed up in my throat, but I swallowed it down and straightened. A wave of dizziness swept me. I leaned against him and buried my face in his chest.

"We need to leave," he said, taking hold of my shoulders and nudging me toward the passenger seat. "Just get in the car, and I'll get us out of here." I obeyed, sitting heavily and dragging my legs in after me. He hurried around to the driver's side, throwing a glance back at the warehouse, as if he expected them to come barreling out at any moment.

He pulled up the mindware to start the car. I touched his shoulder to stop him.

"We need to go." His voice was soft, like he was talking to a child waking from a nightmare.

"No. Wait. I have to wake them up." It didn't seem right to leave them passed out cold on the concrete floor.

"Wake them up?" He peered at the warehouse, draped in shadows. "What happened in there, Kira? I only remember being here in the car. You went in, but I don't remember anything else until I woke up inside. Then everyone was falling down."

Words came out of my mouth explaining how I jacked into people's minds, how Molloy had ordered Raf killed, and how Simon was going to do it. And so, of course, I had to stop Simon. And Molloy. And the others. I watched his eyes go wide as saucers and then shrink with horror and finally settle into pure amazement. I walked him through every step, but it felt like a lecture I was giving to students in a tinny hall far away. *Today, students, I will explain how I knocked out a battalion of mindjacking Clan members. There will be a quiz at the end.*

Sickness rose up again. I had to stop talking to choke it back down.

Raf brushed my cheeks, and they seemed wet. I blinked to clear away the blurriness.

The amazement on Raf's face had tempered to concern. "What do we do now?"

"We should call the police," I said. "No, wait." I tried to clear the fuzziness in my brain. "If I wake them up while the police are there, they'll just jack the officers and escape. Or worse. There has to be some way to stop them. Maybe order them to cooperate with the police and turn themselves in?" I wasn't even sure of that. Somehow I had managed to knock them out, but they weren't expecting it. I caught them by surprise. If they were all awake... and angry...

"I'm not sure it's a good idea to stay until the police arrive," Raf said.

"We can't let them go free," I said. "They'll hurt my family."

Raf pulled his phone out of his pocket. "How about I call the police, and we'll pull over behind those bushes." He pointed to a row of hedges large enough to obscure his car and out of reading range of the warehouse. "Can you do your, um, jacking from there?"

"Yes. I think so." An unreasonable smile broke across my face. Raf gave me a whisper of a smile and then became serious as he focused on his phone. I reached inside the building. The location of each mind was seared into me. They were all still safely unconscious. Raf switched on the car and used the manual joystick to quickly swing the car around and hide us behind the hedge.

The night was still as we waited.

The air was thick with things I needed to say to Raf, but the words wouldn't come out of my mouth. I stared at the green twisting branches of the bush, snarled like all the lies I had told, and searched for the right thing to say. From the corner of my eye, I saw Raf staring at me. It all seemed so silly now, in retrospect. The one person I should have trusted all along was the one I had lied to the most.

"How did you find me?" I asked, stalling while I searched for a way to apologize. Raf gripped the car's joystick. I wasn't sure if he was anxious about the police or if he was angry about the insanity that had just occurred. He didn't look at me.

"I followed you." His voice was quiet, like he was embarrassed.

"From my house?" I asked, not quite putting it all together.

"No, from the school." His whisper hung in the air. Heat crept up my neck as I remembered what Simon and I had been doing, for quite some time, in that school parking lot. Had my mom called Raf? Did he just stumble onto that scene? It didn't matter. Simon's betrayal just fueled the fire on my cheeks.

"I was worried about you, Kira," Raf said, still defending himself.

"Raf." I wanted him to look at me, but he kept staring at the bushes. "I was wrong. About a lot of things. I should have told you the truth." My hands were white from clenching each other in my lap. "I was trying to protect you," I mumbled.

His head snapped to me. "Protect me from *them*?"

"And from me." The words came out a whisper.

He shook his head. "Kira, you wouldn't hurt me. You saved my life tonight."

"I already hurt you once." My final secret came out before I could stop it.

"You mean, in chem lab?" Knowing I had cut down a warehouse full of jackers, he had to know that I had done the same thing to him. He took a deep breath and gazed through the bushes to the building where the bodies still lay. "I knew there was something going on with you, Kira, I just didn't know what. And you wouldn't talk to me. I wish you had let me help you, instead of turning to that guy, Simon." The hurt in his eyes was clear, even in the dim parking lot lights, and it stabbed me.

"Me too," I whispered. My face burned with embarrassment and anger—at Simon, at myself for lying, at the universe for giving me this cursed ability. I had messed things up pretty good and almost gotten my best friend killed.

Twice.

And I had lied to everyone I cared about in the process. There must be something worse than green sludge on cheese, because I had sunk to a new low. I stared at my hands and wondered if Raf could ever trust me again. Then his hand found mine. It was warm and soft, and my fingers automatically sought his and held tight.

"It's going to be all right," he said. But I already knew that from the safe feeling that pulsed from his hands into mine, from the easy forgiveness he gave me with his touch. Although I didn't deserve his trust, I desperately needed it.

The right words had abandoned me again.

As I searched for something to say, a black car careened around the corner of the winding industrial row and screeched to a stop in front of the warehouse. It didn't appear to be a police car, with no lights, siren, or markings. We heard the doors open and hard soled shoes clattering on the pavement. I linked into the two newcomer's minds to see if they were Clan members coming to rescue their fallen crew.

One pushed me out of his head before I could register a name. The second was distracted, thinking about someone inside the warehouse. His name popped up. *Agent Kestrel, FBI.* My eyes went wide. Agent Kestrel pushed me out, hard, and kept pushing all the way back to my impenetrable mind. Except maybe it wasn't. The force of him on my mind was stronger than anything I'd felt before.

"We have to leave!" I said. Raf jumped in his seat. "Now, now, *now!*"

I closed my eyes in concentration. If we stayed any longer, Agent Kestrel might jack into my head, and I was certain that would be a bad thing. I pressed my hands to my temples, as if I could ward Kestrel off that way. Raf threw the car into reverse and flung me forward into the dash. We hurtled backward across the empty parking lot. The pressure on my head lessened. I opened my eyes and braced myself against the dash right as Raf hit the brakes and flung me back into my seat. I struggled with the seat belt as he screeched out of the parking lot.

A squeal of tires sounded behind us. Even though we were tearing away from the warehouse, the pressure on my mind started to grow again.

"He's following us..." I whispered.

"Who's following us?" Raf said hoarsely. "What's going on?"

"They're FBI agents. *Jacker* agents." The pressure grew stronger. I pressed the heel of my hand to my forehead. "We have to get farther away, Raf. Go faster!"

"I am!" he said, but then he started to slow down and pull to the side of the road.

He had slumped against the dash.

"Raf!" I grabbed the joystick and tried to keep us from crashing into the trees lining the street, but it wasn't responding. Agent Kestrel must have jacked into the car's mindware as well as Raf's mind. I reached into the mindware controls and wrestled with Kestrel. Somehow he managed to shut down the engine, and our car crawled to a full stop at the curb.

Raf slumped against the window, too groggy to move. I reached for Kestrel's mind, but he was ready for me and he was too strong. I couldn't even slow him down.

Tires crunched on the road behind us. Kestrel sprang out of his car and stalked toward ours. I shook Raf, trying to get him to move. Too late, I realized I had to run.

I wrenched the door handle up and stumbled out into the cool night air. The grass was slick under my hands as I caught myself. I got three steps before Agent Kestrel's hand clamped around my arm. I wrestled with his mind and body in a flurry of hands and feet and thoughts. His bony hand held me fast against him, like a brick wall with an iron claw.

A sharp pain jabbed my arm, and a haze washed through me. My mind went numb, followed by my limbs, and the wet grass rushed to meet my face.

Run, Raf. But my thoughts were a jumble of words scattered on the lawn.

The darkness fell like a trap slamming shut.

chapter TWENTY-FOUR

Metal support bars dug through the thin, cold mattress, prodding my back as I woke up.

I forced my parched throat to swallow and propped myself up. The room smelled of stale sweat. Grime caked the edges of the walls. Other than the cot and a cracked toilet without a seat tucked in the far corner, the pale gray room was bare.

My head was numb, like it had disconnected from my body. I rubbed the heels of my hands on my temples, but it didn't drive away the fuzziness. An orange aftertaste stung the back of my tongue. I gingerly swung my shaky legs over the edge of the bed and pressed my bare feet to the cold concrete floor. *Why don't I have shoes?*

Pictures flashed through my mind: Raf slumped over the wheel, a pinprick in my arm, my face in the cold grass. *Raf!* I jerked up from the bed and the room spun. Catching myself on the corner of the mattress, I stumbled toward the metallic door.

There was no handle, only a small window I could barely see through, even standing on my tiptoes. The upper half of a concrete hallway was all I could see. I pounded on the door.

"Hey! Let me out!" I fought through the orange haze in my mind. Raf might be in another holding room nearby. I strained my eyes to peer down the featureless corridor. A tall man in a gray uniform lurched into view and strode toward me.

I backed away from the door before the guard pushed it open. He stood with one hand on the knob and the other on a short black stick attached to his belt.

"Don't get testy, princess," he said. "You'll be leaving soon enough."

I reflexively backed away from him. His dark hair was greasy and slicked to the side, contrasting with his neatly pressed uniform. Something in his sharp blue eyes made it seem like he had seen horrible things and liked it. His lips pulled back in the kind of smile a crocodile gives right before it eats you for lunch.

The backs of my knees hit the bed and I nearly tumbled onto it. I straightened and took a deep breath. It didn't matter if Reptile Man was big and frightening and kind of smelly, if I jacked him... I reached toward his mind, but my brain was too fuzzed. I could barely form a coherent thought, much less control his brain from across the room.

He snorted. "Not so tough when you're on the juice, now are you?" Then he leered at me and a shiver convulsed me so hard I almost fell on the bare mattress again.

Abruptly, he swung his head to peer down the hallway. When his eyes returned to me, they had lost their gleam. "Time's up, princess. Come on." He stepped back, but I wasn't so interested in leaving my room anymore.

"Where are we going?" He didn't answer my question, and his ugly smile returned, like he wanted an excuse to come in the room after me. My legs twitched as I slipped out the door, keeping as much distance as possible between me and Reptile Man.

The long gray hallway was lined with doors identical to mine, perhaps twenty of them before a double door at the end. The small high windows kept me from seeing in. My feet pricked with cold from the concrete floor, and the bracing air of the prison soaked into my thin shorts and t-shirt. I hugged myself to keep the shivering to a minimum. The guard stopped just before the end double doors to open a side cell.

The room was the same size as mine. A battered metal table stood in the center with spindly chairs on either side, facing each other in a silent duel. The guard closed the door with a click that sounded like I would be staying put. My throat was still painfully dry, and a plastic cup of water called to me from the table. I picked it up and sniffed. They had already drugged me with whatever they wanted, so I gulped down the entire cup. The vinyl-cushioned chair clung to my legs when I sat down.

I sank my face into my hands. What had happened to Raf?

They must have taken him into custody as well. My brain was so fuzzed that I had to fight to remember what happened. The FBI had found the warehouse with the unconscious Clan members and captured Raf and me. Were we under arrest? It seemed so.

But we didn't do anything wrong.

A bubble of anger boiled through the fog in my mind. Why was I being held prisoner, when Simon and his band of jackers were the real criminals?

I jerked when the door of the room swung open. Only my legs sticking to the red plastic cushion kept me from falling off the chair. I steadied myself by clutching the table. The agent who captured us—Kestrel—closed the door behind him. He sat carefully in the seat across from me.

He had seemed like a wall of iron grip and mental force when he wrestled me into custody on the streets of Glenview, but now he was only a man. His piercing blue eyes returned my stare. He appeared about twenty-five, or maybe a little older. His dark hair was cut short, and his cheeks were so hollowed they almost looked scarred. I desperately wished the orange haze would clear from my mind so I could jack into Kestrel's. For now, I would have to get my answers the old-fashioned way.

"What have you done with Raf?" I asked.

Agent Kestrel drew his thin lips into a line and leaned back in his chair. "Your friend is fine. He's back home, thinking he shouldn't have drunk so much last night."

What is Kestrel talking about? "Did you drug him too?"

"No. We wiped his true memories, and replaced them with a sim of him drowning his sorrows. When he wakes, the last true thing Mr. Lobos Santos will remember is watching you and Mr. Zagan in the parking lot."

I gaped. He had wiped Raf's memory? I supposed it was possible—I had swept clean the conscious thoughts of the minds in the warehouse. If I had reached farther into their minds, I probably could have brushed away their true memories as well. And if Kestrel had erased Raf's memory of last night, everything—my explanation, Raf's forgiveness—was gone. All Raf would remember was Simon and me making out in the parking lot. My hands clenched my knees.

Kestrel's face had gone icy cold. "It makes it easier to explain why you and Mr. Zagan both disappeared on the same night."

"What do you mean, disappeared?"

Kestrel narrowed his eyes. "Surely you don't think you're going home now, Kira."

"You can't... you can't just..." I swallowed. "You can't just hold me here forever."

"Here?" His eyebrows arched. "No, not here." His eyes drifted to the empty cup sitting on the table between us. "Are you thirsty? The juice can quickly dehydrate you. Can I get you some more water?"

I blinked at his conversational tone, as though we were two friends having a nice cup of tea. "Uh, okay," I said slowly. His smile thinned his lips until they almost disappeared. He snatched the cup, and the door opened for him. A guard exchanged the old cup for a new one filled with water. Kestrel returned to the table and carefully set down the cup.

"How did you find us last night?" I asked. "The Clan, I mean. Was it because we called the police?"

"No. We've been monitoring the Clan for some time, but they seldom gather all together. They usually launder money for the New Metro mob. This time they had some new corporate espionage scheme in the works. Our agent inside told us they had brought in someone from an international spy ring, to see if their newest recruit was the asset they needed." He paused. "It was our chance to catch everyone together."

I knew the Clan was up to no good, but espionage? I shook my head, trying to clear the fuzz. "Wait. You had an agent in the Clan?"

"Yes." His cold eyes measured me for a moment. "Mrs. Gomez. She's the—"

"Librarian." It jarred my orange-misted brain: the librarian wasn't simply a jacker. She was an undercover FBI jacker, infiltrating the local jacker mafia. She always seemed so nice, when I needed help at the reference desk.

Kestrel waited for me to piece it together. "So I was supposed to be the new recruit?" I asked. "The asset?"

Kestrel leaned forward and laced his fingers. "Yes. We moved in when we lost contact with our agent. When you linked into my head," he grimaced, "I thought you were just one of the Clan. It wasn't until after I got inside the warehouse that I realized what you were—and what had happened."

What I was. I gulped. *What was I?* A mutant jacker, with an extraordinarily hard head. That much I knew. But I didn't know if Agent Kestrel knew.

"What am I?"

"Well, that is the question, isn't it?" He looked me over. "I've never seen a jacker lay low an entire Clan at once. Whatever you are, Kira, you are unique."

My pulse started to beat on my temples. Being *unique* probably didn't come with a blue-ribbon prize. "What about the Clan?" I asked, stalling while I figured this out. "Did you arrest them?"

"They're all in custody now." His voice was flat, and I imagined Simon juiced up in a smelly holding cell somewhere. I found it hard to muster much sympathy for him. He knew what he was getting into, but he had no right to suck me into it and get Raf caught in the crossfire. The Justice Department could deal with Simon and his law-breaking friends.

Except I stumbled over the idea of Simon standing trial. "Wait, how can you try them?" I asked. "It seems unlikely you could get a jury to convict."

Kestrel's face hardened. "There won't be any trials. We have a special camp for jackers, Kira. You don't want to go there."

My jaw dropped. *Camp?* Images of barbed wire and my Great Grandpa Reilly in the early reader camps flashed through my mind. I shuddered.

Kestrel's eyes bored into mine. "Kira, the only reason you're not under sedation now and on your way to jacker camp is because of what you can do and who your father is."

"My father?" My voice squeaked. "My father works for the Navy..." I stopped because it was getting hard to breathe. My father worked for Naval Intelligence. The Clan had jackers, the FBI had jackers—surely the Navy had jackers too. *My father is a jacker.*

Kestrel watched calmly as my mouth flopped open. My father was a jacker, and he had never said a word. All this time, he knew. *He knew.* Why didn't he *warn* me?

"Officer Patrick Moore is a very important asset for the government." Kestrel lowered his voice. "One we would rather not lose to the camp."

"What are you saying?" Panic crept into my chest. Would Kestrel send my dad to that camp for jackers if I didn't do what he wanted? And what about me?

"I'm saying that you and your father can *both* help the government, Kira. It's a big job, protecting normal citizens." He arched an eyebrow. "I'm sure you understand how dangerous a jacker can be. We can't have them running loose in society."

The sharp edge of his voice scraped against my already panicked nerves. My legs twitched in agitation. I jumped to my feet, startling Kestrel. He jerked back from the table and then deliberately folded his hands in his lap.

I paced the room, my twitchy legs carrying me from the door to the opposite wall, only a half dozen paces. Blood pounded through my head, and it seemed to flush out some of the haze. If only I could think clearly for a minute.

"Kira, sit down." Kestrel's voice was harsh, like he could command me to sit. I kept pacing. He wanted something from me. He said I was unique. *He had never seen someone take out an entire Clan before...*

"Kira. Sit down." This time his tone was softer. I stopped, frozen halfway across the room at the gentle sound of his voice. Just like Simon, he wanted to talk me into something—something he couldn't force me to do, because he couldn't jack me. The Clan wanted me for my hard head, to do some kind of special spy mission. What did the FBI want me for?

The same thing as Kestrel. Catch other jackers.

I tried not to let my eyes go wide. Kestrel gestured encouragingly to the rickety chair. "It's going to be all right, Kira. Let's just talk about it. Sit down."

I slowly sank into the seat.

"Do you want some more water?" he asked. The cup was still full. I shook my head. "It's not as bad as you think. The FBI is giving you a chance to avoid the camp and work for us."

The FBI should only send dangerous criminals to that jacker camp, like Molloy and his Clan. I wasn't a criminal, and neither was my dad. But Kestrel seemed all too happy to send me there—and possibly my dad as well—if I didn't work for him, catching other jackers and sending them to the camp. I gripped my knees to keep my hands from shaking.

Kestrel leaned forward, his face severe again. "Not everyone gets a choice, Kira."

There had to be some way out of this. I didn't want to go to jacker camp, but I didn't want any part of sending other jackers there either. Maybe I could pretend to go along with what he wanted. At least until I figured a way out. I nodded to keep him talking.

His shoulders relaxed. "Good. You're making the right choice, Kira."

He started explaining about the FBI's jacker recruitment program, but I wasn't listening any more. I pretended to weigh his words. The pacing had cleared my head a little, but my thoughts were still fuzzed. Maybe this was what obscura felt like, for readers that wanted to dull their thoughts and everyone else's. Everything in my mind was less distinct, as if parts of my brain had gone numb. As I fought through the haze, I found my brain felt soft...

"Once you go through the training, everything will return to normal," Kestrel was saying. "You'll have a regular life, like your father…"

The Jell-O inside my head was exactly like the squishy material of other people's minds!

I carefully kept my face flat and nodded some more as Kestrel rambled on. The orange mist was infused into the thinking parts of my brain in the front. I could feel it, taste it. Orange and spice, like tea, but it felt like anesthetic.

I told my body to increase the blood flow to that part of my brain. My heart started to race, pumping blood furiously to my head. My face radiated heat as blood coursed through it. I focused momentarily on Kestrel to see if he noticed.

He prattled on. "No one will know you're a jacker. And you'll be helping to put dangerous jackers where they belong, where they won't be able to hurt anyone else…"

The orange mist was clearing, carried away in my bloodstream to some place in my body where it wouldn't affect my ability to jack. My mental strength was coming back. If I could fight off the juice, maybe I could escape. Catch Kestrel off-guard and jack him hard. I would only have one chance. If he saw it coming, he would be too strong for me. I picked up the glass of water and drained it.

"Do you…" He faltered as I smiled at him. "Do you have any questions?"

"Can I get another glass of water?" I kept my face blank, although the heat from it seemed to scorch the air. Kestrel didn't notice.

"Sure."

Whisking the cup off the table, he paused at the door, clearly linking a thought to someone outside. In a moment, it opened for another cup exchange. He returned to the table. "So, what do you think?" He gave me another invisible-lipped smile.

I took a deep breath and jacked into his head with everything I had. The jack felt weak, even as I strained forward and plunged deep into Kestrel's mind. *Stop,* I thought, but it had the strength of a suggestion, not a command.

Kestrel's eyes went wide and he tumbled backward, knocking the chair over and tripping as he scrambled to put distance between us. *Stop! Stop!* I jumped to my feet and crawled over the table. If I got closer to him the intensity would increase. I leaped off the table, trying to grab him, but he batted my hands away. I managed to latch onto his arm and pull him close. It didn't matter. I was too weak to knock him out.

The door burst open. A large guard quickly pinned me to the floor, and another followed right behind him. There were too many of them, all trapping me within my own skull again. The second guard already had a needle in my arm.

Kestrel's stark face loomed over me. "You shouldn't have done that, Kira." His voice faded as the orange mist pumped into my brain and clouded my vision.

His cold blue eyes were the last things I saw before oblivion.

chapter TWENTY-FIVE

I swam up out of unconsciousness to the feel of someone's hands roughly patting me down.

My mind was fuzzed from the orange-mist drug Kestrel's thugs had injected into me, and my eyelids were a heavy curtain I couldn't command open. The warm, rough floor shook underneath me, and sounds of crunching tires and creaking metal bounced along with it.

I wondered where on earth I was, but top priority was stopping the praver who was pawing me as if he expected to find weapons hidden in my thin t-shirt and shorts. I beat at his probing hands, but the juice had made my arms quivery and useless. I jacked into his mind, but he immediately threw me out.

Taking a deep breath, I reached inside my own mind to speed up my heart and clear away the mist. I tolerated about ten more seconds of the groping. As soon as the fuzz cleared enough, I jacked deep into his mind and ordered him to stop. His hands left me, and I heard him hit the metal floor.

I forced my eyes open and grimaced against the harsh light

that streamed in through the truck's high windows. My molester lay like a broken puppet on the dusty floor. He couldn't have been more than thirteen. My stomach curled into a knot. As I contemplated waking him, I heard a sniffle. A girl sat huddled on a metal bench that ran along the wall of the truck. Her face was buried in her arms as they hugged the tops of her knees.

"Are you okay?" My voice rasped with dryness. She didn't answer. The truck swayed underneath me, and I gripped the metal bench to haul myself to my feet. I stood on my tiptoes to peek out the windows. Nothing but blue sky.

Holding the wall to keep steady, I shuffled to the front where a door looked like it might lead to the driver's compartment. The knob twisted easily in my hand, and I flung it open, only to find two empty seats. The truck ambled down a hard-packed dirt road, apparently on an autopath, but there was no mindware interface, no entry point where I could jack in and change the preprogrammed course. Ahead, a huge encampment rose out of the desert, covered with sand-colored camouflage netting and surrounded by metal fences fifteen feet high. Barbed razor wire spiraled along the top. It looked like a prison.

Which, of course, it was.

A tremor ran through my hands as the pieces clicked into place, and I gripped the back of the vacant driver seat to steady them. Kestrel had sent me to the jacker camp, along with these two jacker kids. I licked my cracked lips, parched from the drugs and the desert. He had sent me to prison simply for being who I was.

Anger clawed my stomach like an angry beast.

As we approached the camp gate, it swung open with determined mechanical speed. Sunlight pushed through the netting and mottled the ground under the canopy. Another metallic gridded gate and a second fence waited a hundred feet inside the camp. We rumbled past the first fence, and I strained to see beyond the second one.

Whatever was on the other side, I was sure I wasn't prepared for it.

The truck lurched to a stop, and the girl whimpered. Her dirty face was streaked with tears. She couldn't be any older than the boy. Straggles of brown hair fell across her wide blue eyes, and dirt marred the pink skirt draped over her knees. Her bright white ankle socks were untouched by the desert. If I wasn't prepared, she didn't have a prayer. I found handholds along the truck and crouched down next to her.

"What's your name?"

She leaned away from me. "Laney."

"Okay, Laney. You and I are going to stick together." I tried to smile without cracking my dried lips. She nodded and glanced at the still form of the boy.

"Should we wake him?" I asked, following her gaze.

She shook her head in short, rapid movements. A whining sound came from below the truck, and the view out the front spun until the first gate appeared again. The truck jerked and I almost tumbled over, catching myself on the wall behind Laney's head. We were backing toward the second gate now, and whatever waited for us would soon be here. I searched the dusty floor for a weapon. The truck was bare.

I tentatively reached through the gate with my mind. Hundreds of people milled around inside the fences. I pulled back from the thrumming of all those thoughts and heard the metallic grinding of the second gate opening. The truck lurched to a stop, and I nearly lost my footing again. The gate rattled shut behind us. An audible murmur rose in the distance.

I gave Laney a quick nod and edged toward the back door, hoping to get the jump on whatever lay beyond it. There was scuffling outside the truck, and something heavy slammed against the door. The entire truck shuddered with the impact.

I backed away, keeping between Laney and the door and hoping I could stop whatever would come through. As I stretched my mind forward, the gray door screeched open and there stood Simon.

My mouth fell open, and he threw his head back, as if I hit him. "You!" The word wheezed out of him. "What the..." His eyes went wide, as though finding me in the truck was the worst possible twist on a very bad day.

Behind him a full-on melee raged in the camp. Desert-brown buildings hemmed a large open area jammed with people. They encircled a dozen fighters in the middle, a scrum of fists flying and bodies dropping. I saw a flash of red hair.

Simon cursed under his breath, pulling my attention back to him. He seemed to resolve some debate in his mind. I was afraid to link in and find out what it was.

"Come on, let's go!" He spat the words and held the door wide for us. But there was no way I was trusting Simon Zagan, arch-betrayer of girlfriends and unsuspecting jackers.

I stood straighter and clenched my fists at my side. "I'm not going anywhere with you!"

His jaw dropped, but it quickly set into a hard grinding of muscles. "I don't have time to argue. If you want to live, come with me. *Now!*"

I glanced again at the melee behind him. The ring of on-lookers, some as young as Laney, cheered on the fighters, who seemed older and bigger. The brawl was getting uglier, with fighters falling down and not getting up. I didn't want Laney or myself mixed up in any of that.

My options seemed bad and worse, and bad would have to do.

"Fine. But she's coming with me." I took hold of Laney's hand and pulled her up on shaky legs.

"Okay, okay, let's go." Simon checked over his shoulder.

As Laney and I scooted past the slumped figure of the boy, I asked, "What about him?"

"He's on his own." Another boy lay motionless in the dirt below the door. My mouth flopped open to ask, then I shut it. Simon hoisted Laney out of the truck and over the body. I ignored Simon's hand and hopped over the inert boy myself. Simon shut the truck door behind us, glanced over his shoulder again, and hurried us away from the center square.

The hardscrabble dirt reflected the dots of sun that made it through the canopy. I gripped Laney's hand as Simon weaved us between dizzying arrays of identical sand-weathered barracks. They stood in clustered rows like parked train cars, with large open areas in between. We ran to keep up with him, and he alternated between sprinting and darting looks around corners.

Simon held his arm out to stop us, and I almost crashed into it. Up ahead, between barracks, three girls huddled around a fourth, who was on her knees in the dirt. As we watched, she slumped to the ground. A chill went through me as Simon backed us up, watching the ring of tormenters to see if they noticed us. They were too busy checking the pockets of the fallen girl.

Simon tugged us around another barrack, out of their sight. He dashed across a short alleyway-sized gap and turned down a different row of buildings, each with four doors. At the last building, he pulled open the furthest door. Inside was a space about the size of my living room back home. The air was cooler, but stale. Six cots wrapped tightly with gray blankets lined the bare walls.

He closed the door and pressed against it, listening or maybe reaching for something. Laney dropped my hand and climbed on a bed in the furthest corner. She drew up her knees and clenched them again. Simon exhaled, apparently content that we hadn't been followed.

I linked into his mind. He whipped his head around and shoved me back out. "Don't do that here." His voice was rough and low. "Not if you want to make it through the day."

I took a step back. Maybe I had made a terrible mistake, letting him secret Laney and me away.

He rubbed his face with both hands. "What are you doing here, Kira?" he demanded.

"I didn't want to come here!" I shot back.

"It's your fault we're all here!"

My jaw dropped. "How is it my fault?"

"Don't tell me you're not a mole for the FBI!" He clenched his hands. "Someone had to rat us out, and you and Gomez are the only ones who didn't come with us to the camp. So, did the Feds give up on you? Couldn't break into that hard head of yours?" He took several swift steps and made to tap on my forehead. I cringed away from his touch.

"I..." I swallowed and straightened. "I didn't know anything about the FBI or this place. I didn't know anything at all until you came along and tried to trick me into joining your stupid Clan!"

Simon rocked back on his heels. "There are a lot of people here who think you betrayed them."

"*I* betrayed *them*?"

"Yes! And they're going to want your head for it." His voice was urgent, as though he was trying to shock some sense into me. "Look, just stay hidden here until I can figure this thing out."

He ran his fingers through his dark hair, which had been lightened with ground-in dust. A smudge ran along his cheek, and his clothes were the same that he wore at the warehouse—except the white starched shirt was mostly wrinkles. A fine layer of grit had colored it the same dull brown as the apartment walls.

"I have to go help out with something. Stay here and don't make any noise, and whatever you do, don't jack anyone until I get back." He started to turn away and then stopped. "Unless you have to." He quickly crossed the room, but hesitated again at the door and glanced at Laney. "If I don't come back, stay hidden as long as you can." He slipped out the door and closed it solidly behind him.

I stared at the door for a long time. Laney's head was still hidden in her arms as she clutched her folded legs. I sat next to her and linked, very gently, into her mind. Her mind-scent was sweet, like raspberries.

I guess we're going to be here a while. My name is Kira.

She peeked up and wordlessly showed me a stream of pictures: her fighting with her family about homework; them collapsing on the floor around her; her frantic call to 911 only to have the FBI show up; the FBI saying her family would wake up believing she had run away.

The memories made tears flow down Laney's face again. I wrapped an arm around her, but it didn't quell the shaking. I borrowed blankets from two other cots and wrapped them around us. Her body quieted as our collective heat fought off the chill of the room and our dire situation.

I hoped like crazy that no one would find us before Simon returned.

chapter TWENTY-SIX

Laney fell asleep on my shoulder.

I wriggled out of our cocoon and eased her down to the thin cot, smoothing the stray hairs back from her face so they wouldn't tickle and wake her. The peace of sleep made her seem even younger.

That Kestrel would send someone so young to this lawless camp in the desert made me clench my teeth. Not that I belonged here either. I was trying to figure out our options when Simon burst into the barrack. He gulped in ragged breaths and darted looks all around the room, as though he expected an ambush. If he'd brought back an angry mob with him, the flimsy door he was leaning against wouldn't hold them off.

I put a finger to my lips and slid off the cot, careful not to disturb Laney. If he wouldn't let me link into his head to mindtalk, at least we could discuss things quietly and not wake her up.

And we definitely needed to talk.

He looked considerably worse than when he left, with dirt ground into his face and a dull smear of blood at the corner of his mouth. I reached up to touch his face.

He smacked my hand away.

I pulled back my stinging hand. "Are you hurt?"

He narrowed his eyes. "I'm fine." A purplish bruise was blooming on the side of his face. He must have gone back to the entrance and joined the melee.

I swallowed, my throat still raw from thirst. "What was the fight about?"

"The fight's over. Clan Molloy is now in control of Block C, which means Molloy and the rest of the Clan will be here soon." He hesitated. "I might be able to hide you, Kira, because they can't jack into your head. They won't sense you from the other barracks. But her," he said and flicked a glance to Laney, "they'll notice right away. She's still a changeling."

"Well you can't just turn her over to Molloy!"

Simon grimaced. "She's safer with Molloy than she is with *you*," he said. "And Molloy will be a much better Block chief than that monster Lenny." I guessed Lenny was on the losing end of the fight, but that didn't make Molloy worth trusting.

Reading my skeptical look, Simon sighed. "Molloy's not the bad guy here, Kira. There are a lot worse people out there, and some of them are living in the next Block over." He gestured to the prefab buildings beyond the walls. "You could have been part of the Clan, you know. Everything would have worked out fine if you hadn't lost it at the warehouse."

I gaped. "You were going to kill Raf!"

Anger burst to life on his face. "He was spying on us! I didn't have any choice! Molloy would have done it, if I hadn't."

"What was I supposed to do?" My voice had risen. "Just let you kill him?"

We glared at each other, faces drawn tight and close. A bright red bead of blood formed at the corner of his mouth and trickled down. He wiped it with the back of his hand and turned away, shoulders slumped. With his back to me, voice flat, he said, "Things don't always turn out the way you'd like them to."

I stared hard at the back of his head, tempted to jack in and make him sorry for what he had done. Sorry for trying to kill Raf, sorry for luring me into the Clan, sorry for pretending to care about me all that time, only to trick me into working for Molloy. I wanted to make him regret all he had done, but somehow seeing him trapped in a desert camp, fighting to survive—I didn't have the heart.

After all, he was right. We would all be better off if the FBI hadn't caught up with the Clan. There had to be some way out of this nightmare. I didn't trust Simon, but he had already helped us. And I had more than myself to think about.

"If you bring Laney to Molloy, do you promise he'll keep her safe?" I tried to keep the edge out of my voice.

He hesitated before he turned to me. Weariness dragged his face down. "He will, I promise. His younger brother disappeared a long time ago, when they were trying to escape the Feds. I told you, he has a soft spot for the young ones, and he hates the way no one looks out for them here. He sent me to check the newcomer truck, even though we were taking a thrashing from Lenny's clan, just to make sure we got to any changelings before the others did."

I shifted from one foot to the other. "Okay."

Simon gave me a short nod. His eyes rested on my lips, still chapped from the desert and the drugs. "Look, we should give Molloy some time to get settled." His face twisted in disgust. "There might be some stragglers from Lenny's clan that he needs to decide about."

"Decide what?"

"Well, there's nowhere for a defeated Clan to go. They either get broken up and absorbed into other Clans, or..."

"Or?"

"I don't want to know what happens to them, okay!" The fear on Simon's face sent a chill through me. "Whatever it is, she doesn't need to see it." He glanced at Laney. "It's better if we let the dust settle. In the meantime, I'll get you some water and food. Water shouldn't be a problem, but there's not much food. I'll see what I can do. I'll be back soon."

I didn't want him to leave. It felt like a pack of wild dogs was roaming outside in the brilliant desert heat, and he was the only one that knew how to control them. On his way out the door, he gave me a grim smile and repeated, "I'll be right back."

While he was out, Laney tossed and turned in the rough blankets wrapped around her, letting out occasional soft whimpers. The same scene she had played before, where she accidentally knocked out her entire family, repeated over and over in her mind. I slowly nudged her to a new dream, one where no one was hurt. Her tremors stopped, and she slipped into a deeper, dreamless sleep. The quiet sound of her breathing had me straining to hear beyond the barrack walls, in case anyone might be coming for us. But I didn't reach out with my mind.

A few minutes later, a scuffle of feet outside kicked up my heart rate until Simon pulled open the door and let in a blast of dust and sunshine. He brought bottles of water and dust-coated protein bars. My throat still rasped like sandpaper. He had to stop me from guzzling an entire bottle at once.

"So are you going to tell me how you ended up here?" he asked, when I paused for a breath. I took another swig of water and licked my lips, not sure what to tell him. At this point, there didn't seem to be any sense in lying.

"The FBI caught up to me." At the last second, I left Raf out of it. "They wanted to recruit me." I cocked my head. "Just like you did."

Simon didn't seem to take offense at my accusation. "So why didn't you join them? Why come here?"

"I didn't plan on doing either. My plan was to escape."

He snorted. "I guess that didn't work out for you." His half-grin was more rueful than cruel, but I still didn't appreciate it.

"I almost did," I said. "If I'd had a few more minutes, I could have gotten rid of the last of that orange mist drug, or whatever it was, and taken out Agent Kestrel and his jacker guards."

Simon's face went dead still. "You did what?" He stepped closer to me. I held my ground and shifted so I was between him and Laney, where she lay sleeping on the cot. The look in his eyes made me stammer.

"I... I could have taken him out, but the drug..."

"You said you got rid of the drug." It was a statement, and his eyes bored into mine, daring me to deny it.

"Yes." I cleared my throat. "Yes, I did."

"How?" He leaned toward me, as though our lives hung on the answer to his question.

"I told my brain to pump it out." It sounded a lot more lame than the reality of manipulating my own mind. He took a step back and his eyes widened, as if he had discovered I had a third arm or maybe an alien brain. Too late, I realized I should have kept that to myself.

He quickly regained his composure. "Can you do it again?"

"I did it on the way here. In the truck."

A smile flashed across his face. He closed the space between us, like he was about to hug me. Instead, he took hold of my shoulders. I shrank back from his touch and the fervent look in his eyes. "Kira, if you tell Molloy about this ability of yours, he'll let you stay in the Clan, I'm sure of it."

I didn't really want to be in Clan Molloy, but the rest of the camp wasn't exactly attractive. And Molloy was the devil I knew, so sticking with him seemed smarter than taking my chances with the unknown pravers menacing the camp. Besides, I didn't really trust any of them, and staying in the Clan meant I could keep an eye on Laney. Just in case.

Laney started to stir, her tranquil look lingering as she propped herself up and licked her dry lips. I twisted out of Simon's grasp and brought her one of the water bottles. She greedily slurped it down. She hadn't entirely awoken to our nightmarish situation in the camp, and a surreal look of happiness crossed her face as the water hit its mark.

I met Simon's expectant look. "Fine. Take us to Molloy."

chapter TWENTY-SEVEN

Simon led Laney and me back out into the blistering sun.

Our barrack was at the tail end of a row of eight identical buildings. Simon took us toward the front and around a corner, where a hundred-foot space opened between our cluster of barracks and the next group of military-style structures. The gap between blocks had been empty before, but now that the fighting was done, several groups of jackers lounged outside the weathered doors of their barracks.

A knot of four boys my age swung their heads in our direction. Their clothes were frayed and torn, some holes patched and others left gaping. They looked like they'd been wearing the same thing for months. Each had a strip of black cloth tied around their arm.

Their minds pressed on mine. Simon said not to jack in here, but these pravers seemed to have no compunction. Laney's hand trembled in mine.

"Can they jack from there?" I asked Simon.

"Most can't bridge the gap between blocks to do more than

link in. That's why they're set so far apart." The boys stared like wolves sizing up which sheep to eat first. Simon must have linked some thought to them, because they switched focus to him, and the light pressure on my mind evaporated. They gave Laney and me another lingering look filled with nasty promise, then the apparent leader shoved his hands in his pockets, and they turned their backs on us.

Simon hurried us forward. We quickly reached the center barrack in the block, identical to all the others except the letter C had been etched above the first door.

"Just let me do the talking." Simon walked in, and we trailed behind him.

The room had been stripped of cots, leaving more space for the two dozen Clan members. Molloy's red head towered over them as they gathered around him. The Clan was in much the same shape as Simon—dusty, beaten, and faces lit up with their apparent victory. Molloy's broad smile extended to Simon, but instantly twisted to a snarl when he saw me.

"Wha—?" He growled and parted the crowd of Clan members as he moved more quickly than a giant should. "What is she doing here?" he demanded. I was afraid he would run us over, with the speed he was picking up.

"Wait!" Simon leaped in front of me. "Let me explain."

Molloy hesitated, but seemed ready to pummel me into the ground like the rival gang of jackers he had destroyed minutes ago. Simon felt like a thin barrier to the wrath that was coming off the Red Giant. His eyes flicked to Simon, back to me, and then finally noticed Laney tucked behind me. Molloy's eyes narrowed as he took in my protective stance.

"She came in the truck with the newcomers," Simon was saying. "This changeling was there, and another boy, but I couldn't help him."

Molloy's eyes swung back to Simon. "Why not?"

"He was unconscious." Simon glanced at me, and I wished he hadn't. Molloy could probably figure out who had made him that way. "I had to fight off Lenny's crew just to get to the truck. I didn't have time to haul the kid out."

"So you brought *her* instead." The intensity of Molloy's stare on my face was matched by the pressure of him trying to jack into my mind. "A fine choice. Now we can pay her back." The rest of the Clan members had slowly circled around us. Pasty Man, Molloy's international spook friend, stood by the door. His face was imprinted with a red boot mark. There was no way we were leaving the room.

I was a match in the middle of a keg of gunpowder.

"That wasn't her fault!" Simon held up his hands. "She didn't know anything about the Feds. Gomez must have been the rat. Right? Otherwise why would Kira be here?"

"Perhaps the Feds sent her to spy on us again." Molloy leaned to the side to peer at Laney. "What about the little one?" He was talking to me now. "Is she a snitch like you, Kira?"

I swallowed. "She's just a kid. She needs protection."

Molloy didn't seem to expect that response from me. Simon cut in. "She's just a changeling."

Molloy jutted his chin out to the Clan members hovering behind us. "We'll take the girl into the Clan. But not the traitor."

Hands reached out of the crowd and tugged Laney away from me. She gasped and gripped my hand with both of hers. Her best chance was probably with the Clan, but I had a hard time convincing myself to let go.

I stood straighter and stared down the hatred on Molloy's face. "Do you promise to keep her safe?"

"My quarrel isn't with her." His shark smile hollowed out my stomach.

Laney's wide-eyed look stabbed through me.

"Laney, it's okay. I promise." I linked into her head. *I don't want you mixed up in my mess, okay? I need you to go with them. To be safe.*

Fear gave her mind a bitter aftertaste. She slowly released her death-grip. Her small eyes grew large and round as she was swallowed by the crowd.

Molloy's meaty hand clamped on my arm and jerked me around. My knees softened as he loomed over me, probably deciding how best to take his revenge. Before I could open my mouth, Simon grabbed Molloy's wrist. "She can help us."

"I've heard that from you before." Molloy released me and focused on Simon. Pasty Man appeared by his side.

Simon seemed to stagger under a great weight, and I realized that they must be fighting in his mind. Simon buckled and fell to the floor, landing on his knees but managing to stay upright. A cruel smile curled one side of Pasty Man's face as Simon swayed under their assault. I remembered the force that Pasty Man had pressed on my mind in the warehouse. With the two of them combined, Simon didn't have a chance.

"I know how to fight the gas." I stepped next to Simon. "Let him go, and I'll tell you how." I didn't like Simon. Not even a little bit. But he was trying to help me, and it wasn't right for him to take Molloy's wrath.

In the warehouse, Molloy and his Clan had been unprepared. I had caught them by surprise and knocked them out before they knew what was happening. But now, I doubted I could even overpower Molloy, much less a room full of angry Clan members. Maybe I could bargain our way out of this.

Molloy ignored me and fixed his eyes on Simon. His whole body trembled, and he squeezed his eyes shut, as if he could keep Molloy out by the power of his eyelids. I clenched my hands. If I attacked Molloy, neither of us would likely make it out of the room. But if they didn't release Simon soon, I would have to at least try to shove Molloy out of Simon's mind, before he did any permanent damage.

Right as I was about to jack in, Molloy released his mental grip on Simon, and Pasty Man sneered his disgust at some unspoken command. Simon fell forward on his hands and gasped for air. I gingerly pressed into Simon's mind, afraid of what I would find. There was no sign of Molloy's presence. *Are you okay?*

Yes. Simon's response was weak.

"So," said Molloy. "Simon here seems to believe you're telling the truth about this ability to control the effects of the gas."

"That's right." I stood taller.

Molloy eyed me with curiosity, the hatred having vanished with his interrogation of Simon's mind. "Well, now, little Kira.

It seems you may make a useful addition to the Clan yet." Some of the hardness returned to his face. "But Simon is much more trusting than I am. And much more enamored with you than he should be."

I refused to look at Simon. He had forfeited the right to any feelings for me the moment we walked into that warehouse. And my feelings for him were closer to hatred than anything else.

"I can tell you how it works."

"Oh, you'll need to do much better than that, little Kira. I'll believe you can defeat the gas when I see you do it."

Considering I had the Impenetrable Mind, and Molloy couldn't get into my head for a truth examination, there was a certain logic to proving my newfound talent by demonstration. But I still didn't like the sound of it.

"Uh, okay."

Molloy smirked at my discomfort. "According to information from a few, ah, *recruits* from Lenny's Clan, we're due for another supply drop." Pasty Man seemed like he enjoyed extracting that information from the minds of Lenny's crew.

"When the Feds come in, they gas the camp first. Everyone goes down and wakes up with fresh food and water supplies to fight over."

"Why don't they just send in the truck?" Given that I had been delivered on an autotruck to the camp, gassing everyone seemed like a lot of effort merely to supply food and water.

Molloy's face turned cold. "Because they take a few *volunteers* with them when they leave."

The Feds took people *out* of the camp? I had assumed it was a one-way trip. Why send us all to jacker camp, only to take us back out again, a few at a time? It didn't make any sense. "Where do they take them?"

"According to Lenny's Clan, somewhere worse than here," Molloy said with dead seriousness. What could possibly be worse than the camp? "If you're able to fight off the gas, little Kira, then perhaps you could be useful after all." He loomed over me with his giant frame, but his words were more frightening than his hulking presence. "I don't want to lose any of my Clan to the Feds and their ghoulish experiments."

My jaw dropped. The Feds were experimenting on jackers? It was like the early days of the change, when they pushed probes into my Great Grandpa Reilly's brain like he was a lab rat. How could they possibly justify that? Anger boiled in my stomach.

"Like I said," Molloy continued, "I'll believe you can control the gas when I see it. If you can, we'll talk about putting your ability to good use. Like getting out of the Fed's cozy prison. But I'm not going to risk any of my Clan members based on your *good word*," he said, the words sounding like they tasted bitter, "and Simon's misplaced trust." He folded his arms to study me. "If you can fight the gas when the drop comes, you should be able to bring back food from the depot before the rest of the camp awakes. If you can't do that much, well, you're not much use to us then, are you? And if the Feds catch you, then we'll see you when you come back in the newcomer truck with a few pieces missing." He leaned closer, looming over me. "Either way, I expect you to use that unique head of yours to keep my Clan safe. If there's anyone missing after the drop, it had better be *you*."

I leaned away from him. Either Molloy thought I could fight through the mist and hold off the Feds all on my own, or he was hoping I would get caught trying and end up in one of the Fed's experiments. I had a chance of fighting off the gas, but I didn't have much hope of holding the Feds at bay. I hoped like crazy that they wouldn't come looking for any Clan Molloy members during the next drop.

Because it seemed there was a place worse than the camp after all.

chapter TWENTY-EIGHT

Molloy had learned much from interrogating Lenny's crew. Andre, Molloy's pasty second-in-command, was briefing me and seemed to enjoy talking to me about as much as I liked his beady stares. We each wore the red armband that identified us as Block C now, like the rest of the Clan, but I didn't make the mistake of assuming we were on the same side. "The supply drops happen randomly," he said. "Before the drop, the camp is gassed. It comes in through an underground piping system. The barracks, the washrooms, the depot. Even outside." His grin was filled with evil, and I was sure he hoped I would fail miserably in combating the gas and the Feds.

Only that was exactly what Molloy expected me to do. "How many prisoners do they take?" I tried to not bow under Pasty Man's antagonism.

"Usually only two or three."

Maybe luck would be on my side. Block C could hold about 400 people, but it was relatively empty, with most of Lenny's Clan fleeing after the fight. If the other Blocks were even half full, and with seven Blocks spread around the camp, my rough calculations put the camp at over a thousand inmates. The odds seemed low that any Clan Molloy members would go missing.

The idea of a thousand jackers made my mind fuzz out a bit. There must be many more jackers in the world than I ever imagined. With a thousand in the camp, there had to be many times that amount hiding among the readers of the world.

Andre was distracted by Simon hopping around on one foot and making a squawking noise. I had convinced Simon to let Laney practice her jacking skills on him, since she couldn't jack into my Impenetrable Mind. I linked a thought to her. *Don't make Simon mad. We're going to need his help.*

She pouted. *Can I make him sing?*

No.

How about cartwheels?

I threw out my hands. *Just practice linking your thoughts.*

She rolled her eyes, but Simon stumbled to a stop and glared at me from across the room. I ignored him. "So," I said to Andre, "as long as no Clan Molloy members go missing and I bring back some food, we're good. Right?"

Andre hesitated, but gave me a short nod. "As soon as the drop is finished and the camp awakens from the gas, the depot will be overrun. Each Block sends its strongest jackers at harvest time. Some don't come back." His evil smile returned. I narrowed my eyes. "If, however, you can remain awake, it should be no problem for you to bring back food for the Clan." He lifted a dusty pillow from the cot next to us. "A pillowcase full should be enough to convince Mr. Molloy."

I snatched the pillow from him and started to tug the pillowcase off. "No problem." But I wasn't at all sure about any of it. If I could keep the gas at bay, I should be able to get to the depot after the Feds left and before anyone else woke up. But if the FBI agents came after any Clan Molloy members, I was in serious trouble. Maybe I would be able to knock them out, if they weren't expecting me. And if I was on the losing end of that jack? No, if they came looking for *volunteers* from Clan Molloy, I'd be better off finding another Clan to join. Which made me realize how little I knew about the rest of the Clans and the layout of the camp, much less where the food was held. "Where's the depot?"

"I'm sure Simon can help you with that."

I had a sick feeling that I had stepped into some kind of trap. We both glanced at Simon, who was doing pushups on the floor next to a grinning Laney. I let out a long sigh.

After Andre left and I convinced Laney to apologize to Simon, I planned to check out the rest of the camp, find the depot, and possibly scout out ways to escape and take Laney with me. Simon insisted on coming along. I told him I didn't want to leave Laney alone, that I was concerned about the less savory members of Clan Molloy, including Andre. Simon insisted she would be fine as long as she stayed in Block C.

I lightly brushed Simon's mind, just a bare whisper of a link so I could read his thoughts without him being aware of my presence. I had learned how to do this shortly after Molloy gave us temporary sanctuary in the Clan. Jacking into someone's mind was the same as asking for a fight, but only if they knew you were there. Trusting Simon wasn't high on my priority list, but he seemed to only be thinking of keeping me safe outside Block C. And I didn't see a way to leave him behind.

As it turned out, I was glad Simon came with me as soon as we left Block C. A gang of jackers drifted away from Block B to follow us. They were the four guys from before, they knew my head was as hard as a rock, and they had brought more friends with black armbands. They might have figured out I was unique or maybe they wanted to finish whatever praver thoughts they had from before.

Simon didn't have to tell me to pick up the pace.

We started jogging and then flat out ran to the depot when they kept pace. We avoided territory staked out by other Clans by staying in the wide-open areas between Blocks. The depot was hard to miss. If there hadn't been a melee when I first arrived, I would have seen it. The sand-colored walls enclosed racks and racks of empty shelving that stood in rows down the warehouse-sized depot. We shut the heavy double doors and locked ourselves inside.

"Do you know those guys?" My voice was strained from the run and the panic.

"Yeah," Simon said. "They're some of Lenny's old crew." His voice was even more wheezy than mine. "Block B must have taken them in. They're not very nice." Simon dragged an empty rack over, metal screeching against concrete, and braced it against the door. I reached out to lightly check on our followers. They were gathered in the open space where the fight had gone down.

"They're waiting for us to come out," I said. "They're

planning to attack us then. They want to take us prisoner, not kill us." They really wanted to take *me* prisoner, not so much Simon, but I left that part out.

Simon straightened. "How do you know that?"

Oops.

"How do you think?" I retorted. Simon may be on my side for the moment, but I wasn't on a sharing-secrets basis with him, even if he had saved me from Molloy's wrath. Simon shook his head and searched for other things to stack against the door. He settled on an empty 55-gallon drum that he wheeled over and shoved against the rack.

"So, are we going to hole up here until they go away?"

Simon brushed the dust from his hands and opened his mouth to answer, then sagged toward the ground. I lunged forward and barely got my arm under him to keep him from cracking his head on the concrete floor.

"Simon!" I jacked fast into his mind. Three of the Block B gang were deep inside and tunneling deeper to slow his heart and breathing. They had a change of plans. Now they decided if they killed Simon, it would be easier to take me without a fight. My quick survey outside the warehouse showed all six had crept up to the door.

I pushed them out of Simon's head, slamming them back into their own minds and knocking the weakest one out, but the others were too strong for me. When the body hit the dirt outside, the others were momentarily distracted.

I gritted my teeth and dragged Simon away from the door. I needed to put distance between him and the gang to revive him. He groggily squirmed in my arms, which didn't help much. Then he snapped awake with a gasp and twisted out of my hands altogether. He crouched on the floor, wild-eyed.

Follow me! I ordered his limbs to move while his mind sorted things out. *They're right outside the door!*

The back of the warehouse was a good seventy feet from the door, far enough to lessen their ability to jack Simon. I reached back to lightly tap their thoughts. They still didn't realize I was listening in and couldn't seem to find the blank spot of my mind. But they could sense Simon. They revived their crewmate and planned to split up, one group going around the side of the warehouse to seek us out, while the others worked on opening the door.

I slammed into the weakened one and sent him collapsing back to the ground again. Their outrage and confusion derailed their plans for a moment, but we were running out of time. I scouted the warehouse for another door. There was only a row of high windows letting in camouflage-dappled light and a bunch of empty shelving. That would have to do.

I flashed a picture of our escape route to Simon. Together we tipped a shelving rack until it banged loudly against the wall and formed a metallic ladder of sorts. I grabbed a discarded coffee can and clambered up the scaffolding with Simon close on my heels. The sharp edge of the can dug into my hand as I slammed it against the window. It made a terrific noise and achieved nothing. Simon climbed up next to me and twisted around so he was balanced on the top shelf with his feet braced on the window. He kicked a hole straight through, sending the shattered pieces of glass flying outward. Several dagger-sized pieces still rimmed the edges. He kept kicking until there was a hole we could climb through without slicing ourselves to shreds.

I reached for the minds of our stalkers. They had heard the sound of the window smashing. Simon's shoes protected his feet as he perched on the edge of the window, but tiny rivers of blood flowed down from the gashes in his leg. He leaped down to the ground, and I scuttled up to the window to jump after him, wincing as the glass bit into my hands. When I hit the ground, Simon steadied me so I didn't topple into the glass-littered dirt.

The pravers had heard us, but we had a head start. Simon took my hand, and we ran like our feet were on fire all the way back to Block C.

After that, I crossed Block B off the list of Clans I would seek refuge in if things went south with the Feds during the supply drop. I might not survive joining another Clan, but it had to be better than being taken by the Feds. I was still hoping I'd get lucky and the Feds wouldn't come looking for any Clan Molloy members. Then maybe, with the help of Clan Molloy, Laney and I could escape. In the meantime, there was nothing to do but wait for the drop to come.

After my nightmarish trip to the depot, I kept to our barrack room, well within the protective zone that surrounded Block C. If the waking periods in the camp were nightmarish, the actual nights weren't any better.

I was dead asleep when something jabbed me in the stomach. My eyelids dragged open. It was only Laney, rolling around in her restless, dream-haunted sleep again. I gingerly moved her elbow away and linked into her mind.

The last three nights, the same dream had played like a sim-cast on an endless loop. Laney ran through a maze of empty hallways, searching barren white rooms for her mom. At the end of the dream, Laney would find her mom sprawled on the floor next to Laney's dad and little brother, all motionless like broken dolls. I was pretty sure she had only knocked them out, considering the FBI had told her they wiped her family's true memories, but Laney didn't know for sure. The FBI had hauled her off before she saw them wake up.

I intercepted her dream-self and steered her to a park filled with sunshine. I conjured her family waiting at a picnic table. Having seen the pallid versions of their faces in her nightmares, it was easy to create the outline of their features—Laney filled in the rest.

Her body quieted and her features smoothed. She rolled away from me and sighed. A kid like Laney didn't belong in a place like this. And neither did I.

If I could find a way out, I vowed to go home and set a few things straight—starting with my dad. *My dad the jacker*. Since Agent Kestrel dropped that little bombshell, a rumbling anger had filled me. Why hadn't my dad warned me? He must have known it was possible I might be a jacker, not a zero after all. And what did he really do for the Navy, anyway? At some point, he must have taken the option to work for the government, rather than going to the camp. I couldn't believe he would round up other innocent jackers. He wasn't like Kestrel. Maybe all those childhood sims my dad told us were true, and he was using his jacker abilities to catch the bad guys.

Except I wasn't sure who the bad guys were anymore.

If my dad had simply told me the truth, I wouldn't be lying in a concentration camp, trying to find a way to break out. If I ever did get out, he would have some answering to do.

And I would make things right with Raf as well. No more lies. He deserved to know the truth, and now I knew he would understand. It made me cringe to think his last true memory of me was with Simon, in the car, making out.

Simon wheezed as he pulled air into his lungs. It made me shudder. He'd had been beaten pretty good in the fight with Lenny's Clan, and the gashes on his leg from yesterday turned out to be pretty deep. I had cleaned and bandaged them as best I could, but there weren't any doctors or real medical supplies in our little Camp of the Flies. I hoped his injuries could heal on their own.

Simon moaned and then coughed as the sound rumbled through his chest. I linked into his mind to see if he was awake and found him caught in a dream that was all too real. A pack of older jackers crowded around a kid no bigger than Laney, menacing him with their looks and their minds. The boy quickly crumpled under the mental duress. Simon's arm twitched against the rough blanket of his cot, but in the dream it was Molloy that held him back, saying *Too late, too late.*

That image was washed away by another where Simon ran past rows of barracks. He threw open every single door, searching for someone he was afraid to find. At the last door, he discovered a girl with brown hair collapsed on the floor. He rushed to her and pulled her into his arms. Her hair fell back from her face.

I jerked out of his head. The shock of seeing my face on that girl—that dead girl in his arms—chilled me to the bone. Simon writhed on the bed again and then curled on his side, a small whimper escaping him. I could jack his nightmare away, like I had Laney's, but I didn't relish the idea of seeing myself dead again.

I stared at the ceiling and tried to ignore my racing heart and the quiet sounds of pain from Simon's cot. Either he was upset about my dream-death or the thrashing around was causing him physical pain. Regardless, I wouldn't get any sleep with him moaning. I took a deep breath and linked back in.

He was still kneeling in the room where he had found me. Thankfully, my body was gone. Except now his hands were covered in blood, and he was smearing them all over his shirt and pants. He wasn't getting them clean, just making a disastrous mess.

I needed to pull him out of his wild guilt dream before it drove us both mad. I erased the blood and the room from his mind and replaced it with a meadow in moonlight. Simon filled the meadow in with a giant boulder and his car parked beside it, recreating that night when we snuck out and met his reader friends for some pretend dipping.

These were safe true memories.

The faint smell of wild grass filled me. At first, it seemed like the scent of the meadow, recreated by Simon. Then I realized it was his mind-scent. I had been in his mind several times, but always under duress, never quite like this, where I had time to notice it.

Simon leaned against the boulder in his dream and a girl walked up to him. It was me, and when the dream-me reached up to kiss him, I jerked out of his mind again. I wasn't ready to replay that bit of disaster—the moment when I decided to be Simon Zagan's girlfriend. Not the best choice I've ever made.

Simon's body calmed, but his legs were still crooked from his earlier trauma. His breathing evened out, and the wheezing seemed less pronounced. My muscles relaxed from the constant tension of the last three days, and I sank deeper into the thin cot. I closed my eyes and tried to summon my own safe dreams to lull me into a peaceful sleep.

Something that didn't involve someone dying.

I imagined Raf, holding my hand in the car as we hid behind the hedge. In my daydream, Kestrel never came careening around the corner, and Raf slowly leaned toward me. He was going to kiss me, and this time I wouldn't stop him. This time I would find out if his lips were as soft as they looked.

A hiss whispered in my ear. I cursed inwardly and added snakes to the perils that haunted us in the Camp of the Flies. Then I caught a faint whiff of orange spice and opened my eyes. Mist rose from the floor.

The gas.

I rolled out of the cot I shared with Laney and onto my feet. The mist was already numbing my mind, its tendrils winding through the room and seeming to come from everywhere. I focused inward and sped up my heart rate from jittery panic to full-blown pounding. My head throbbed, but the extra blood pumped out the juice that was clouding my thinking. Unfortunately, each new rasping breath brought another lungful of gas. I ripped off my pillowcase and covered my nose and mouth. It already smelled of orange spice.

I couldn't hold my breath and make my heart beat out of my chest at the same time. I had to get out of the barrack and dilute the gas somehow. I linked gently into Laney and Simon's minds. They were well under the influence of the gas, deep in an unconscious state. Hopefully the rest of the camp was as well.

I tore open the barrack door and lurched out into the moonlit gap between the buildings. The gas was less concentrated outside, but it still swirled in an orange fog around my bare feet as I strode toward the common space between Block C and Block B. I kept the pillowcase over my nose and mouth and slinked into the shadows close to the barrack wall. Bodies of the Block B crew lay crumpled on the ground. The gas must have claimed them while they kept watch.

Even through the pillowcase, my gasping breaths sounded loud in the quiet night air. My heart was pounding a pulse in my head that raced to keep the gas at bay. I sprinted down the wide corridors between blocks, and the desert rocks bit into the soles of my feet. I scanned for any movement from jackers who might have eluded the gas. There was nothing but stillness until I arrived at the depot.

Men garbed in black poured from one of the two trucks parked by the gate. Gas masks obscured their faces, making them look like freakish insects. They formed a protective circle around both vehicles. Their rifles glinted in their hands as they scanned for jackers that might be resisting the effects of the gas.

Like me.

I skittered into the shadow of a nearby barrack and lightly probed the minds of the well-armed guards. They were wary, but not overly anxious. No one had overcome the effects of the gas before, yet they were prepared for the unexpected. Although most of them were readers, there was one jacker in the lead. Their thoughts overlapped, like one beast with ten pairs of eyes that could see in every direction. I could easily jack the readers but the jacker guard was like a live-wire waiting to trip. I pulled back in case he sensed me lurking at the edge of his mind.

The second truck pulled up to the depot door, and a thick mechanical tongue extended to where two rifle-less guards stood waiting. Crates about the size of my cot slowly started to travel down the conveyor belt.

A man in a long black coat, face also obscured by a gas mask, stepped around the first truck. He grasped an e-slate in his hand and set off toward the closest barrack, accompanied by two armed guards. No doubt searching for fresh victims for the government's experiments.

I stayed in the shadows.

Slate Man and his two goons returned with the limp body of a young jacker in their arms. She couldn't be any more than fourteen. My throat closed up as I watched them load her into the first truck. Then they headed straight toward me.

I scurried back along the wall and around the corner, out of their view. Their boots scuffed the ground nearby, and I muffled my heavy breathing with the pillowcase. The trio's determined steps faded. What if they were heading to Block C? I huddled out of sight and strained to listen. I didn't dare brush into their minds in case they were jackers and could sense me so close by.

The pounding of my heart was starting to take a toll. I leaned against the wall as a wave of dizziness swept through me. My chest ached. Was I giving myself a heart attack? I pressed my forehead against the cool wall and focused on slowing my heart a little, enough to keep the dizziness under control. Only each gulping breath brought more gas, and my mind was starting to fuzz out.

I wasn't going to last until the guards finished unloading.

I edged back around the barrack to check the progress at the depot. Maybe I could jack the guards unloading the crates to look the other way while I slipped inside. I brushed their minds, but pulled back quickly. *Jackers.*

The rough scraping of boots on dirt sounded to my right, and I flattened myself against the wall. The footsteps shuffled along, and when the guards swung into view, they carried a fresh victim between them, another girl, even younger this time. With dark brown hair.

Laney.

No! I lurched out from the shadows before I could stop myself. My hands twitched with the need to do something, anything, but what? Before they could catch sight of me, I ordered the two guards carrying her to *Put her down!* I would knock all three of them out as soon as Laney was safely on the ground. They readily obeyed my command, stopping in their tracks and slowly lowering her to the ground. But Slate Man was a jacker. *Keep going!* he overrode my command and quickly cast his mind out searching for me. I glimpsed two piercing blue eyes behind the mask. *Kestrel!* I tried to disappear back into the shadows and hoped he wouldn't detect the blank spot of my mind, but it was the movement that caught his eye and gave me away.

Kestrel grabbed a pistol from the guard's holster, and the pop of the gun split the quiet air.

A sharp pain stabbed my leg, and I fell to the ground. Two more jabbed my back, but I hardly felt them.

I slipped into a deep orange-colored haze.

chapter TWENTY-NINE

I struggled through the orange-flavored fuzz, but couldn't pry open my eyes. My dry tongue scraped uselessly against the roof of my mouth. I groaned my frustration and a hand clasped my arm. Instinctively, I gasped and lunged out with my mind.

Hey! It's just me, Simon thought as I plunged into his mind. I stilled and tried again to force open my eyes.

What happened? I linked the thought to him, unable to form words with my drug-disabled mouth.

I found you by Block E, near the depot, he thought. *You must have been some kind of raging elephant, because it took three darts for them to take you down.* There was a strange undercurrent of pride in his thoughts that didn't make any sense to me.

Darts? I recalled Kestrel and his victims. *Laney!*

I jerked upright, yanked my eyes open, and cringed against the barrack lights and morning sun. Half-blind, I patted the cot next to me, but I knew Laney wasn't there.

Laney's gone, Simon thought.

No!

Maybe I distracted them. Maybe they dropped her and left after they shot me. I stretched my mind out, roaming lightly over all the Clan members in Block C. She wasn't there. Maybe some other Clan had taken her in. I stretched and found I could reach Block B. I skimmed across the dozens of minds packed into the safety of their barracks. Still nothing. I kept stretching. It didn't seem like I should be able to reach so far, but then I had never really tried before. There had been no reason to. But now I reached and scanned every barrack in the camp, stopping at each of the thousand minds long enough to know they weren't Laney. They weren't the little girl who had already suffered too much for the non-crime of being a jacker kid.

No! No. But I couldn't find her anywhere in the camp.

I'm sorry, thought Simon.

Why? The thought ripped through me and came out as an animal sound in my parched throat. *Why did they take her and not me?*

I don't know. Simon's thoughts were genuinely puzzled, like he knew as well as I did that it was some kind of cruel joke. Some horrible trick to take little Laney, who was too young to have even broken curfew, and yet leave me behind, probably the most mutant jacker of all. I hung my head and tried to swallow down the pain of that thought.

Simon hesitantly put his hand on my shoulder. When I didn't shove his hand away, he lightly rubbed my back. *I'm so sorry, Kira.*

It's not right. I retreated from his mind to my own, where no one could hear the thoughts running through it. Thoughts about how I had failed—failed to conquer the gas, failed to get the food from the depot, failed to stop them from taking Laney.

"None of it's right," Simon said softly. He tipped my chin up with his finger. "But you did a pretty good job of convincing Molloy to keep you around."

"What? But..." The words caught on the dryness of my throat and made me cough.

Simon hopped off my cot and fetched a water bottle from our meager stash of supplies by the door. I gulped it down, washing away the dirt and the orange aftertaste. I wished I could wash away my guilt for losing Laney along with it.

When my mouth could function again, I rasped out, "What are you talking about? I didn't get the food. And they took Laney!"

Simon rested his hand on mine. "Laney was probably the only other Clan member, besides yourself, that they could have taken and Molloy would have forgiven you for." He cracked a smile. "Although he probably wouldn't have missed me much."

It still didn't make sense. Laney was new to the Clan, but her disappearance only proved that I had failed. Simon cocked his head. "Molloy's not a monster," he said. "Well, not completely a monster. He knows you were trying to protect Laney, and that means something to him. The fact that you made it out to the depot, and they had to stop you with darts, convinced him pretty well that you were the real deal."

"So." I had to stop to take another drink of water. "So, he's letting me stay in Block C?"

"Yeah," he said. "And Molloy's put the word out to the Clans seeking to ally with Block C to search for Laney. He thinks one of the others might have taken her in."

My shoulders sagged. "She's gone." Although it was reassuring that Molloy was at least trying to find her. He really did look out for the changelings, as well as the rest of his Clan. I understood a little better what he meant by "family" now.

Simon gently squeezed my shoulder. "Don't give up hope. They may have forgotten about her, once they had you to contend with."

"No, you don't understand," I said. "I searched the camp. She's not here."

He drew back. "You've been out for hours, Kira. Ever since I found you near the depot." His eyes went wide. "Wait. You mean you searched with your *mind*? How far can you *reach*?"

"Far enough." Simon probably saved my life by bringing me back before some praver found me lying in the dirt. Yet I couldn't bring myself to trust him.

He seemed to think my brain was still fuzzed on juice. "You're sure she's not here?" The answer was plain on my face. "You searched the *entire* camp?" There was a new wonder in his voice. "Kira, that's..." The gears were turning in his head, but what did it matter? "The camp's over a thousand feet per side, Kira. Can you really reach that far? How about control? Can you jack that far?"

I looked away from him. It didn't matter. All it meant was that Laney was gone. And I was an even a bigger freak. Why hadn't they taken me? Why did Kestrel leave me behind, while taking Laney for some hideous experiment? My body shook with a cold-sweat chill. It wasn't right.

"Because if you can," he said, pulling my face back to his, "we might have a way out of here."

That got my attention. "What do you mean?"

Furious thinking and giddy excitement warred on his face. "The camp is surrounded by electrified fences. They're buried below the ground level, too. The only way in or out is through the gates."

"Why doesn't someone hijack the newcomer truck and ride that back out?"

"The truck and the perimeter are gassed whenever the newcomer truck leaves. Everything's remote-controlled, and they must have cameras somewhere because if someone tries to escape through the gate, they turn on the gas. But," he said, his voice rising a notch, "you can defeat the gas. You could get outside the fences." There was a gleam in his eye.

"Couldn't someone just hold their breath to get through?" The trip through the gates didn't seem that long. Mostly, I didn't want Simon to know my ability to fight off the gas had an upper limit in terms of time.

"No, the gas is too powerful. Even if someone could make it past the electrified fences and the gas, they'd still have to contend with the outer perimeter fence and the guards. Plus they have guns. There are four guard stations around the perimeter, but there's only one gate, where they bring in the newcomer truck."

"Maybe they could jack the guards?" I asked, realizing the *they* we were talking about now was likely *me*.

"The guard gate is at least a half a mile away, far outside

anyone's range to jack. Except maybe *you*." He smirked. "The guards could be readers or jackers or both. If you could jack at a thousand feet away, then maybe... if you could reach the guard gate from here, you could jack them to open the gates. Even if you can't reach that far, you could fight off the gas in the truck, get close enough, and even if they were jackers, if they didn't see you coming..."

"I could jack them before they knew what had happened."

He seemed like he wanted to hug me, but kept his hands to himself, which was a good move on his part. His plan was entirely demens, and the idea that I could jack someone half a mile away was far-fetched at best. Maybe I wouldn't have to jack that far. Maybe I could ride the truck right to the gate and catch them by surprise.

"Do you think it could work?" I asked.

"I think we need to find out what you can do." His grin seemed to crack his dust-covered face.

It didn't take long to discover I had more range than I ever imagined. Not only could I reach people at the other end of camp, but if I concentrated, I could jack them as well. But I couldn't reach the outer perimeter. Somewhere between a thousand feet and a half mile was the limits of my abilities.

Simon pressed me on. "Focus on the jack. It's like a muscle— the more you use it, the stronger you get."

My eyes were closed, but I felt the intensity of his stare. "Yeah. Except when you're distracting me."

"Sorry," he said, his voice hushed.

I reached out and brushed several minds at the far side of

the camp. They didn't sense me, so I could easily knock out the weaker ones before they knew what happened. Some were so weak they could barely push back. I practiced on a few of those first, making sure they were already sitting down. No need for concussions.

"How far out are you?" His voice was impatient.

"I'm in Block D." I snapped my eyes open. "Is that far enough for you?" Block D was at the farthest corner of the camp from Block C. Whoever had laid out the Camp of the Flies had no respect for alphabetical order.

His laser focus didn't waver. "Yes, but can you jack there?"

"I just knocked out two inmates." A smug edge crawled into my voice and it made me queasy. "They weren't very strong."

"Some of the jackers here are practically linkers."

"Linkers?"

"Jackers that aren't very strong. They can link thoughts but not much else."

"How did they end up here?"

"How did any of us end up here?" he asked with a snort. "Extreme bad luck. Anyway, did the linkers you jacked know you were there?"

"No."

"A jacker can only resist you if he knows you're there. If you catch them unaware and move fast, even the strongest jacker can be knocked out. But if you hesitate or if he's expecting you... Well, that's when you end up on the losing side of the jack."

"I've got the Impenetrable Mind, remember?"

He gave a short laugh. "Right. Okay, so maybe it won't be a

problem for you." He gave me an unexpected soft look that made me close my eyes again.

"Okay," I said. "What next, Master Zagan?"

"Next, Little One, you need to jack the strongest one you can find." I killed the smile that threatened to break out on my face. Simon was right—the more I practiced, the stronger I got. Although some jackers seemed naturally stronger than others, regardless of how old they were. I wondered if my dad was a unique like I was—did he have an Impenetrable Mind, too? Could he reach a thousand feet? If he had simply told me the truth, I wouldn't have to rely on Simon to find out what my abilities were.

As I brushed across the minds in Block D, I could tell which jackers were the strongest by the feel of their brain barriers. It was the difference between Jell-O and cream cheese—the cheese would give, but I had to push harder. Even with all the jacking I had done, it still grossed me out.

I was growing stronger, but I was no match for the strongest ones—plus they more quickly sensed me and pushed me back out. The leader of Block D threw me out after a fraction of a second. His second-in-command was even stronger. I retreated and left them sparring with each other. At least they didn't know who I was. I kept trying, jacking in and grappling with fairly strong jackers. Unless I caught them completely unprepared, I couldn't knock them out. And all the strongest jackers in the Camp of the Flies were constantly on edge.

After we had practiced enough to satisfy Simon, he brought me to Molloy.

Molloy verified my long range ability by sending Andre and a couple other members of Clan Molloy to the far side of the camp. Even at that range, Andre had a hard time keeping me out of his head, which brought a smile to my face. But I could only knock out the weaker jackers he had with him. Still, that delighted Molloy to no end and convinced him even more that my skills were worth keeping around.

"Okay, there's this skinny weasel named Jackson in Block D," Molloy said, hunched on the cot next to me. "Can you find him?"

I closed my eyes and reached out to Block D. "Does Jackson have dark brown hair and an abiding love of beets?" Jackson was holed up in a corner with a pile of beet cans, his recent booty from the food frenzy. I had been lucky that Simon had found me before the jackers who knew I was a bigger prize than beets.

"That's the one," said Molloy, like a kid with a shiny new toy. Only I was the toy. "Can you kill him? Even at this range?"

I popped my eyes open. "We talked about this. No killing." I had made my terms clear as soon as we came to Molloy with my new skills.

"Okay, okay. Just knock him out for me. Wait, wait!" Molloy held up his hands. "Make him dump out all the beets on the floor first. Then knock him out." I closed my eyes to block out the smirk on Molloy's face as he got his thrills at Jackson's expense. But I did as he asked.

"Okay," I said. "It will take a while to empty out twenty-three cans."

"Take your time," said Molloy, with a self-satisfied tone. I kept my eyes closed as Jackson methodically opened his cans and poured them onto the dirty barrack floor. I did another sweep through Block D and the next Block over, still hoping that I had missed Laney that first time. I didn't find her, but there were plenty of other horrible things happening.

In Block G, four older boys were tormenting a thirteen-year-old named Daniel by taking turns inflicting phantom pain. Since pain was in the brain, not the body, all they had to do was jack an imaginary broken arm or bruised kidney into his mind. The injuries weren't real, but the pain was. I gritted my teeth and concentrated on reflecting the miseries back on the senders. Each time a praver jacked into Daniel's mind to inflict some imagined injury, I recreated the same one in the tormenter's mind. Daniel wasn't a linker, but he wasn't a very strong jacker either. They quickly backed off, confused at this new mind trickery.

They had no idea it was me, which made me smile.

I jacked Daniel to take advantage of their confusion and run. I planted the idea in his head to find his way to Block C. Hopefully, Molloy would take him in.

"Kira!" Molloy's voice was filled with impatience.

My eyes snapped open. "Huh?"

"Did you get lost there, lassie, counting cans?" He was suspicious. I quickly checked on Jackson and sure enough, he was done. I knocked him out.

"Nope. Jackson is sleeping on his pile of beets now."

Molloy's grin sent a buzz through the room. "Well done, lassie!" Molloy slapped Andre's back, but Andre was far less amused with my parlor tricks. He had been trying to pierce me with his steel-gray eyes the entire time. Probably still sore that I had jacked him into doing the chicken dance earlier. I ignored him.

"So, let's talk about this plan of yours." Molloy motioned to Simon, who had been leaning against the far wall. Simon strode over and gave me wink on the way to let me know I had done well. I scowled at him.

Molloy's face grew serious. "The Clan can give you cover when the next newcomer truck arrives. Blocks E and F are already allied with us, and we may have others by the time the truck comes. Could be any day, we don't know when. When the truck arrives, we'll retrieve the newcomers and slip you two in," Molloy motioned to Simon and me, "before anyone can give serious notice."

"Wait," I said, interrupting him. "I thought I was doing this alone."

Molloy's face became granite. "Seeing as how I can't tap into that hard little head of yours, lassie," he said, reaching over to thump my forehead, "I'll not be trusting you to do this alone. Simon here will be along to make sure you keep your promise to come back for the rest of us." Molloy's shark teeth were back and glinting.

The plan was that I would break out, overpower the guards, and then release the gates so that all the prisoners would be freed, including Molloy and his Clan. If I was lucky enough to make it out, I wasn't sure letting the rest of them loose was a great idea. The camp held a lot of changelings like Laney that shouldn't be locked up in a prison, but there were just as many camp-hardened pravers that gave me the creeps. Obviously, I couldn't let Molloy know my thoughts on that subject, or I'd never get the chance to escape. Having Simon along was a liability.

"What if I don't agree?"

Molloy stood and loomed over me. "Either you're a part of the Clan or you're not, lassie. If you're in, you stay in. If you betray us again, I won't stop next time to ask why."

"I'm in," I said, without hesitation. I didn't have any other options.

"Right," said Molloy. He narrowed his eyes. "And don't be thinking about letting the gas take Simon, little Kira. If he comes back in the truck alone, I'll make sure he regrets the day he met you."

I gulped. I didn't like Simon, but he didn't deserve whatever punishment Molloy would dish out. When Simon had tried to kill Raf, he had jacked in deep to slow his heart rate. I should be able to do the opposite and speed up Simon's heart to keep pace with the gas, like I did my own. It would slow me down, but it would work. I gave Molloy a short nod.

Molloy's shark teeth receded, replaced by a real smile. "Now, there's this right nuisance, Samson, a part of Lenny's old crew." He settled back into his spot across from me. "I think he's in Block D now. Can you find him?"

"Sure." I went hunting for the unfortunate Samson. Simon nodded as though this was all according to plan. He did save my life on more than one occasion, so I didn't mind breaking him out of the camp. But, like Molloy said, Simon was more likely to come back for the rest of them.

I had no intention of being a part of Clan Molloy once I was free. I yearned to go home and set things right with Raf, maybe get my life back again. My dad was a jacker and a high-ranking Naval Intelligence officer. He had to know how to keep the Feds at bay. If Clan Molloy were stuck in the camp, I wouldn't have to worry about them menacing my family on top of everything else.

But if I left Clan Molloy behind, I would be dooming all the changelings that were trapped in the camp as well. Changelings that hadn't done a thing wrong in their lives, like Laney.

I tried not to think about what was happening to her.

My top priority was getting out of the camp. If Simon insisted on opening the gates for Molloy, I wasn't sure I would stop him. But if he tried to stop me from leaving Clan Molloy behind, I wouldn't hesitate to overpower him and leave him with his friends in the desert.

chapter THIRTY

It wasn't long before Daniel-the-changeling found his way to Block C. He was smart enough to shed his armband along the way, but his tattered shirt betrayed that he had been in the camp for a while.

Molloy raised his eyebrows. "You wouldn't have anything to do with this, would you, lassie?"

I shrugged and feigned innocence. Since Molloy couldn't scrub my mind, he set Andre on Daniel to make sure he wasn't a spy. I cringed as Daniel suffered through Andre's interrogation.

"Is that necessary?" Maybe bringing Daniel to Block C had been a mistake. Molloy didn't answer, and Andre released Daniel after a few more moments.

"He's just a changeling." Andre glared at me, but didn't say any more. If he'd found any evidence that I had been involved, he wouldn't hesitate to say so.

Molloy offered Daniel a hand up from the floor. "Sorry about that, lad. You understand, don't you?" The boy nodded so hard, I was afraid his head would fall off. I didn't care much for Molloy's methods, but once he had accepted Daniel into the Clan, it seemed like Molloy would take care of him. And he didn't raise any more eyebrows when changelings started showing up at Block C after that.

At least, I didn't think he suspected me.

Nearly a week passed before the newcomer truck brought fresh inmates to the camp. Word traveled fast about the truck's impending arrival, the linked whispers of the Camp of the Flies rivaling the thought-speed rumor mill of Warren Township High. However, sitting on a rough cot in the middle of Block C, surrounded by anxious members of Clan Molloy, couldn't have been more different than walking the halls of my school. And Shark Boy could only dream of being as ruthless as the pravers in the camp.

I knew without brushing any minds that the newcomer truck had stopped at the first gate. After a week of practice, my reach easily swept beyond the camp fences to the surrounding desert. I kept checking whether I could extend out to the guards at the outer perimeter (still no) or detect the incoming shipment of new inmates before anyone else (yes).

Molloy gathered his people so we could travel as a group to intercept the truck. The plan included myself and Simon, Molloy, Andre, and a half dozen other Clan members, plus a few strong jackers from Blocks E and F. We needed a large group, partly to ensure our own safety and that of the newcomers, and also so Simon and I would not be missed when we slipped inside the truck. Our Allied Clans were in on the escape effort, but alerting the other inmates to our plans would be problematic at best.

I gave a short nod to Simon, indicating the newcomer truck had passed the first gate. The truck held returnees from whatever government facility was used for the Feds' heinous experiments. The girls were both fourteen and changelings. So much like Laney, but neither was her. Their thoughts were fuzzed, even though their minds were clear of the juice. I felt the parts of their brains that had been damaged, like soft dead spots where the doctors had targeted their destruction.

A sour taste in the back of my throat threatened to bring up my lunch of protein bars. I hoped that someday Kestrel would suffer a painful payback for what he had done.

Simon signaled Molloy that it was time to leave, and soon we were striding past weathered barracks and wary onlookers. We moved as a pack toward the entrance gate and sported a rainbow of armbands, with me and Simon surrounded by the strongest jackers in the Allied Clans.

No one messed with us.

The inner gate creaked to a metallic stop, and the truck slowly backed into the camp on its autopath. In theory, we could walk straight past the open gates into the hundred-foot gap between the fences. When Molloy scrubbed the minds of several veteran inmates, searching for true memories about escaping the camp, he found out that a few desperate prisoners had tried to escape that way. None had survived. Any movement between the fences triggered a wave of gas and trapped the escapee in that no man's land until the next drop shipment or newcomer truck.

I shook that mental image out of my head as the truck lurched to a stop. Molloy's crew formed a brigade at the rear end.

Simon and I pulled open the dust-covered doors and climbed inside. The wide-eyed pair of changelings cowered together on the bench, holding hands. Either they were friends, or they had already made an alliance. I cringed when I told them to get out. They were in no state to deal with the camp, but at least Molloy would look out for them. And maybe they wouldn't be there long. If we were successful.

The door slammed closed behind them.

I took their place on the warm metal bench, and Simon sat next to me. When the gas struck, I would have to speed up his heart to fight it off, in addition to controlling my own heart rate and reaching out to the guards. I preferred that he stayed on the other side of the truck, but it would take less effort to control his heart rate if he was nearby. He, on the other hand, didn't seem to mind being close.

We waited for the truck to start its autopath out of the camp. Our plan was to survive the gas, ride the truck to the perimeter gate, and knock out the guards. Then we would open the camp gates and release the prisoners. That part was Simon's job. I planned on being long gone before any jackers reached the perimeter. But Simon didn't need to know that until the time came.

Simon seemed like he had something to say, only he wouldn't spit it out. There was nothing left to discuss, but the stifling heat of the truck left me with little patience.

"What?" I asked. I would save linking into his mind until it was necessary.

He studied his hands. "I shouldn't have lied to you, Kira. I should have told you the truth, about the Clan. About all of it."

I nodded but didn't offer any more than that. I wouldn't be facing a truck full of gas and trying to escape the Camp of the Flies if he hadn't lied to me almost every step of the way. I still couldn't figure out when the lies had begun, but they probably ended at the warehouse. By that point, it was a little late for the truth.

Simon stared at the metal riveted floor of the truck. "All of this could have been avoided. If I'd told you the truth, maybe you would have joined the Clan willingly. Maybe I could have convinced you..."

I snorted, causing him to look up. "It would have taken a lot more than kisses from you to convince me join the Clan."

His face twisted into a pained smile. "Well, at least there was some fun along the way."

It was my turn to stare at the rivets snaking along the floor and try to order away the blush rising up my face. How could I control my own heart rate, but not keep my cheeks from lighting up every time I was embarrassed? Simon scooted closer, so that our knees brushed. Mine were exposed by the shorts I had on when I was captured. We both had on the same clothes from the last time we kissed, in his car a lifetime ago.

"We can still make this work, Kira." His voiced dropped to that soft, rich sound he used when he was trying to convince me of something. He ran his fingers along my hair and tucked it behind my ear. "Just the two of us. Once we're out of here, we can run away. Forget the Clan. We'll go somewhere no one knows us and start over. We can pass as readers, and no one will ever know the difference."

His soft, urgent words tugged at me. I didn't have to link into his head to know that was what he had wanted all along. Pretend to have a normal life, live off our ill-gotten gains, lie to everyone we knew. I dreamed of a normal life once, too, complete with boyfriends and college. Only Simon's face was never the one that filled those dreams. If we got out of this alive, Simon could make his own way in the world. I was going home and seeing if I could get my life back and put things right with Raf.

Simon took my silence for something else and leaned in to kiss me. I turned my face at the last moment, so that his lips landed on my cheek instead. They were as searing hot as always, even in the desert heat of the truck.

Puffs from his laugh caressed my cheek. "I guess I deserved that."

The truck lurched and sent me crashing into him. He righted us, holding me gently by the shoulder. I took his hand and linked into his mind. *You don't deserve this. Neither of us does.* Just because Simon had lied and betrayed me didn't mean he deserved the camp. But his thoughts made more of that statement than I intended.

A hiss announced the beginning of the gas, so I jacked in further to step up both our heart rates before the first whiff of orange scent reached us. Adrenaline made me want to pace the tight confines of the truck, but I stayed with Simon, my hand locked with his, and kept tabs on the state of his mind. As the mist surrounded us, I pulled the neck of my t-shirt up to cover my mouth and nose, and Simon did the same. It wasn't much use. The intensity of the gas was overwhelming.

The truck swayed to a stop and waited for the gates behind us to close and the ones ahead to open. Metal creaked over the hiss of the gas. When the outer gate was fully open, the truck still sat in the perimeter no-man's-land between the electrified fences. My heart was already trying to pound out of my chest or it would have raced from worry that something had gone wrong. *Why isn't the truck moving?*

I reached out and searched again for a mindware interface, but found nothing, like my first trip in the truck. Finally, the truck jerked forward and lumbered through the outer gate. I leaned off the bench and squinted at the desert glare coming through the dusty windows in front. A guard tower shimmered in the heat. A half mile seemed a reasonable estimate.

Simon's face shone bright red around his dirt-stained shirt. He heaved breaths through the thin fabric, and his eyelids blinked very slowly. *Stay with me, Simon.* I commanded him to a jittery wakefulness and struggled to keep my own eyes open as the juice seeped into my brain.

The truck bounced and crunched on the dirt path leading away from the camp. I peeked again at the hard-packed line that was hardly a road. The desert was clear ahead of us, but impossibly, the guard tower didn't seem any closer. The truck trundled along at a maddeningly slow speed. I reached as far as I could. There was nothing but scrub brush ahead of us. If we didn't pick up the pace, we'd both pass out before we got close enough to knock out the guards.

For a moment I considered letting the gas take Simon. My

range was shortened by having to fight the gas for both of us. After I knocked out the guards, reviving Simon from a full juice dose would take time, maybe more time than I would have before the guards from the other perimeter stations reached the gate. Perhaps I could take them all, but it would be tough if they were jackers. I might need Simon's help. And as much as I didn't dream of a jacker life with him, I couldn't leave him behind to face whatever Molloy had in store for him.

Simon's sweaty hand clenched in mine. I was jacked deep in his mind to control his heart rate and couldn't help hearing all his thoughts, even the ones he was trying not to think. Thoughts about after the escape. His longing for a normal life. With me. If only he had more time, he might be able to change my mind. Convince me.

I refrained from wiping those thoughts out of his head and concentrated on keeping our hearts pounding fast enough to keep up with the gas. It was a losing battle. Maybe we could crack a window and let some of it out. I pulled him off the bench and we shuffled toward the front. The side windows were sealed tight. Simon climbed into the passenger seat and kicked at the flexiglass with his uninjured leg, but no luck.

I tipped my head to the back, and a wave of dizziness swept over me. Whether it was from the gas or the heart palpitations, we were running out of time. The only way to keep from passing out was to vent the gas out the back doors—or leave the truck altogether.

The guards at the perimeter gate had guns. Big guns. Molloy had scrubbed a true memory about one jacker who had shorted out the fences and cut his way through, somehow sprinting across the gas in the no-man's-land to saw a hole through the outer fence. He was shot. He died right at the fence line and lay there until the next drop shipment when the Feds took his body away.

I didn't want to mess with a gun that picked off escaping prisoners half a mile away.

That meant staying in the truck as long as possible. But we had to reduce the intensity of the gas. If we opened the doors a crack, maybe that would vent enough of the gas to keep us awake. If not, we would have to get out. The truck was slow enough that we could follow along behind and use it as a shield. Then we'd be free of the gas, and I could reach farther and knock out the tower guards sooner.

I pulled Simon toward the rear of the truck. He stumbled a bit on the way, but caught himself before he fell. *We should open the doors, just a crack,* I linked the thought to him. *So the guards can't see, in case they're watching.*

Okay, Simon thought, but the orange mist was fuzzing his brain. Sweat made our hands slippery. I laced my fingers through his for a better grip, and he gave me a smile in return. He was willing to go along with the plan, which was good enough.

Wrapping my fingers around the hot metal handle of the rear door, I slowly pulled it down, careful to only open it a couple of inches and holding tight in case the door went flapping wide and alerted the guards.

A blaring horn startled me into losing my grip on the handle. The truck lurched to a stop, sending Simon and me flying toward the front and banging the door shut again. The alarm reverberated through the truck a second time.

Oh no.

Any element of surprise was gone; the truck was stopped dead in its tracks and screaming in distress. I scrambled to my feet and towed Simon to the back door. As I flung it open, a wave of hot desert air swept into the truck. I leaped down and brought Simon with me, still tethered by our joined hands. Our hearts continued to pound blood through our brains, and each lungful of gas-free desert air brought more relief. My head started to clear and Simon was more alert.

What now? he asked as we crouched behind the open back of the truck. I pulled out of Simon's mind and let the adrenaline pumping through our systems keep our hearts racing. Free of controlling our heart rates, I stretched forward to the limits of my reach, but I couldn't sense the guards. The dusty windows of the truck obscured the hard-packed road ahead, so I peeked through the slit between the flung-open door and the truck body. The guard post floated on a shimmering layer of desert-heated air. It was tough to gauge how far it was. A thousand feet? Two? Either way, I had to get closer and the truck wasn't going to help anymore.

I linked back into Simon's head. *I'll have to run.* I licked away the dryness on my lips from the desert dust and the gas. *I'm not close enough yet.*

He shook his head. *Not without me.*

His injured leg was still wrapped with the homemade bandages I had made. Simon was in no condition to run, and he would only slow me down. *I'll come back for you once I knock the guards out.* I checked the slit again. *We don't have much time. They know something's wrong.*

Simon shook his head again, and an image of me fleeing the gate without him popped into his mind. I swiped dust out of my eyes. *I'm not going to leave you. I promise.*

His thoughts switched to the danger from the guns. Of course, it was risky to leave the truck, but there wasn't much choice. We weren't going to escape at all if I didn't get close enough to knock out the guards. Simon tried to push me out of his head. I didn't understand why, but I pulled out anyway.

"I don't want you to get shot," he said. "Ruins my chances for escape, you know?" He gave me a half smile, and I couldn't help returning it.

"Yeah, well, I don't want to get shot either. If I don't get moving, we're never getting out of here."

He bit his lip and leaned over me to peek through the slit. "Okay. Run back and forth, not straight at the gate. Make it harder for them to target you. And run fast."

I gave him a cockeyed look.

"Just be careful." He gave my hand a squeeze before slipping his fingers out from mine.

I shuffled to the end of the open door and curled my fingers around the hot metal edge. I focused my mind forward one more time, but I still couldn't sense anything. Taking two large gulps of gas-free air, I gave Simon a nod and tore around the corner of the door.

The heat of the sun-baked ground burned through the soles

of my shoes as they pounded the dirt. I veered off to the right, then left, trying to change direction as randomly as I could. The running and surge of adrenaline pounded my heart, allowing me to focus on stretching farther and farther forward.

Still nothing.

It seemed as if the guard gate must not be real, an actual mirage floating above the desert. I kept reaching anyway.

A rumbling sound rolled across the hard-baked desert floor, and I checked the clear blue sky above. It seemed demens to have thunder without clouds, but I didn't have time to think about it. A small cloud of dirt rose from the ground to my left, making me jump, and then a second later another roll of thunder.

I skittered to the right and another puff of dust exploded out of the ground, even closer than before, followed by another rumbling across the desert. My brain finally put it together—they were shooting at me. My legs had new energy down to the soles of my feet, ignoring the burn in my muscles and hopping me back and forth like a crazed jackrabbit. I reached even further forward, until I sensed the barest whisper of the minds of the guards. Still not close enough to jack. Another roll of thunder sounded, but there were no more clouds of dust. The sniper's aim must be getting worse with my fancy footwork.

I strained to see details of the guard post through the glare of the desert. Maybe if I could see the guards, I could hone in on those phantom whispers.

Two more air-crackling peals of rifle shots split the air before I found the mind of the sniper. I made his eyes cross while I sprinted a few more yards, bringing me just close enough. His mind shut down as I knocked him out.

The thunder booms stopped, but I kept running. I flitted across the minds of the guards, who were now in a full state of panic. *Eight.* I found one on the radio, calling another guard post for backup. He was a reader, along with the other two guards in the command tower, so I easily knocked them out. That left four more: one wrestling to reload the sniper's gun, the others manning their own rifles and trying to find me with their scopes.

None of them were jackers. I knocked them all out.

I slowed my pace and scanned again for more guards. There were none, but the others would be on the way, and soon. I braced my hands on my knees, wheezing from the run, and reached back to the truck to tell Simon the coast was clear.

He wasn't there.

My head snapped up. The truck sat abandoned on the dirt road a few hundred feet behind me. I scanned twice, three times. There was no one there. Had he run? I swept my mind and eyes out, searching for any sign of him. I found him lying motionless in the dirt a hundred feet away. His mind was a shadow of its normal strength.

My legs were carrying me to him before I could think what do to. I stumbled and fell forward, skinning my knees and grinding stones into my hands. I scrambled back to my feet, praying he only tripped and fell. When I reached him, his leg was bent back and his eyes were squeezed shut.

There were no thoughts in his mind. It was hollow like an abandoned room, and when I tried to jack him awake, my efforts only echoed uselessly against the edges. I knelt down to shake

him physically as well as mentally, desperate to reach him.
"Simon!"

Then a red pool started to spread underneath him. *No.* My
hands fluttered over him, landing where the bullet had gone in. A
deep red circle spread from the dark hole. I pressed my hands to
the spot and searched through his mind to find a way to fix him.
Stop the bleeding! Stop! I commanded his brain, but I couldn't
make it comply. His mind was becoming less substantial with
every passing second, as if it was fading away.

Simon, please wake up! His mind was more ghostly with
each failing heartbeat. It sucked me in like a vacuum, deeper
and deeper into nothingness. I had to pull back or be dragged
into that blackness with him.

I was staring at him, hands pressed to his chest, when his last
breath escaped him.

A shudder rippled through my arms. I stood and stepped
back from Simon's body. Anger, red and raw, boiled inside me.
My hands clenched, sweaty and wet.

They should pay for what they had done.

I reached toward the guard tower, seeking out the sniper, but
I was too far away. My legs sprinted forward, my arms pumping
and my mind stretching. When I was close enough, I found the
guard who had shot Simon. Who *killed* Simon.

He was still unconscious. I tunneled deep into his mind
and slowed his heart. I wondered if he would die slowly like
Simon, life leaking out of him, never knowing what happened.
The gunman's heart thudded, a slow gong in his chest, and his
mind began to soften and grow empty, like Simon's. Pictures

of a young girl and a woman with brown, shining hair flashed through it. *His daughter. His wife.* He wanted to keep them safe from the dangerous jackers in the camp.

I jerked back out of his head and stumbled over a rock I couldn't see through the blur of tears in my eyes. I fell and scraped my hands on the hard-baked ground. The pain raked through my mind like a razor-sharp claw.

What am I doing?

I wanted him to pay for killing Simon. But... those images... I couldn't. I ground my hands into the fire-hot dirt as I pushed off the ground, standing and rubbing my eyes with the backs of my hands. Reaching forward again, I sped up the guard's heart until it was beating normally.

Simon's body lay in the dirt behind me. It was wrong that he was dead. Wrong that he was lying in the dust and would never get up again.

My feet were glued to the desert floor.

Simon should be coming with me. To convince me to live a life of lies with him. To start over somewhere new. To pretend that we were normal. He should be next to me, trying to get me to open the gates and free the Clan and the rest of the jackers the Feds had sent here.

The camp was a shrouded, desert-camouflaged mound in the distance. If I jacked the tower guard to open the inner gates, Molloy and his Clan would almost certainly kill the guards. And then the entire camp would be loose, heading to whatever town was closest in this desert wasteland. A thousand camp-hardened jackers descending on a town full of defenseless readers. A chill rippled through me, picturing what some of those jackers might do, then the chill settled into a cold pool in my stomach. Daniel and the other changelings like Laney—how could I leave them behind, stuck in prison full of monsters?

In the distance, a dust cloud trailed from a pair of trucks racing along the periphery of the fence. *The other guards.* They were coming, and I was still a thousand feet from the gate.

I promised I would let all the prisoners all go.

I lied.

My legs unlocked, and I raced toward the command tower, waking the guard and ordering him to open the outer perimeter gate. The oncoming trucks were much faster than me, but they were stuck hugging the edge of the fence. My legs burned as I ran, but a single thought seared into my head. A promise. *I'll come back for you.* Somehow, I would free the changelings I was leaving trapped behind the camp's fence. Somehow, I would make the Feds pay for killing Simon.

By the time I flew through the outer gates, the approaching trucks still weren't close enough for me to reach. A truck parked near the gate had a passkey dangling from the dash. I jacked into the mindware interface, and the metallic taste stung the back of my tongue as I switched the truck to manual controls.

I climbed in and gripped the joystick, pulling onto the make-shift dirt road leading away from the guard tower. My hands felt slippery, like the joystick was greased. I glanced down to find it smeared with something dark and red. My stomach lurched, and I used my shirt to hastily wipe away Simon's blood from the hard, plastic grip. I rubbed my hands on my shirt until the slippery feeling was gone. My chest was so tight that I could barely pull in a breath.

I left the jacker camp behind as fast as the truck would take me.

chapter THIRTY-ONE

It had taken four washings, with soap, to get Simon's blood off my hands.

The blood had seeped into my cuticles and under my fingernails and dried while I drove like mad away from the camp. I stuffed my blood-smeared t-shirt deep in the trash can of the Navajo Lutheran Thrift Shop bathroom and slipped my arms through the shirt I had stolen. My hands shook so badly, it was difficult to get the hot pink t-shirt over my head. Then I sat on the cold, miniature-tiled floor and hugged myself hard. My teeth chattered from the shaking, so I clamped my hand over my mouth and focused on breathing through my nose.

Simon was dead.

I couldn't stop the bleeding. I couldn't even wake him. He died alone on the desert floor. My stomach lurched, as it had countless times since I left the camp.

Simon had run out and gotten himself killed. *But why?* Why did he leave the truck, where he was safe, when all he had to do was wait for me to jack the guards?

I knew why, but the truth made me want to twist up my pink shirt and scream. He had told me why. *"I don't want you to get shot."* He had tried to draw their fire, by running out after me.

And it worked.

Tears spilled down my face, and I bunched my knees tighter to my chest, rocking back and banging against the tiled wall of the bathroom. He had sacrificed himself to make sure I got out, but it didn't make sense that he would run out to catch a sniper's bullet for me. We weren't Romeo and Juliet in some demens tragedy. Or did he actually love me after all of the lies and betrayals?

Simon had lied to me from the beginning. He knew long before I did that I was different—that my Impenetrable Mind was unique, something he had never seen before. That my hard head and extra range gave me an edge over other jackers and the Feds. That I was something they didn't expect.

That maybe I was the one who could change things.

Someone needed to free the changelings that were still trapped in the camp. And someone had to stop the experiments the Feds were conducting on kids like Laney. With my Impenetrable Mind and my dad's help, maybe I could do more than just make things right at home. Maybe I could do something about those horrors. Then Simon's death would count for something.

I suspected that Simon knew that too.

I angrily brushed the tears away to clear my vision. Simon had paid a huge price to make sure I got out of the camp. I wouldn't waste that by crying in the bathroom and letting myself get caught again. The Feds were probably tracking me already.

I pushed myself up from the floor, clenching and unclenching my fists. Avoiding the mirror above the sink, I splashed my face several times and then cupped my hands, gulping down water to soothe my gas-ravaged throat. My hand didn't shake so badly when I pulled open the bathroom door.

When I came into the thrift shop, I made sure the short Navajo woman behind the counter was busy folding scarves and the even shorter Navajo grandma was focused on sorting clothes in the back room, jacking them to ignore me as I left in my new hot pink t-shirt.

As I stepped out of the thrift shop, a blast of dry desert air whipped the tears off my face. When I had left the camp, the truck's navigator had directed me northeast, across the hard-baked desert to a paved road, and fifteen miles later, I came upon the tiny town of Rock Point, Arizona. The Navajo Lutheran Church complex dominated the town, with a church and school in addition to the thrift shop. The buildings were old and too close together, as if frozen in time and covered with a hundred years of desert dust.

Patches of scrub brush were scattered between a half dozen trailers and a hydrogen charger station. I had left the truck where I had crashed it—smashed into a pole by the charger station that had appeared out of nowhere when I had tried to park under a covered awning. Driving was a lot simpler than parking, it seemed.

Maybe the Feds would come after me once they revived the guards and made sure there wasn't a full-scale prison break. At the very least, they could track the truck's navigator. I needed to keep moving, and for that I had to get a new vehicle.

I rounded the corner of the Thrift Shop, and my heart stuttered. A camouflage-colored military-style truck had parked behind my crashed one, half under the awning. I ducked back out of sight and tentatively reached out with my mind. One of the reinforcement guards from the camp was heading toward the charger-station shop. He was a reader, and I almost reflexively knocked him out, but that would only alert the Feds to my presence. And there might be more guards on the way.

I reached into the mind of the shop owner, an older Navajo man, and planted a sim. I made him believe he had seen me come in with the truck. I was driving erratically, as if maybe I had been shot. He saw my bloody hands when I came in, and I forced him to give me some food and water. Then I left out the back, heading out on foot into the scrub brush. When the guard entered his shop, the older man relayed my carefully crafted sim and conjectured that I must be heading out to the nearby sandstone bluffs to hole up in the caves there.

I quieted my gasping breaths while the guard hurried out of the shop, jumped in his truck, and chased my sim across the desert. I had bought myself a little time, but I didn't know how much.

I reached back into the Thrift Shop to scan the minds of the two ladies. The younger one always left her rusted electric car unlocked and parked in back. I edged around the building and started it up. The manual joystick was difficult to turn, but I managed to quietly slide out onto Highway 191. Her relic of a vehicle didn't have a navigator, so I lifted from her mind that civilization was to the south. The Feds shouldn't be searching for me in an ancient electric car. I tried to drive like I hadn't just broken out of prison.

The laser-straight road went on for an endless hour. I kept glancing behind me, expecting to see a military vehicle bearing down on me, but there were only scrub brush and low sandstone mesas to break up the scenery. At the first micro town, filled with whitewashed trailers and an enormous school in the middle of nowhere, I ditched the electric car and stole another one. I quickly got back on the road, but it seemed like I wasn't moving at all, only replaying the same bit of dry, desert highway mile after mile. The brilliant blue sky was the same one I had seen overhead for the last two weeks in the camp, only now it wasn't broken up by camouflage netting and it seemed almost too blue—like it had scared away the clouds with its brilliance.

The car was running out of charge, so I stopped at the next tiny Navajo town and switched vehicles again. The Feds seemed to have been thrown off, at least temporarily. The next car had a navigator and more range with its hydro power. I jacked into the mindware and set an autopath to Route 40 and got back on the road.

Route 40 seemed like a tremendously large highway on the navigator, yet it was only slightly wider than Route 191. Still, I headed west toward Winslow, which the navigator insisted had some decent rail transportation. I wasn't sure where I was headed, only that I needed to be somewhere with people so I could hide among them until I figured out a plan.

It was one thing to want to take on the Feds and another thing altogether to know what to do. I was sure the Feds would keep looking for me, even if they were delayed by my sim. After all, by escaping their high-security camp, I had just proven I was a dangerous, new breed of jacker that could defeat their security measures.

Simon's last breath kept playing over and over in my mind. I wished he had said something, or I could have read the remnants of his mind. At least linked in to let him know he wasn't alone. And to say goodbye.

The afternoon sun blinded me with its glare. An hour later, arriving at Winslow seemed like returning to civilization. Terracotta shingle roofs and rows of slender adobe-colored houses spaced to meet the range codes sang of order and normal life. People bustled along the tourist shops and restaurants.

When I switched to manual controls and pulled up to a parking lot at the edge of downtown, I stopped at the entrance. How was I supposed to park in these tiny spaces that seemed barely big enough for a scooter? I was the clear master of pre-programmed autopaths on open stretches of desert road devoid of other cars, but I hadn't taken any actual driving lessons. That was supposed to happen next summer, before I got my license. The idea of driving lessons seemed to belong to another lifetime. I circled the lot several times until I found three spaces together. I barely made it into the spot without crashing.

Before I left the car, I reached out to all the minds around me to turn their focus elsewhere. The tourist at the parking meter, the t-shirt vendor tending his cart, the waitress taking an order at the café—anyone that could possibly see or hear me. I was about to step out of the car when I realized that one man, the docent at the trading-post-turned-visitor-center, was a jacker.

Even in tiny Winslow, Arizona, there were jackers hiding in plain sight. It made me wonder how many thousands of us there were, all hidden in the reader world.

His mind barrier was weak, and I could have easily jacked in and controlled him. Instead, I slipped out of the car and padded across the parking lot in the opposite direction from the visitors' center. If I avoided his notice, he wouldn't detect the blank spot of my mind in the presence of all the readers.

Trinket shops and art galleries lined the main street, which traced old Route 66. I turned people's heads away as I walked past. I couldn't remember the last time I'd eaten, and an old-fashioned red-and-white diner beckoned from down the street. A bell tinkled as I opened the door. I made sure all seven occupants—including the fry cook—thought their hearing was impaired and kept their eyes away from the door where I stood.

Cherry pie rotated on a display on the counter. I took a slice and sat on one of the red vinyl stools welded to the floor in front of the bar. The waitress passed by without a glance and took a plate to one of the customers that she could see.

I was the Invisible Girl—again.

Maybe someday I would have a normal life, where I could walk into a diner and be served like everyone else. Simon had joined a gang of criminals and lied to everyone he knew, just to have a chance at that. Laney never had the chance to lie, her abilities betraying her before she could even try to pretend.

Now she was in a government medical facility somewhere, and no one knew about it. No one knew Simon was dead. Only the Feds, with their secret jacker camp, had any idea what was going on. And if they caught up to me, I would disappear for real, like Laney and Simon.

They probably had an all-points bulletin out for me already.

Cameras!

I scanned the room wildly for a moment and let out a long low breath when I saw there were no cameras in this tiny diner off Route 66. But that wouldn't be true everywhere. I needed to be more careful.

I went to find a fork and grabbed a glass of water from the half dozen the busboy had queued up. My throat was still recovering from the gas and the desert and the hours of driving, so I took my time with the bites and sips. When I was done, I stacked my dishes by the busboy's pile and opened the door slowly to avoid ringing the bell.

Across the street from the diner was the Posada Hotel, which the navigator had told me was also the train station. Crossing the red cobbled road, I ducked into the shaded arches that framed the train station entrance. I shoved open the green dust-covered doors and stepped into the dark polished-wood interior.

The schedule board showed two daily trains out of Winslow—one heading west to Los Angeles, and one heading east to... Chicago. An empty feeling hollowed out my bones.

Chicago.

Home.

It was dangerous to go home. Probably the worst place I

could pick. But I needed my dad's help to figure out a plan. And part of me still wanted to know why he hadn't told me the truth, leaving me to the mercy of Simon and the Clan.

I focused on the schedule. The eastbound train came once each day at six in the morning. That was more than twelve hours away. The empty train depot had no cameras, only southwestern artwork on the walls. I slipped through the doors connecting the train station to the hotel. As long as there were no cameras, I could persuade the hotel clerk to give me a room. I would hole up until the train came and hope the Feds didn't find me before morning.

Then I would go home and make things right.

chapter THIRTY-TWO

The rumbling sounded like far-off thunder, but I knew it was only the crack of the rifle.

A changeling zigzagged across the desert, her bare feet kicking up puffs of dust as she ran. I lined up my sights, correcting for the distance, the rippling atmospheric effects of the heat, and the motion of my target: a dangerous mutant jacker escaping from prison. All I had to do was gently squeeze the trigger and her blood would soak into the parched ground...

I gasped and bolted upright on the fold-out sleeper bench. I reflexively reached out to scan the occupants of the train, but there were still no jackers on board. Fields of prairie grass whipped past the window.

I wasn't a sniper. I didn't kill anyone. I was heading home.

The night before had been a fitful struggle to sleep as I twisted myself up in the hotel sheets only to wake and untwist them again. Fatigue pulled on me the next morning, so I opted for a sleeper cabin on the train. Jacking an image of my Grandma O'Donnell into the conductor's mind, along with a postcard I had stolen and ripped into the size of a train ticket, had won me a tip of his hat and an escort to my room. He offered the seventy-five-year-old woman he saw before him a bottle of water and left me in a room that was slightly larger than my closet at home. I locked the thin, metal door and sank deep into the sofa. The motion of the bullet train lulled me into a stupor, while we rocketed toward Chicago. Sleep must have claimed me... until the nightmare had startled me awake.

I pressed the heels of my hands against my eyes to clear the remnants of sleep and swung my feet over the edge of the sofa.

So far, the Feds hadn't come crashing through the door of my micro-sized cabin. Maybe they had given up looking for me altogether. Or maybe they were waiting at Chicago's Union Station to arrest me when I disembarked. My luck didn't go so far as to have no cameras at the guard gate back at the camp. They could probably figure out who had escaped, in spite of not doing a regular attendance roll-call at the camp.

Even if I wasn't caught on camera, they might piece it together once they found the dead boy in the desert. I wondered what they had done with Simon's body. My stomach twisted as I pictured him dying under my hands. The true memories of the smiles and kisses were swallowed up by that last moment. At least my memories of Simon were in my mind somewhere and hadn't been stolen.

Unlike Raf, whose memory had been wiped by Agent Kestrel. Raf remembered nothing of that night at the warehouse when he found out my secret and held my hand and told me that everything would be fine. But that memory was emblazoned in my mind. Someday, I hoped Kestrel would pay for stealing Raf's true memories. In the meantime, I wanted Raf to know the truth.

About me. About everything.

I lay back on the foam-cushioned bench and imagined the words that I would use to explain. Hours of train ride lay ahead of me, plenty of time to choose my words and plan for station cameras and transportation. I only hoped there wouldn't be jacker FBI agents waiting.

~ ✱ ~

I stole a Cubs baseball hat from a poor kid who was coming to Chicago New Metro to visit his grandma. There was no way to make up for it, so I erased the memory of the hat from his mind. I shuffled through the Union Station crowd, clutching a stolen jacket and ducking my head away from potential cameras. Halfway to the transfer station, I changed my mind and reached back to restore the boy's true memory. Better to think he lost it, than to have a memory stolen from him, no matter how small.

I gave a fake tally card to the station attendant and got a transfer ticket that would take me out on the T-94, with a switch to the T-41 taking me all the way to Gurnee. Ancient brownstones whizzed past my window seat, jammed up against one another. I shuddered at the idea of so many people living so close together. The sun sank below the horizon and transformed the Chicago skyline into jagged glittering teeth. I was glad I would be out of the city before it got dark.

When I finally reached the Gurnee stop on the T-41, I was momentarily confounded. The autocab wouldn't accept a fake tally card, and I didn't have any real unos on me, so I ended up walking. The trim, neat yards and equally-spaced, spindly houses of my town looked the same, but my skin prickled as though every darkening shadow held a jacker agent. I reached out and swept the neighboring streets, just to be sure.

I stopped several blocks away from my house at a park where Raf and I used to play as kids. I reached across the suburban houses to scan my home. It was one thing to suspect the Feds might stake out my house, and quite another to find two jacker agents parked outside. I slumped into a swing and pumped my legs. The street lights flickered on to hem the edges of the park with spotlights. The swings and I were hidden in the gloom.

I brushed the agents' minds, keeping it light so they wouldn't sense me. They were watching the Cubs game on their phones and not paying much attention to their stakeout. I flitted across the minds inside my house and was surprised to find Seamus home, as well as my mom and dad. Of course they would have recalled my dad back from his overseas duty when this whole thing went down, but Seamus should be at school. Mom seemed to agree, as she was deep in an argument with him about returning to West Point.

The hard marbles of the agents' presence were jacked into both their minds, yet were strangely absent from my dad's mind. It wasn't because he had an Impenetrable Mind like me. I could easily have pushed past his medium-hard mind barrier, if I wanted. My dad wasn't a linker, but he wasn't the strongest jacker I'd come across either.

Just average.

My shoulders sagged. Maybe my dad wouldn't have the answers I needed after all.

The agents probably stayed out of my dad's mind by the same kind of jacker code that existed in the camp—jacking into a jacker's mind was asking for a fight. Unless he was working with them. A shiver ran down my back. *No.* My dad seemed to tolerate the agents' presence in Mom's and Seamus's minds as a condition of staying in our home.

I swallowed. The Feds might arrest my family too.

I couldn't reach any deeper into Mom's or Seamus's minds without alerting the agents. They weren't very strong jackers, and I could probably knock them out before they suspected my presence. But why wouldn't the Feds put their strongest jackers on surveillance duty? Maybe it was a trap. If I knocked them out, the Feds would swoop in and capture me. Or worse, take my family, once they knew I was watching. Make me turn myself in.

The park grew darker as the last of the sun's light disappeared from the day. The agents couldn't know I was home, but I needed help and answers from my dad. He paced alone in his room, and his thoughts skittered between hatred for Agent Kestrel and ways to convince him to release me from the camp. Well, we had our feelings for Agent Kestrel in common. My dad sat down on the edge of the bed and nervously bounced his leg.

I hesitated, afraid he might inadvertently tip off the surveillance crew outside. I took a deep breath and linked a thought to him. *Dad.* His mind-scent reminded me of early morning dew.

He jerked up from the bed. *Kira!* The thought was so strong, I was afraid he had said it aloud.

Be quiet! They might hear you. I almost jacked in and made it a command, which made my stomach clench. I wanted answers, but not the way Molloy got them out of Simon.

It's okay. The agents outside aren't monitoring my thoughts.

I know. I wanted to explain, yet at the last second, I held back. If my dad knew what I was capable of, Kestrel could drill through his mind to find it. It was dangerous to talk to my dad at all, but I needed his help.

Kira, where are you? he thought. *I've been trying to get you released. How did you get out?* His mind was a jumble of guesses, but I couldn't tell him anything about that without tipping my hand to Kestrel.

That's not important. He reached out and searched for me, but he couldn't sense me three blocks away in the park. His reach was the same as an ordinary jacker. *And you should stop reaching for me, in case you alert the agents.*

Right. He pulled back and tried to figure out how I reached him if he couldn't reach me. Then a dread filled him, as he wondered what else I could do that he couldn't.

This sparked a flare of anger that I threw at him. *Why didn't you tell me you were a jacker?*

He cringed under the force of my thoughts, and I pulled back a little. *I'm sorry, Kira! We didn't think... your mom and I thought it would be best if you didn't know. Until you were older. And then you didn't change, and we thought maybe...*

You thought I would be a zero, like Grandma. I didn't try to hide my bitterness. No sense letting the family mental reject in on the big family secret: hey Kira, not only aren't you a reader, you're not a jacker either! Sorry about your luck. In some twisted way, maybe they were trying to spare my feelings, but it only felt like lies.

Grandma O'Donnell was a jacker, Kira, he thought.

My thoughts turned upside down. *What?*

She was one of the very first ones, and a strong jacker, too, he thought. *But she saw what happened to her dad. You remember the experiments the government did on Great-Grandpa Reilly and the other early readers—she didn't want that happening to her.*

So, she pretended to be a zero? For her whole life?

Yes, he thought. *It upset your mom a lot.*

Because she was embarrassed. I know. The bitterness came back, a foul taste in my mouth. No one had ever said it out loud, but I had always known. Appearances were important to my mom, even in her semi-heremita lifestyle. I had embarrassed her, just like her mom.

No! Anger colored his thoughts. *Because your mom had to keep it a secret from everyone. You know how hard it is for readers to keep secrets.*

A dull ache pulled at my chest.

My reader-mom had to keep Grandma O'Donnell's jacker-secret her entire life. No wonder my mom kept her distance from people outside the family. Grandma's secret had cost my mom a lot.

The stars peeked through the nighttime haze at the park. If

I had known my mom was so good at keeping secrets, I would have trusted her with mine. And if she knew Grandma's secret, then she must have known Dad's too.

So when Mom met you...

I knew she could keep my secret as well, he finished.

But you didn't think I could! Never mind that I had lied to them; they had lied to me first.

You were young, and we thought you might still change, he thought. *It's hard enough for adult readers to keep secrets, but for changelings it's practically impossible. We couldn't have your changeling thoughts running around the school.*

Well, thanks for nothing! I pulled out of his head, all the way back to my own. The swing had come to a rest, and my feet dragged in the wood chips piled below it. I kicked them, and they flew out and disappeared into the millions of wood chips filling the park. I knew Dad was right, but that didn't make it hurt any less. I curled my fists around the swing chains and wondered if they had told Seamus. Did he know the big Moore family secret, all this time? That generations of mutant jackers filled our family tree?

My mouth fell open. *Family tree.*

I reached across the quiet suburban blocks and linked back into my dad's mind. *Dad...*

Kira! Oh, thank god! Kira, please, please don't leave again! His mind was in a full-blown state of panic. *I almost lost you before. Please don't disappear like that. I'm sorry we didn't tell you the truth. We should have. We should have warned you...*

Dad! I cut off his rambling thoughts. *Dad, it's okay. I get it. You didn't know if I could keep the secret or not.* My mind raced ahead. *I think I understand now. Why I'm...* I didn't want to say what I was. There were some secrets I had to keep. *Why I'm different. Jackers don't always have jacker parents, right?* Laney and Simon's parents hadn't been jackers, but apparently my family was filled with them.

Right, he thought. *The government's not sure if it's genetic or not. It could be the environment changing everyone again, like the first readers. Or maybe both—maybe the genetic component only gets expressed under certain conditions.*

But Seamus isn't a jacker, right? I needed to make sure my miniature theory held up to the facts. *And neither is Mom.*

That's true... he thought. *What are you getting at, Kira?*

I'm the only female in our family that has jackers on both sides of the family.

The same gears were clicking into place in my dad's head. *So, if there was such a thing as a jacker gene, and it was carried on the female X chromosome...*

I just got a double dose of it. Finally, something was making sense in the world. *Which is why my abilities are... different.*

My dad's mind raced as he agreed it was possible. A picture of Agent Kestrel flashed through his mind, which reminded me I didn't actually know what my dad did for the Navy.

Don't tell me you're working with Agent Kestrel. He's the one who sent me to the camp in the first place.

Of course not! A wave of disgust flavored his thoughts.

Can't you do something to stop him? Use some of your Navy connections to keep him from sending jackers to the camp?

Kestrel's too powerful, he thought. *I couldn't even convince the FBI to release you! Kestrel's the head of a Task Force conducting experiments on jackers.*

Experiments. Maybe my dad knew where Kestrel had sent Laney. *Dad, where does Kestrel take the jackers he experiments on?*

I don't know, he thought. *All I know is that he's in charge of the program, and he's on a personal mission to stop jackers. He's been searching for a genetic link for some time. The government wants to keep more jackers from being made, or born, or whatever. They want to control it.* My dad's mind filled with horror. *Kira, you could be the genetic link he's looking for.*

The temperature around me seemed to drop ten degrees. I had just put the biggest secret of all into my dad's mind. Right where Kestrel could find it.

Dad... I didn't want to link what I was thinking to him.

My dad's mind was cranking to a panicked state again. *Kira!* he thought. *Kira, he can't find out about this.*

Dad, no... I couldn't do it. My stomach clenched just thinking about it.

You have to erase that idea from my mind. His thoughts were firm, resolute.

My mouth had gone dry in the cool New Metro night air. I didn't want to do it. Not even a little.

Can you do it, Kira? my dad insisted.

I swallowed down the dryness. *Yes.*

Then do it. Now.

I tried desperately to find some other way to keep the idea

from falling into Kestrel's hands. My father's thoughts showed that Kestrel paid him regular visits to see what he knew. Kestrel had too much power over him. There would be no keeping it a secret.

So I did it. My stomach twisted as I unwound our conversation, back to the point where my dad was apologizing profusely about keeping dangerous secrets from his baby girl. The one he had tried so hard to protect. The one he was protecting now, by having me erase part of his mind. A lump rose in my throat.

Kira, please, please don't leave again! His mind had rewound back into panic. *I almost lost you before. Please don't disappear like that. I'm sorry we didn't tell you the truth. We should have. We should have warned you...*

Dad, it's okay. You didn't know if I could keep the secret or not.

The relief in his mind tore at me. That he didn't know what secret I was keeping. That he couldn't ever know. *I know you can keep these secrets now, Kira,* he thought. *You could still join the jacker bureau. I'm sure they would take you. It's the only way; you know that, right? You could even work with me in Naval Intelligence. We need strong jackers there, and you could do good things. Positive things. You would be a tremendous asset to your country, Kira. But you need to turn yourself in.*

The tears in my eyes made all the woodchips run together, like one big lumpy mass of destroyed trees lurking outside the spotlights of the street lamps. *I can't do that, Dad. Give Mom my love, okay? Seamus, too.* I pulled out of his mind so I wouldn't have to listen to any more of his impassioned pleas.

My heart sank like a stone, and tears rolled off my cheeks onto my dirt-stained shorts.

Going home wasn't an option for me anymore.

~*~

I wasn't quite sure how I ended up in front of Raf's house.

The walk from the park was a haze, as though my mind had been emptied of everything but echoes. Like Simon's mind before his death. Like I was fading away. I shivered and pulled my oversized cargo jacket tighter around me.

My dad couldn't help me. I couldn't go home. I was on my own.

Simon was right after all. The best we could hope for was a life on the run. Go somewhere and disappear. Blend in. Pass for a reader. Hope that the Feds never caught up to me.

Anger boiled some life into me. Maybe I couldn't go home. Maybe Kestrel had too much power for my dad to stop him. But I was something Kestrel didn't expect.

I was different.

It was time to make that count. Time to stop the horrors that Kestrel was putting the changelings through. I'd made a promise, and I was going to do everything I could to keep it. I wasn't at all sure I could find Laney or get the others out of the camp without getting sent back there myself. But I was going to try.

Before I did, I had to make things right with Raf. I might not get another chance.

The brightly lit windows on the top floor of Raf's house told me he was awake. There were no jacker agents keeping guard over Raf. Maybe they didn't think Raf meant that much to me.

They were wrong.

I brushed the minds inside Raf's house. Mrs. Santos was watching a Brazilian soap opera and weeping at some awful love scene. She probably wouldn't notice me sneaking up the front stairs, even if I didn't jack her thoughts away. Raf was on the third floor in his room, listening to that crazy synchrony music he likes. *Cantos Syn.*

I swept the neighborhood as well, finding nothing and no one out of place. Just to be sure, I pulled my hat lower and tucked in my chin as I crossed the empty street. Stymied for a moment by the locked front door, I sighed and jacked Mrs. Santos to come downstairs to unlock it. Once she returned to the star-crossed lovers on the sim-cast, I opened the door and tiptoed up the three flights to Raf's room.

He hadn't heard me come up, with his wireless ear buds cranked to eardrum-damage mode. He hummed the song in his mind, some musically tortured thing about loving and losing. The scent of linen and fresh spring air seeped into my mind, and somehow it fit him perfectly. All the words I had conjured on the train had vanished.

I took a deep breath and stepped into his room.

His mouth dropped open. "Kira!" He jumped up from the bed where he had been sprawled and tugged the ear buds out. They stopped buzzing when he tapped them. "What...? How did you...?" He wavered, then stood straighter. "You're back." The last part was an accusation. An image sprung up in his mind of me and Simon, kissing and running our hands over each other. Seeing Simon alive again, if only in Raf's mind, made my throat close up.

There was no point putting off the inevitable, so I linked a thought to him. *I'm back.*

Raf's eyes went wide. He took a half step back and bumped into the bed. *I can read you now...* His thoughts swirled around questions he had been asking himself ever since I had disappeared. Why had I run away with Simon? Why had I picked Simon over him? He tried to push those thoughts aside and directed one thought to me. *So, did Simon get tired of you and send you home?* His thoughts were like tiny knives stabbing my heart.

Simon's dead. I blinked back the tears that pricked my eyes. Crying over Simon in front of Raf would be a tragic mistake.

What? Raf took a tentative step toward me, then stopped. I wished he would close the five feet between us and hold me in his arms, but anger and confusion held him back. *What happened? Are you okay?*

Was I okay? No, I wasn't. Not in the slightest. I pulled away from the stray daggers of thoughts in his mind and struggled with what to tell him. He frowned like he was trying to hear my thoughts, but of course he couldn't. He never would unless I wanted him to. I shivered and wrapped my arms around myself. My mind sputtered, and I tried to summon the right thing to say by staring at the floor.

"Kira, I can't hear you anymore. What's wrong? I don't understand."

I couldn't keep the tears from falling in small splats on the wooden floor, and suddenly Raf was wrapping his arms around me. I sobbed into his shirt, bunching it in my fists and pressing it into my eyes. "It's okay. It's okay," he said softly, holding me tighter. "Whatever's wrong, we'll figure it out."

There were so many things I needed to tell him, I didn't even know where to begin. I was a jacker. No, I was a mutant jacker. The FBI was after me and I couldn't go home and the world had gone demens because kids like Laney were being experimented on and jackers like Simon were dead. I sucked in a breath and tried to control the sobs, and slowly the warmth of Raf's arms calmed me. I laid my head on his chest and pressed my ear over his heart. Its beat was strong and a little too quick.

I linked back into his mind, and his thoughts were a jumbled mess—happiness that he was holding me, anger at whatever trouble Simon had gotten me into, confusion about what to say and do to help me. I ached to soothe his mind, but anything I told him would do the opposite. So I lingered for a moment, resting against his chest and gathering my courage to tell him all the truths I had been hiding for so long.

Finally, I picked my head up and leaned away from him so I could see his face. *I'm not really a reader, Raf. I'm something different.*

His eyebrows arched slightly. *Well, I can read you again now. Does it just fade on and off like that?*

No. I don't read minds at all. I control them. It's called mindjacking... I stopped at the incredulous look on his face, and then anger flashed across his mind.

Is this some kind of joke? he thought. His arms had loosened their hold on me, and I missed the feeling immediately.

The joke was on me. *No. I really can control minds.*

Raf dropped his arms away from me. *What kind of game is this?*

It hadn't occurred to me that Raf wouldn't believe me. Before, at the warehouse, he had understood, but then he had seen it in action. I reached down to the living room and jacked Mrs. Santos to bring Raf a glass of water. She jumped up from the sofa and hurried to the kitchen.

This is no game, Raf. I wish it was. I'll prove it to you.

Okay...

I just told your mom to bring you a glass of water. She's on her way. Her footsteps were coming lightly up the two flights of stairs. We both turned to the open doorway. *She won't see me, because I control what she sees and hears.*

Mrs. Santos' thin frame appeared in the doorway, and I jacked her to ignore me. She stepped quickly past me to hand Raf the glass of water. Her eyes had the purposeful look of someone whose actions were being commandeered, and her thoughts were the endless loop of a jacked mind. And Raf could hear that. *Bring Raf some water. Bring Raf some water. Some water...*

Raf stared after her as she left his room. His face had lost some of its color. He backed all the way to the bed again and shakily set the water down on the end table. His fear was a bitter taste on my tongue. All of a sudden, I wasn't the girl he had always known and loved. I was some kind of monster instead. His thoughts made me cringe. Raf was more right than he knew.

Stay away from me, he thought as he edged around the bed to put even more distance between us.

Raf, I'm not going to hurt you...

He clenched his hands to his head. "Stay out of my head!" The harshness of his voice made me step back. I pulled out of his mind, mostly because his thoughts were slashing through my heart. That he should have known there was something wrong with me. That he should never have trusted me.

"Raf, please..." The words stopped in my throat. He didn't trust me, and why should he? I had done nothing but lie to him all along. He didn't remember when I had finally told him the truth and that I was sorry. He didn't remember any of it.

The shiny wooden floor blurred as the tears returned to my eyes. I shuffled toward the door, but the doorway seemed to sway, so I held on to the doorjamb for a moment. I stumbled over the threshold, and my feet seemed to catch on the hallway carpet. I gripped the stair rail with both hands so my unsteady legs wouldn't send me tumbling to my death.

When I was halfway down the steps, Raf called out behind me. "Kira, wait!"

I froze and slowly turned to look up at him. Mrs. Santos had heard him, so I commanded her to ignore any sounds from the third floor and redirected her to the soap opera. Raf teetered at the top of the stairs. I held my breath and waited for him to speak.

He bit his lip. "You can control me. Make me do what you want."

I nodded, but didn't say anything.

"But you're not, right now, right?" I shook my head, still holding my breath. "You could hurt me. But you're not. Why?"

I let out an exasperated breath. "Why would I hurt you, Raf?"

His face twisted, and I knew his thoughts without peering into his head. I had already hurt him. By choosing Simon, by not trusting him. By leaving.

"I... I never meant to hurt you, Raf, I swear it." My voice was cracking but I pushed on. I had to get it all out, while I had the chance. Before he sent me away for good. "I was trying to protect you. There are others jackers, like me, and some of them are dangerous. I didn't want you to get hurt, so I lied. But I shouldn't have. I don't want to." My voice was rising as the hysteria climbed out of my chest. "All the lies are causing all the problems. I want it all to stop, Raf. That's why I came back!" I was nearly shouting by the time I was done. I stopped and tried to get control of my ragged breathing.

"Will you tell me truth?" he asked. "All of it? Without that..." He stumbled over the word. "...*jacking* thing that you do?"

I nodded so hard my brain wobbled inside my head.

"Okay, well, come on up. We can, um, talk in my room." He backed toward his room, not taking his eyes off me and keeping his distance, like I was a wild animal that might strike at any moment. I didn't care. I was so elated, I nearly floated up the steps. Back in his room, he carefully sat at the head of his bed. I perched at the end of it, waiting.

"So, how does this jacking thing work?" he asked.

I took a deep breath and told him everything. How I discovered I could jack when I accidentally knocked him out. How

Simon found out and convinced me he was the only one I could trust with my secret. How he lured me to the warehouse and tried to get me to join his Clan of criminal jackers.

Raf's eyes grew wide when I told him how I had saved him from the Clan, but we had been caught by Agent Kestrel. I explained that Kestrel had stolen his true memories, so he didn't remember any of it. He was looking pretty shaken, so I stopped there.

I edged toward him. He watched me closely, keeping his back braced against the headboard and his legs folded underneath him. I stopped moving. "I can't give you your true memories back," I said, "because I wasn't the one who erased them. But I can show you what happened that night. If you want."

"You'd have to get into my head to do that, right?" he asked.

"Yes. If you don't want me to, that's fine."

"No. I want to see it." He tensed, as though it might hurt. I scooted closer and took his hand, relieved when he didn't flinch. I could have jacked the images into his head from the next street over—I just wanted an excuse to touch him again.

I replayed what I could remember of that night. Knocking out the Clan members was etched in my mind, but Raf pulling me out of the warehouse was kind of fuzzed out. I clearly remembered the warmth of his hand on mine and his forgiveness like a warm blanket after an endless time in the barren cold.

When I was done, I pulled out of his mind. His face pinched in as he puzzled through it. "So, Agent Kestrel erased my true memory of this. Made me think you had run away with Simon?"

"I hope to make him pay for that." That earned me a smile

that filled my entire body with sunshine. I wanted to tell Raf everything—every ability I had and every horror I'd seen. But I needed to be careful. I could only tell him things that Kestrel already knew. Raf would be even more helpless to keep secrets from Kestrel than my dad.

At least I could be honest about the lying.

"Raf, there are some things that I can't tell you. Not many, but some." I talked faster. "It's not that I don't want to. It's just that Kestrel might find out—and that would be bad. For a lot of people."

"Okay. I was never any good at keeping secrets anyway." He smiled again, and I became very aware that my hand still held his. Raf had always told me how he felt, even though he didn't have to and it probably hurt him when he did. My face ran hot with embarrassment for all the lies I had told, when he had never been anything but honest with me.

I pulled away and twisted my hands in my lap. "I'm sorry I wasn't honest with you before, Raf."

"Hey." He edged closer. "Everything's going to be all right. Just tell me what you can."

And so I did. All about the horror that was jacker camp and Laney and breaking out. I went light on the details there, so Kestrel wouldn't learn anything new. I told Raf how Laney had been kidnapped, and they were experimenting on her, and how I hated leaving behind the other changelings like her in the camp. I didn't tell him how I had vowed to help them, if I could, because I didn't want Kestrel to know.

I told him how the guard killed Simon, and he died bleeding

in the desert, and there was nothing I could do to stop it. Raf's hand stole over mine when I paused and fought through the tears, not wanting to cry over Simon in front of him. When I had composed myself again, I wondered how I had ever doubted that Raf was the one I could trust.

I pressed on and told him how I'd been on the run, trying to stay invisible. The less Kestrel knew about the visit to my family, the better, so I left that out. And I didn't tell him about my extra range or fighting off the gas—nothing that would show me to be different from any other jacker. Although Kestrel already knew some of it.

Raf was nodding when I finished. I was empty in a good way, like things that I had kept inside too long were finally out.

It made me light-headed.

"So, what are you going to do now?" Raf asked, his face wrinkled with concern. I had an urge to touch his forehead and smooth out the worry lines. But I kept my hand in my lap, not sure if he wanted my touch.

"I'm not sure." I gave him a sheepish smile. "Actually, I have an idea, but I can't tell you." While I was explaining it all to Raf, a plan had slowly formed in my head. I would need some help to get the changelings freed from the camp, but that wasn't the dangerous part, if you didn't count the demens idea of going into the city late at night. Finding Laney would be the tricky bit, where things could go south in a hurry.

The less Raf knew about my plans, the better. For his own safety and to have any hope of pulling it off.

He refrained from asking me for more. He trusted me to tell

him if I could. It was so much more than I deserved, but it was exactly what I needed.

That, and a change of clothes.

Raf let me use his shower and borrow his mom's clothes. Mrs. Santos's frilly red shirt and black skin-tight pants weren't exactly my style. But they fit and weren't caked with Arizona dust. Add in the Cubs hat and the oversized jacket, and I looked ridiculous. At least I was clean.

We stood at the top of the stairs to the front door, awkwardly wondering how to say goodbye. Mama Santos had gone to bed, never realizing that I had been in her house. Raf pressed a wad of unos into my hand.

I stuffed the bills in the pocket of his shirt. "I'm good." There was very little chance I was coming back. Even if all my plans worked out, I couldn't return home. It was too dangerous—for me and for everyone I loved. After I was through doing what I could for the changelings and Laney, I would go away somewhere. Start over. That was the best possible case—the worst being any number of ways I could get caught and sent back to the camp.

Besides, I owed Raf too much to take his money as well.

His face twisted. "Why won't you let me help you?"

I decided to smooth away his worry lines this time and hoped he didn't mind my touch. I wanted to kiss him but was afraid it might be too much. "You've already helped me so much." Just having a plan and spending time with Raf had left me with a strange sense of elation. It was hard to contain my smile.

"Will you come back soon?" The longing in his eyes

made my breath catch.

I wanted to say yes, but I didn't want to lie to him anymore. "If it's possible. If it's safe." At least that much was the truth.

"That's a lot of ifs." He gave me an uncertain smile.

"I want to, Raf."

He nodded, but the worried look was back. I reached up to hug him and then scurried out the door before I lost my nerve to leave him at all.

chapter THIRTY-THREE

The vacant T-94 train car reminded me that the city at night was literally for the demens.

Once I arrived at Union Station, my transfer ticket put me on a bus, but I wished I had taken Raf's unos so I could pay for an autocab instead. The bus to Tribune Tower was like a Halloween spook ride come to life. It was on autopath, probably because they couldn't pay anyone to drive it.

Only impoverished fuzzheads or the demens lived in the crowded slums of the city, where the apartments were seldom up to range codes and people heard their neighbors' thoughts in their sleep. The fuzzheads were usually harmless—the obscura dulled the part of their minds that received thought waves, but it also fuzzed out any other coherent thought. It was the demens that could be dangerous, with their brain chemistry permanently altered by the barrage of thought waves.

The scrawny guy with the backward t-shirt and hollowed-out eyes seemed too fuzzed out to be dangerous. The gnarled guy with the tin foil hat and the baggy coat was almost certainly demens. But he stuck to mumbling in the back of the bus, and I stayed up front. It was the lady in the skin-tight pink pants who kept wandering the length of the bus that had me the most worried. She talked out loud to someone named Freddie and had very colorful names to describe his unfaithfulness.

After about ten minutes, she finally lunged for me, thinking I was her phantom boyfriend, and I had to jack into the craziness inside her head. She dropped to the floor like a stone. The rest of the demens on the bus barely noticed. I pulled out of Pink Pants's head quickly, but the demens state of her mind left a strange peppermint taste that burned my mouth. I stood up near the door of the bus, as far from the rest of them as I could. I was staying out of their heads, if at all possible.

I gathered my oversized jacket tight around me, warding off the crisp fall air, and skittered off the bus at my stop. The black glass towers of the city still sparkled with the lights of late-night workers. The Tribune Tower's limestone blocks loomed above me, a grand building from Chicago's past, with ornate buttresses lit up and garish at the top. Windows on several floors above the arched entryway shone with promise. My plan would only work if one of those late-night workers was a hard-working reporter looking for a tru-cast.

Reaching inside, I found a single guard in the lobby. I jacked his attention firmly on the ball game, which wasn't hard since the game was in extra innings. The revolving brass doors gave way to a flush of warm air that brushed off the cold of the street.

The guard's large, black hands clutched a palm screen whispering the game. Security cameras glared at me from three different corners of the lobby. I pulled my cap down as I scurried past the guard, keeping my footfalls quiet through the metal detectors and to the elevators beyond.

The directory was a maze of names I didn't recognize, but the reporters all seemed to be on the middle floors, in between the ground-level cast station and the executive suites above the 24th floor. I scanned the floors above me and found a couple of journalists on the fifth floor, some maintenance workers on floors seven and eight, and a lone reporter on the tenth floor, researching an article about pollution in the Chicago River. Dealing with one reporter seemed easier, so I punched the button for floor ten.

The tenth floor was only half-lit, in energy-saving mode. I wove through several darkened hallways before I found the reporter in a bright castroom with about two dozen workpods crammed together. She hunched in her chair and gazed at her screen, using mindware to sift through the Tribune's archives.

I stepped quietly to her desk and skimmed her mind while I waited for her to notice me. Her name was Maria Lopez, and she had been a tru-cast reporter with the Trib for about ten years. When she finally realized I was standing next to her desk, she started so badly that she nearly fell off her chair.

Sweet Mother, you scared me! she thought, and then eyed me warily. Of course, she couldn't read my thoughts, which instantly pegged me as a not-to-be-trusted zero. I linked into her mind quickly, because I didn't want to lose her trust before I even got started.

I'm sorry. I didn't mean to frighten you.

Relieved that I wasn't a zero, she thought, *It's all right.* I tasted her sour nervousness. Through her eyes, I looked demens, with my wacky outfit and the Cubs cap. My fellow bus travelers had probably thought I was one of them too. I resisted adding to the effect by laughing and took off my hat instead. Her shoulders relaxed.

Good. Because I have a tru-cast for you. I held back from jacking into her mind and making it a command. I wanted her to help me out, but only if she was willing. Otherwise, I would need to find someone else. *It's about people who can control minds.*

Her eyebrows arched. She decided I was definitely demens, and she needed to call security. Well, maybe I could use that to make my point.

I think maybe you should leave, she thought, reaching for her phone.

You can call the security guard, but it won't matter.

She directed her mindware phone to send a scrit to the security guard that she needed help with a guest on the tenth floor. She decided to keep me calm until he arrived.

Why won't it matter? If you don't mind me asking, she thought.

Because I'm one of the people that can control your mind. Her eyes widened slightly. She tried to keep her thoughts and face a calm mask, but her mind couldn't help flitting around. Mostly wondering what flavor of demens thought they could control minds, and if that made them more or less dangerous. She shoved those thoughts to the back of her mind, still trying to appear calm. *Oh? You can control minds? That's very interesting.*

More so than you can imagine. The elevator dinged its arrival in the distance. I lifted the name of the security guard from his mind. *When George arrives, he won't be able to see me.*

Are you invisible? She decided I was probably a harmless flavor of demens.

Only when I want to be. It was one thing to misdirect people's minds so they didn't see or hear me, but something different to make myself completely invisible. I had changed my appearance before by jacking in a different image, but never made myself disappear altogether. Yet I was pretty sure I could do it. The mind was good at filling in things it thought it saw—or didn't.

Maria smiled indulgently, waiting for George to take this somewhat entertaining demens off her hands so she could continue her research. As George entered the castroom, I jacked him to ignore me. I stepped to the side, flush against a wall covered with tru-cast awards, hoping that would make it easier for George's mind to blend me out of existence. I jacked the command to him hard: I was invisible, nothing but air. When he approached the desk, his mind was already compensating for my appearance, like filling in a blind spot.

Did you need something, Ms. Lopez? His large frame filled the short entrance to the workspace, and his dark face glistened with the slight sweat he had worked up in his hurry.

Would you please escort my friend back to the lobby? I think we're done here. Maria gave me that indulgent smile again and hoped that I would go willingly.

George scanned her workspace quickly. *Sure, Ms. Lopez.*

Where's your friend?

Maria's smile died. *She's right there, George.* She pointed and George's eyes followed her finger and looked right at me. Or rather through me. His mind had decided I didn't exist, so he only saw a wall filled with tru-cast accolades. He peered over the short workpod wall and scanned the rest of the castroom, looking for the mysterious guest.

I'm controlling what he can see. She jerked back from her desk as if I'd shocked her. She tentatively stood, hands rigid at her side.

George, is this a joke? Maria thought, her dark eyebrows pulled tight.

Joke? George echoed, still looking for the supposed intruder. Maria heard his echoing jacked thoughts, *no one here, no one here.* She unclenched her fists. George was searching her face now, wondering if she was all right.

Maria hastily thought, *I must just be tired. I thought I saw someone. It's okay, George, you can go now.*

Are you sure, Ms. Lopez? George was genuinely concerned that she might be working too hard. She smiled in a reassuring way and tried to keep her thoughts focused on her apology.

I'm sorry to drag you all the way up here, she thought. *I'm fine. I'll be going home soon.*

Okay, George thought. *I'm gonna make sure to call you an autocab when you're ready, Ms. Lopez. You know a nice lady like you shouldn't be working late in the city.* He slowly made his way out of the castroom, looking around to be sure he hadn't missed something.

I had Maria's full attention now. *What's going on?* she demanded.

Can we sit down? This might take some time to explain. She narrowed her eyes, and motioned me to a chair in the corner of her workpod, which I dragged over to her desk. I had started the morning in Arizona, and fatigue was making my legs ache.

I settled heavily into the chair and started from the beginning. Somewhere partway through, Maria remembered she was a reporter and started taking notes on her computer. Doubts haunted the edges of her mind, but when I told her about the camp, she stopped writing altogether.

"Do you have any proof this place exists?" We had resorted to spoken language once she realized I was linking thoughts into her head. She didn't care for that any more than Raf did.

"I know where it's located."

Her eyes went wide. "Coordinates?"

"Not exact, but it's about 15 miles southwest of Rock Point, Arizona."

Maria used mindware to pull up the latest satellite images of the area. She gaped at the screen. "There's nothing 15 miles southwest of Rock Point."

"Well, there's camouflage netting over the camp. Maybe the satellites can't see it? You should at least see the perimeter fence."

She rotated the screen toward me. "No, I mean there's *nothing* there."

A grayed out area of the screen labeled *Information Not Available* spanned several miles of the desert southwest of Rock

Point. I panicked for a moment, wondering if somehow I had it wrong, but Maria was shaking her head in amazement. "You've stepped into something serious here, Kira."

"It's really there! I know it is."

"There's definitely *something* there," she said. "This is the satellite blockage that usually pops up over military facilities."

I leaned back in the chair. She believed me. And while the camp was blocked from view, she knew that meant there was something to hide. I pictured all the trucks that went in and out of the facility. The Feds must not want any evidence of movement in the area.

"I'll have to get someone out there. Maybe Mack could use that crazy new camera of his with the satellite linkage." She was thinking out loud now. She was all-in.

"You need to be careful," I said. "If the Feds find out what you're doing, they may come in and wipe your mind, not to mention your computer."

She blanched and pulled her hands back to her lap. "They can do that?"

"Yes." If I linked into her mind, I could see if the hesitation on her face meant she was going to back out. But I'd promised not to do that, unless she asked.

She nodded to herself. "Then I better make some extra copies."

She focused on the computer, making backups and sending files off to someone named Haggerty. I didn't ask and waited a minute before I said, "I also need you to hold off for a couple days before you go public with this."

She paused in her file manipulations. "Why? You said they were abusing kids in this camp? Don't you want to stop that?"

I grimaced. "Of course!" The whole point of telling Maria about the camp was so she would blow the Feds' cover, and they would have to release the changelings trapped inside. "But they're also experimenting on kids somewhere else, and I need to find out where. That's where I need your help." She was still logged in, and I could reach into the mindware to retrieve the information I needed myself. But I didn't want to abuse Maria's trust if I didn't have to.

"What do you need?" Her shoulders tensed again. She had probably been waiting for the other shoe to drop the whole time we were talking.

"I need the home address of Agent Kestrel. He works for the FBI in Chicago New Metro. He knows where the experiments are being conducted, and I need to find out where they're keeping my friend Laney."

She bit her lip. "You're not going to hurt him, are you?"

"I only want the information." It was a small lie, and I hoped it didn't show. I wanted much more than information from Kestrel. Some payback for all he'd done would be nice. Maria didn't need to know about that, and anyway I didn't have it in me to kill him.

She focused on pulling the information from her system. I was probably asking her to break several laws to get it, but I didn't care. If there was any chance of finding Laney and getting her out, I was taking it.

"Okay, here it is. He's in Lincoln Park. Not too far, in fact."

She showed me the address on the screen, and I memorized it, briefly wondering why an FBI agent would live in the city with the demens.

"Thanks," I said, getting up from my chair.

"Wait, you're leaving?" she asked. "But I have more questions!"

"I need to go. If you don't hear back from me in a couple days, it means they caught me. Maybe even sent me back to the camp. Go ahead and cast everything then. If you expose what they're doing to the jacker kids in the camp, maybe you can even rescue *me*." I put on a fake smile. It seemed all too likely that was how things would turn out.

She pulled a tiny ear-mount camera out of the drawer of her desk and clipped it on. "At least let me get you on camera before you go." She tapped it and a small green light showed it was filming. "Tell me your name first, and then you can give me your true memories about the camp."

I reached over and gently tapped the camera off. "You can't show my face, Maria. Or mention my name." I wanted to free the changelings, but what would the Feds would do to my dad if I went public with everything I knew? That was why I needed Maria. Besides, after this was all over, I planned to disappear. If my face was all over the tru-casts, exposing the camp and outing jackers everywhere, there would be nowhere I could hide.

"If I make it," I said, "I'll call you and answer all the questions you like."

She slowly slid me her card. She obviously didn't approve, but I didn't need her approval, and I already had Kestrel's address.

I tucked her card in my pocket and left.

~*~

I didn't want to deal with another bus ride, but taking an autocab to Lincoln Park would cost real money. An all-night store next door to the Trib Tower made Simon's beer-stop seem upscale. I stole a disposable phone and jacked the attendant to load a tally card with real unos, hoping the cameras didn't get a good shot of me. After memorizing Maria's number, I threw her card away. If I got caught again, I didn't want them tracking back to her before she had a chance to do the tru-cast.

After hailing an autocab with the small, silver phone, I swiped my tally card to pay for the fare and programmed an autopath to Kestrel's address. Turned out he lived in one of the rehabbed brownstones that had been brought up to range codes by reducing the number of occupants and restructuring the floors so there was additional space between them. That kind of rebuilt housing didn't normally come cheap, but then Lincoln Park was still in the city, surrounded by crammed apartments and wacky neighbors. Maybe it was affordable on an FBI salary. I guessed Kestrel didn't worry about living with the demens since he was a jacker.

I rubbed the fatigue from my eyes and scanned the ten levels of the apartment building. Only five were occupied, and Kestrel was asleep on the top floor in a light, scattered dream state. I was tempted to run a few nasty guilt-inducing dreams through his mind. Instead, I jacked him deep into unconsciousness, so he wouldn't wake until I was ready. I convinced the bellman to accompany me to the tenth floor and unlock Kestrel's apartment, erasing the memory from his mind once he was back in the elevator.

I hesitated at the open front door. Since Kestrel couldn't get into my head, he couldn't control me mentally. Yet I wasn't strong enough to simply extract Laney's location from his mind without help. And physically, I was still a sixteen-year-old girl up against a grown man, and I didn't like those odds.

I carefully stepped into the tiny apartment. Apparently, an FBI salary didn't buy you much floor space, even in the city. I checked that Kestrel was safely unconscious in the bedroom as I poked around his apartment. Maybe I could jack into his e-slate for information about Laney, if I could find it.

The apartment was immaculate, and I couldn't find anything at all related to his work. He must keep his e-slate in his bedroom. And maybe his gun. I edged my way back to the bedroom. He was still breathing the deep, slow breaths of the unconscious. I switched on the light, knowing it wouldn't wake him.

The bedroom was likewise spotless. I searched the walk-in closet, lined with identical navy G-man jackets and white, collared shirts. I was about to give up when I found his gun holster and cuffs hanging on the door. I took them down. Maybe I could use the gun to threaten him. Make him to tell me where Laney was without fighting him in his head. The hefty gun was cold and simply looking at it was making my hands sweat.

Maybe not. Plus, I didn't want him to get ahold of it and shoot me.

I searched for a place to hide the gun where he wouldn't find it, but where I could still grab it if things went badly. I pulled open a dresser drawer and started to stuff it under some t-shirts. Something dark and heavy was buried there.

Another gun.

I pulled the large-muzzled weapon slowly out of the drawer. It was a dart gun.

Kestrel may not be afraid of the demens, but he seemed to fear jackers. Which made sense, given all the ones he had sent to the Camp of the Flies.

I quickly checked all the other drawers and the nightstand by his bed. He didn't have any more weapons stashed away. I buried his holstered gun deep in the bottom dresser drawer and dragged Kestrel across the bed to handcuff his limp arm to the bedpost. Dart gun in hand, I perched on the edge of the dresser facing him.

Time to wake up.

I jacked into Kestrel's mind to bring him up from that deep unconscious state. It took him a minute to come to. He squinted at the lights shining behind me. When he realized he was cuffed to the bed, fear pulsed through his mind. He pushed me out of his head, and the pressure of his mind built on mine.

"You!" he hissed, and I wasn't sure if he was angry or frightened. I didn't care.

I shot him.

He stared in horror at the dart that had stabbed him in the chest, right through his navy-striped pajamas. It only took a few seconds for the juice to pull him under. *Not so fast, Kestrel.*

I reached into his mind and sped up his heart. As it pounded blood through his system, it cleared out some of the drug. His mind-scent was pungent and made me gag on the peppery smell.

He awoke gasping for breath. Mentally hindered by the drug, he gave me a wild-eyed look and clutched his chest. He was convinced that I was giving him a heart attack. I figured now was a good time to ask.

"Where's Laney?"

He couldn't catch his breath to answer out loud. *Don't know anyone named Laney,* he thought. With the drug inhibiting his brain, I could tunnel in and pull out the information I needed. I remembered the agonized look on Simon's face when Molloy and Andre scoured his brain for the truth, and it wasn't pretty. If Kestrel didn't tell me soon, I'd do exactly that.

"Where are all the inmates you perform experiments on?" I slowed his heart rate a bit, so he didn't burn through the juice too fast. I needed him impaired if I was going to dig through his mind. Red splotches mottled his face, and his breathing slowed.

He decided I didn't have the stomach for killing. *I'm not telling you anything, Kira.* His hatred for me was like an acid stinging the back of my throat, and he struggled to push me out of his head again, but he was too weak. His eyes went wide and fear sped up his heart. I slowed it back down again, and he blinked, confused about what I was doing.

You're lucky I'm not a monster like you, Kestrel. Although it was surprisingly satisfying to shoot you.

I'm not a monster, he thought. *I send the monsters to the camp.*

Is that how you justify sending little kids to that place? You're one of us, Kestrel. How can you think that's okay? I was wasting time talking to him, but I couldn't seem to stop. Part of me wanted to know how he could do this to his own kind.

You don't know what kinds of monsters are out there.

Oh, I have a pretty good idea. And I'm looking at one of them.

Surprisingly, he didn't disagree, but the drug dose was fuzzing his thoughts. A picture flashed through Kestrel's mind of his mother and father broken on the floor, eerily like Laney's nightmares. Only this image was true, and the people were dead. Kestrel struggled to push me out of his mind again, his face twisting from the exertion.

I supposed that image of his family explained something about Kestrel, but I didn't care. I only wanted to find Laney. *Tell me where you keep them,* I commanded. A picture of a familiar hospital floated up through his mind. The Great Lakes Naval Hospital, where my brother and I were born. My stomach flipped.

The hospital was enormous, filled with people and probably cameras. Not to mention it was on the base. Getting in would not be easy. I needed to know precisely where the prisoners were, if I had any hope of getting them out. *Where?* I commanded him again.

Kestrel resisted much harder this time. I jacked deeper into his brain. He let out a moan but couldn't stop me from sifting through his true memories to find what I needed.

Kestrel walking down the stairs to the basement. There

was a secure door, 1B, requiring the wave of a special passring he wore and entering a code. 0309. Someone's birthday. No biometric IDs, so that would help. A hallway with holding cells and a room with double glass doors at the end. An experiment room. The smell of antiseptic choked me. A tray of needles and a girl strapped to a table. She had dark hair poking out of a cap on her head. Laney! A technician injected her with something. It was the second dose they had given her. She was unconscious and didn't flinch when the needle went in.

I pulled out of the depths of his mind. They were already experimenting on Laney. I didn't have any time to waste with Kestrel. I needed to get her out of the hospital *now*. If she was still there. If it wasn't already too late.

You can't stop them, Kira, Kestrel thought. *This is bigger than just a few changelings. The people in charge of this... they won't stop until they get what they're after, no matter what you do.*

Who were these *people in charge*, and what did they want? My mind flashed to the possibility that what they were after was *me*, the genetic link. But why? Were they just trying to stop more jackers from being made or born? Or was it something more than that? But Kestrel was stalling and I needed to get to Laney before it was too late.

No? Then maybe I'll just stop you. I pulled completely out of his mind and waited until he opened his eyes.

Then I shot him again. "That's for stealing Raf's true memories," I said as his mouth dropped open. I shot the final dart into his chest. "And that's for killing Simon."

Kestrel's head lolled to the side as the drug took him.

"It's better than you deserve." As he slipped into unconsciousness, I wiped my entire visit from his mind. Part of me
wanted him to remember that *I* had been the one to shoot him,
to make him regret what he had done to Simon and Raf. But I
needed to buy some time to get Laney out, and it wouldn't help
if he woke up knowing where I was headed.

I tossed the dart gun onto the bed. Dashing into the closet, I
grabbed one of Kestrel's jackets and a white dress shirt. I tugged
the silver and blue passring off his limp hand and at the last
minute, decided to wipe my prints off the dart gun and the other
gun I had buried in the dresser drawer. I sprinted out of his
apartment and took the stairs to the basement two at a time.

Laney was running out of time.

chapter THIRTY-FOUR

Cold frosted the air in the basement parking garage.

I used Kestrel's passring to unlock his tiny blue hydro car, and I slipped inside to change into his clothes, tucking my disposable silver phone into the pocket of his oversized coat. I kept the Cubs hat, wrapping my hair into a knot and tucking it up under the cap. Even with rolling up the sleeves, his coat was still way too big, and of course, I looked nothing like Kestrel. But if I kept the hat low on my face, I might not raise alarms on the base surveillance cameras.

I linked into the mindware and set an autopath to the naval station. The adrenaline from my encounter with Kestrel faded on the way, and my eyelids drooped. The house lights blurred as the car wove through an endless stream of side streets. I forced my eyes wide-open again. Nodding off wasn't a good idea.

I'd given Kestrel a triple dose of the juice, like I'd gotten in the camp, but his body had already fought off half the first dart. When he woke up, the cuffs and lack of memory would slow him down, but he would surely notice his passring was missing. I cursed myself for forgetting to take his phone. He might piece it together and call ahead to warn them.

In any event, I had to get Laney before they injected her with any more "medicine." A midnight sneak-and-rescue wasn't the best idea I'd ever had, but daytime on base property wouldn't be any better.

The hospital was right off the main drive, easy to find, and my dad had brought us on base a few times, mostly for trips to the hospital for broken bones (my brother) and appendicitis (me). But that was different than spiriting someone out of a secure prison in the basement.

I switched to manual controls as I got close. The front drive looped around and ran past the main gate and a smaller entrance that led to the hospital. I turned into the guard station and hoped that a late-night visit by Kestrel wasn't enough to draw the portly guard out of his comfortable shack.

Keeping my head down so that the hat shielded my face, I waved Kestrel's passring at the ID scanner and jacked an image of his smiling face into the guard's head. The guard gave me an uncertain wave as the scanner flashed green. I reminded myself that Kestrel wasn't exactly the friendly type and killed the smile. I took the guard's wave as a pass to move on.

The hospital stood a couple hundred yards past the gate, spotlights lighting up the white bricks and leaving the corners in jagged shadows. I clenched the joystick. The parking lot to the right was nearly empty and I managed to avoid crashing into the few cars there.

The hospital was close enough that I could reach all fifteen levels from the car. I quickly located two guards that knew classified things happened in the basement—a reader at the front desk scanning a bank of camera images and a jacker guarding a corridor in the basement. The jacker's mind barrier was the hardest I'd ever felt, like granite under my whisper reach. I jerked back when he had a glimmer of awareness of my presence.

I wished I had saved one of those darts I used on Kestrel.

Besides the guard, the basement held two medical personnel and eight inmates. The prisoners were all unconscious, with six sleeping under a light dose of the juice and other two under heavy sedation. They were all changelings, and I searched each one until I found Laney.

I gently probed for those soft dead spots that I had felt in the returnees to the camp. Only her typical nightmares raged through her head as she slept. Whatever they had injected her with so far hadn't done any major damage. I sighed in relief and nudged her dreams toward a happy park scene with her family. I projected myself into her dream and told her I was coming for her. Soon. I would check the rest of the changelings after I got them out.

The jacker guard in the basement was going to be a problem. And getting eight kids out unnoticed? I had no idea how that was going to work. Especially when two of them were knocked out. Besides, the eight of them wouldn't fit into Kestrel's tiny car.

As I sat in the parking lot, pondering my options, the answer drove past my nose. A linen service truck rumbled by, headed away from the hospital. I jacked into the driver's mind and ordered him to return to the loading dock, which was deserted.

I put him under a command to fold sheets in the back of the truck, but I wasn't sure how long that would last. All the more reason to get in and out quickly, before our ride remembered he had somewhere else to be. I hustled to the main entrance of the hospital where the camera-watching guard was stationed.

People milled about in the reception area, visitors and patients waiting for their appointments or to see their loved ones. It was surprisingly busy for so late at night, but I guess sickness didn't have a schedule.

A janitor was cleaning the glass windows of the gift shop, and a guard and receptionist waited at a large, central check-in desk. I easily jacked the dozen people in the lobby to look the other way, but I nearly stumbled over my own feet when I linked into the janitor's mind and he struggled unsuccessfully to push me back out. We locked stares for a moment before I pulled out of his mind and he slowly turned back to his window and resumed cleaning. I lightly brushed his mind, and it was soft like a changeling's, even though he looked at least thirty-five.

Linker. That explained why he hadn't reacted to my feather touch before and I must have missed him. He seemed willing to ignore me, and I certainly didn't need any extra trouble.

I focused on the guard and receptionist. They needed to believe I was Kestrel, just checking in on the patients in the basement. That way I wouldn't have to jack the camera guard all the time while I was busy rescuing changelings. If he saw me on camera, traveling through the hospital, and he thought I was Kestrel, he wouldn't sound any alarms. It might buy me a little time.

I kept my cap low and waved Kestrel's passring by the scanner. When I jacked Kestrel's image into the receptionist's mind, I didn't smile or wave and planned to brusquely stride past.

But she smiled instead of waving me through. *Late night, Agent Kestrel?* There was a casual flirtation in her thoughts and a background hope that he might stop for coffee this time. I cringed internally and tried to figure out Kestrel's most likely response.

A tight smile seemed about right. *Yeah. Never ends, does it?*

She flashed a brighter smile, not expecting that much. *Maybe some coffee when you're done?*

I put some warmth into Kestrel's smile, but my stomach was a hard knot. *Maybe next time. I'll be a while tonight.* She was only mildly disappointed. Luckily, the whole interchange had the effect of making the camera-watching guard avert his eyes and return his attention to the celebrity magazine on his tablet.

I kept my pace measured, but quickly turned the corner to the central elevator bank. There were no stairwells. In the cancer ward next door, the minds of the attendants told me the stairs I needed were in the back corner of the hospital. That would work well for my plan to sneak the inmates out through the loading dock and must be how secret patients were usually transported in and out of the hospital.

I pulled open the ward's double doors and jacked minds to look the other way as I strode past curtained beds and medical equipment. To have any hope of taking on Granite Guard downstairs, I needed help. A nurse hurried past, making rounds and administering medications. I commandeered her and her tray of meds, but none of them were high-powered sedatives. She had the authority to sign meds out of the lockup, which I directed her to do. She estimated it would take several minutes for a syringe full of sedatives to take effect.

I was really regretting not bringing the dart gun. I decided to commandeer a very large orderly as well.

The three of us—the nurse armed with her syringe, the burly orderly, and me with my Impenetrable Mind—left the ward together. I hoped that Granite Guard wouldn't sense me coming. The blank spot of my mind should be invisible next to the nurse and orderly, as long as he didn't detect my presence in their minds. Kestrel's passring got us past the scanner at the stairwell door, and we descended the metal staircase, our footsteps echoing loudly off the white concrete walls. I reached back to check that the camera-watching guard wasn't alarmed by my unusual escorts. Then again, maybe Kestrel brought people down here all the time.

Down one flight of stairs was a door labeled 1B. The stairs continued down another level, but this was the door from Kestrel's forced memories. I very gingerly reached out to brush Granite Guard's mind and yanked back when he immediately sensed my presence. That might have lost us the element of surprise, which was almost all we had in our favor. I quickly pressed the passring to the door scanner and punched in the code. It opened to a short, gray concrete hallway with Granite Guard sitting in a chair at the far end, propped up against a metal door. His fatigues complemented the military weapons magazine he was reading.

His head snapped up as soon as we stepped through the door.

I needed to get closer before he figured out what was wrong, but it was too late. We'd only gone a few steps down the thirty foot hallway, when he pushed me out of the nurse and orderly's minds and pressed on mine. I jacked back in, and they stopped in their tracks, while he and I wrestled in their minds. The guard charged toward me. I could barely press on his mind barrier, much less control him.

I grabbed the syringe out of the nurse's hand. When Granite Guard reached me, I whirled and shoved the syringe into his neck, hoping to get lucky and hit a vein. He roared and yanked out the syringe, and it clattered on the concrete floor. He closed his enormous hand around my throat and pinned me against the wall. All of his attention was focused on trying to jack into my mind. Stars swam before my eyes, but instead of fighting Granite Guard, I jacked the orderly, who grabbed the guard from behind and caused him to lose his grip on me.

I fell hard to the floor and scrambled away. The nurse stood like a frozen mannequin, so I commanded her to grab the guard as well. While the orderly and nurse clung to him like errant children, I sprinted down the corridor to the door. I waved Kestrel's passring by the control pad and punched in the code as quickly as I could.

Then I saw the gun.

The guard had managed to pull it out while wrestling with the nurse and orderly. I yanked open the door, flung myself inside, and pulled it shut behind me. I didn't hear any shots.

Safe behind the locked door, I jacked with all my might into the guard's mind. The sedative must have gone in, because his mind was slowly weakening as it took hold. He kept trying to work himself free of the orderly and nurse's grip, but it was a losing battle between my jacking and the sedative, and he soon slumped to the floor. I ordered the nurse to take the gun and keep watch over him until I got back.

The next time I infiltrated a jacker prison, I was definitely bringing a dart gun.

My gasping breaths echoed down the hallway, which appeared identical to the image in Kestrel's mind. Doors with small, high windows lined the corridor, and the smell of antiseptic pervaded the air. A frosted-glass double door loomed at the end.

I ran from door to door, using the passring to unlock them, and threw the doors open. Each room held a changeling, four boys and three girls, except for one with an empty bed. None were Laney. She must be already in the medical room. I swiped Kestrel's passring to open the glass doors and surprised the two camouflage-clad technicians inside. They were readers, so I froze them, not wanting to knock them out in case I needed them.

Laney lay strapped to a gurney and hooked to an IV. An array of probes was attached to a skullcap on her head, and the med techs had been preparing to inject something into her. I tugged off the cap and shoved the tray of syringes away from her bedside. She was still under the effects of the gas, but it was muted. I slowly jacked her out of her gas-induced sleep while I unhooked the IV and started undoing the straps.

"Kira?" she said when she opened her eyes. "You're really here? I had a dream about you."

"Yeah. I'm really here." My throat choked up, so I didn't try to explain any further. I gently probed her mind to see if they had injected anything other than the juice. She seemed fine.

I cleared my throat. "Can you walk?" She nodded, and I helped her up from the bed. An alarm blared through the room and startled us both so much we almost toppled over. Keeping my grip on Laney, I reached with my mind up to the main floor. The camera-watching guard had seen a video sweep of the disabled guard in the hallway and sounded a security alert. I jacked him to disable the alarm, but I was sure it was too late. This was a military base, and other security personnel would be on the way soon. I knocked him out.

"What was that?" Laney asked.

"Time for us to go." I ordered the med techs to come with us as I hurried to the double glass doors. A large sign hung on a refrigerator next to the door: "No Food or Drink." I remembered Kestrel's warning that I couldn't stop them, that they would keep doing their research no matter what. I could save these changelings, but there would always be others to take their place.

I yanked open the refrigerator door, and racks of liquid filled vials clinked together. The labels were covered with medical terms I didn't understand, but one rack stood separate from the rest on the top shelf. Messy handwriting had scrawled across it: *K. Moore.*

A chill ran through me. My blood... or something... my DNA for sure. How could they have possibly gotten it? Then I remembered I had already been through a similar gray corridor with doors. Doors with small, high windows.

I had been here before.

When Kestrel interrogated me, I had assumed I was in an FBI building, but I wasn't. I was here in the hospital. I jacked into the minds of the med techs and found that there was another holding facility—directly below us. The stairwell past door 1B must lead down to another level where they kept prisoners.

I reached down one floor—there wasn't anyone in the holding rooms below.

The polished steel cabinets and cold, tiled floor of the medical room felt familiar. Had I been in this room? Had they taken me here, unconscious like Laney, and experimented on me? A shiver ran up my back and made my hair stand up. Was I different because Kestrel did something to me?

Someone like me, or even stronger, in Kestrel's hands... it had to be stopped.

I grabbed the chilled vials with my name on them and slipped them into Kestrel's coat pocket, trading them for the silver phone I had stolen. I dialed the number I had memorized.

Maria answered on the first ring. "Hello?"

"I found them." My voice squeaked, so I cleared it. "But it's even worse than I thought." I switched the phone to video streaming mode and panned the room, so she could see the gurney with the straps, the trays of syringes, the two camouflaged med-techs standing still with their glassy-eyed looks.

"Did you get that?" I spoke quietly.

"What am I looking at?"

"It's the basement of the Naval hospital, where they've been experimenting on the changelings." I pointed the phone at the still open refrigerator, filled with racks of vials. "You need to stop them, Maria. Make sure everyone knows what's going on here."

"I need a witness. Someone to verify this before I can tru-cast it. Turn the camera on your face. Talk to me. Tell me what you've found."

"Are you recording all this?" I asked.

"Yes."

I imagined what Kestrel would do to my dad if he found out I had exposed his crimes. My plan was to run, hide, make a new life after freeing the changelings. If I went on camera, there would be no hiding after that. And that was assuming we got out alive, which wasn't going to happen if I stuck around doing an exposé on the medical torment chamber.

I swallowed hard. "I can't."

"But..."

I clicked off the phone and then swept my arm through the refrigerator and dumped racks of vials on the floor. Maybe I could slow Kestrel down. Some of them broke on impact, and some went skittering across the floor, making a hazardous mess. I stomped the vials closest to me and ground the glass under the heel of my shoe, but I quickly realized I didn't have time to destroy them all.

Laney tugged on my arm. "Kira."

I mind-swept the floors above us. Additional security guards gathered around the camera-watching guard, trying to decipher why he had switched on the alarm, then turned it off, only to pass out. They were all readers, so I knocked them out as well.

That added to the general mayhem and would hopefully keep people busy—and away from the loading dock—for a little while.

I ordered the two med techs to smash the remaining vials and let Laney tug me out of the experiment room. The alarm and the open doors had woken the changelings and drawn them out into the hallway. Two remained in their cots, under heavy sedation. We would need help to get them out, so I redirected the med techs to retrieve the changelings from their cells and linked into the minds of the other six dazed inmates, including Laney.

Follow me, and I'll get you out of here.

Their bare feet padded behind me as I raced to the exit door. The nurse still held the gun on the downed jacker guard. I took the gun and ordered her and the orderly to help the med techs, struggling with their burden of the heavily sedated changelings. They gripped each of the limp inmates by the shoulders and feet, like dead bodies.

Yeah, not suspicious-looking at all.

The gun was cold and creepy in my hand as I led the small posse of jacker kids, an orderly, a nurse, and two med techs out of the medical prison and up the stairs.

If anyone was watching the cameras, they'd have quite a show.

But chaos reigned above as medical personnel swarmed around the guards. Some had donned gas masks, thinking there had been an attack that caused the mass fainting. Some set up a perimeter to keep patients and visitors away from the security desk.

Our shuffling group neared the loading dock doors, and I peered through the window to see a military police jeep come to a screeching halt behind the linen service van.

Oh no.

Two camouflage-clad guards with large, shiny black guns hopped out of the jeep and stalked toward the loading dock. I didn't know if they were jackers or not, but I couldn't take the chance of probing them to find out. I threw my hands out to stop our group in its tracks and edged backward, praying the guards hadn't seen us. We shuffled down the hall as fast as a group of barefoot kids and two unconscious changelings carried by adults can go. We stuck out like a troupe of clowns at a funeral.

I shoved open the cancer ward's doors, retracing my steps through the hospital. Maybe we could make it out the front to Kestrel's car. There was no way I could fit all the changelings into one car, but maybe we could steal another ride. We had to move fast. The heavy footsteps of the guards pounded in the corridor behind us, but they passed by the cancer ward and kept going.

We stumbled through the double doors and past the elevators out to the lobby. I jammed to a stop again, with changelings bumping and jostling into me. There were a half dozen armed guards and two jacker agents charging through the lobby. Before I had a chance to think, they spotted us, and eight weapons targeted our heads. Their shiny barrels were narrow and lethal. These were not dart guns. I suddenly remembered I had a gun in my hand and reflexively pointed it back at them.

At the same time, an intense pressure pounded my head. The

jacker agents had shoved me back into my own head, and the six changelings were struggling to fight them off. The nurse, orderly, and med-techs slowly came out of their daze, and started to put the two changelings they were carrying on the floor.

The agents crept toward us, guns still aimed at our group of barefoot children.

"Stop there!" I held my gun straight out, hoping they couldn't see the tip of it shaking like a leaf in the fall breeze. They paused, still trying to jack into my head. After a moment, they seemed to realize that they couldn't, so they switched tactics. The orderly straightened up and lunged toward me. I danced out of the way, and struggled to jack into his mind, ordering him to stay down where he had stumbled to the lobby floor. He staggered and then collapsed on the floor as two changelings grabbed hold of him. I mentally wrestled with the two agents as they jacked into the nurse's and the med-techs' minds. The nurse teetered in her white-soled shoes, uncertain whether she should attack me or have a seat, but the med-techs rushed at me. The other four changelings, still struggling under the assault from the jacker agents, latched onto them and pulled them to the floor.

"Stop or I'll shoot!" I screamed across the lobby, still keeping my gun trained on the lead agent's head. But I wouldn't shoot, I knew that. And the agent seemed to know it too.

Out of the corner of my eye, I saw the janitor, still standing by the gift shop. I didn't have to reach into his mind to know he understood. He knew who we were, and that we were hopelessly outgunned. Outjacked. He held my gaze for a moment, then dropped his eyes to the floor and turned his back on us.

I looked back to the agent and a triumphant smile had crept onto his face. To him, all of this was containable. Once the agents had us under control, they could wipe the minds of everyone here, mop up after they had returned us to the experiment room in the basement prison below. We would disappear, like Simon and all the others in the camp. And no one would come looking for us, because no one would even know that it had happened.

My hand with the gun twitched and a red haze of anger clouded my mind. I wanted to shoot the lead agent before the changelings and I lost the mental and physical wrestling match we were locked in. Make him pay for everything the Feds had done. Pay for the experiments. Pay for killing Simon. If I killed him fast enough, maybe I could shoot the other agent as well. Then it would be easy to jack the reader guards long enough for us to escape. But it was much more likely that I would end up with a bullet in me, like Simon. Bleeding out on the hospital floor was no different than bleeding into desert dust. Dead was dead. Worse, some of the changelings might get shot too. Even the patients and visitors, frozen in fear at the periphery of the lobby where they had shrunk back as far as the room would allow, might be caught in the cross fire.

It was too much. I couldn't risk getting them all killed.

I turned my gun sideways, my finger off the trigger, and held both hands up in front of me, the universal sign of surrender. The agent's smile curved higher.

An image of Raf floated through my mind. I should have kissed him when I had the chance. I wondered if his lips were as soft as they looked or if they would sear mine like Simon's always had.

Now I would never find out.

That's when I realized I still had the phone in my other hand. With the push of a button, I could expose Kestrel, the Feds, and everything they had done to us. I could stop them from taking me and the changelings back down to the basement, to disappear forever. But if Kestrel knew I had blown the cover on his experiments, he was sure to make my dad pay for it. And I would be spilling the biggest secret of all, the one my family had spent their entire lives keeping. There would be no pretending, no hiding among readers. No normal life for me, for any of us. Ever again.

The lies would stop.

With my eyes still locked on the lead agent, I linked into the phone's mindware and dialed Maria, giving silent thanks to whoever invented the speakerphone option.

"Thank God, Kira! It's about time you..." She cut herself off, probably taking in the scene, which I was now streaming to her.

"Are you getting a good signal, Maria?" I asked.

The speakerphone drew the sharp attention of everyone in the room. The smile on the agent's face died.

"Yes." Her voice was cautious, slow.

"I have a tru-cast story for the Trib. It's about an agent of the federal government who threatened to shoot a group of children in a hospital. Are you getting all this?"

"Yes, I have a very good visual on the gun."

The agent's gun wavered. I didn't have to link into his mind to know what he was thinking. Did he want to be on a tru-cast, trying to explain why he was going to shoot down a group of innocent children in a hospital? Did he want to be responsible for that?

"These kids were being held in a basement prison, right here at the Naval hospital," I continued for the benefit of Maria's trucast and for the agent whose gun was still pointed at my head. "They were being held for no other reason than having a special ability, a new ability to link into other people's heads. Just because they have an ability we don't understand, doesn't mean they deserve to be in prison. To be experimented on. It's like the old days when the first readers were discovered. What did we do? We put them in prison. We tortured them with experiments. Well, we're doing it again, to these kids, today."

I swept the phone around, so it had a good shot of my face, and the changelings sprawled on the floor behind me. I took a jittery breath for courage. "My name's Kira Moore, and I'm just like them. I was kidnapped by the FBI, brought here, and then sent to a prison with hundreds of other kids just like me. For no other reason than who I am." I panned across the changelings, slowly. I could only imagine what it must look like to Maria, barefoot changelings in their hospital gowns, still holding onto the med-techs and the orderly to keep them down while mentally wrestling with the agents to control the readers' minds.

"I'm taking these kids out of here, back home to their families, where they belong."

I rotated the camera back to the lead agent and I could see the decision had settled into his face. This was above his pay grade. "This is Kestrel's mess," he said, loud enough that it could be captured on my phone. I was pretty sure he did that on purpose. "Let him clean it up." He slowly lowered his gun. Louder, he said, "A simple misunderstanding, I'm sure." The second agent looked warily at him, but he lowered his weapon, and the guards did the same.

The agents left the changelings' minds and everyone slowly stood up, faces not quite sure. The guards and agents stepped aside, making a path for us to walk out the front door.

For a moment, I was terrified it was a trap. But if they took us down now, it would all be on camera. I linked into the nurse, orderly, and med-techs' minds, our unwitting accomplices in the escape. *Please. Help us.* I would let them decide. If they didn't want to help, I wouldn't force them. Somehow, between the changelings and me, we would manage to get the two unconscious kids out the door. I wasn't exactly sure where we would go from there, but if nothing else, we could walk. We just needed to get off base property before the agent changed his mind about letting us loose.

The orderly lifted one changeling over his shoulder, and the nurse and two changelings managed to pick up the other. The med techs hung back, edging their way back to the elevators. I didn't envy them when Kestrel found out what had happened.

We shuffled and limped past the crowd of readers and guards and agents. I held my phone out toward them, like the weapon of truth that it was. I didn't turn my back on them until everyone was through both sliding glass doors at the entrance. Once we were outside, we stood still for a moment, the changelings shivering as the cool night air swept past their bare feet.

I surveyed the few cars in the parking lot, wondering how

long it would take us to jack into one and whether any of the changelings knew how to drive. I could barely drive, and we would probably be risking someone's life by putting any of the changelings behind a joystick. Maybe I could program an auto-path for them. At least I knew where we had to go next.

As I was about to step off the curb, a delivery van came careening around the corner of the building, pulling quickly up to the front. The driver was the linker janitor from inside. I don't know how or when he slipped away, but he must have made it to the loading dock. The linen delivery driver was nowhere to be seen.

"Need a lift?" he said with a grin. Relief flooded into me, and my knees barely held me up.

Maybe we would make it after all.

chapter THIRTY-FIVE

The truth magistrate touched me with his leathery hand and examined me with his watery eyes.

I tried not to shiver.

Maria had cleared out the castroom floor, and half the changelings were passed out while the other half chomped on vending machine food. But Maria wanted me on camera as soon as possible to explain what we were and what we could do. It was the middle of the night, but our story would probably be playing for days.

I linked my thoughts to the camera crew to keep them calm. Demonstrations would only freak people out. The truth magistrate sat across from me, sincerely believing he could get my true thoughts by holding my hand and asking probing questions. The cameras were trained on us, and a boom dangled over our heads to pick up our thought-waves and translate them into a scrolling scrit at the bottom the tru-cast. I linked into the mindware interface to make sure it captured my thought responses.

Is your name Kira Moore? the truth magistrate asked.

Yes.

His brow creased, probably expecting a rush of emotions. Of course he wouldn't get anything from me unless I jacked it into his head, and I was determined not to do anything but link.

Are you sixteen years old?

Yes.

Do you live on Manor Road in Gurnee, Illinois?

Right now, I'm living in a castroom in the Tribune Tower. That got a twitter of mental laughter from everyone in the room.

Were you born in 2090? This question had more edge. If I was born in 2090, I would be twenty years old, not sixteen. I could jack in any answer I wished, and it would seem like a true thought. But that wouldn't help.

No.

Do you believe you can control other people's minds?

Yes. This visibly shook him. There were no thoughts or emotional responses from me that would indicate lying.

Have you ever been diagnosed demens? Okay, that one irked me.

No. Although I might be demens for outing myself as a jacker. More laughter.

The magistrate's glasses rode up. *Are you controlling my mind right now?*

No. Which was true. I had already explained that I could tell him anything and jack him to believe it, but that I would only link thoughts to him. Whatever he decided was his own choice.

Can you control my mind?

Yes. He paused and contemplated asking for a demonstration.

I didn't want to, but if he asked, I would.

Instead he asked, *How long have you been able to control minds?*

About six weeks.

I imagined Raf waking up in the morning and seeing me on the tru-cast at home. I was glad I had already told him everything, so he wouldn't hear how long I had been lying to him on a tru-cast. If only I had trusted Raf from the beginning, maybe I would be with him now, holding hands and looking into those deep brown eyes, instead of crammed into a cubicle with a leathery old man and a camera crew. Which was almost as bad as it sounded.

The truth magistrate's questioning went on at length, and eventually he was satisfied. Or at least unwilling to admit that he couldn't tell my true thoughts from my sims.

Maria's people interviewed each of the changelings as well, and their faces cycled on all the chat-casts and tru-casts. We had nowhere to go, so we stayed in the Trib Tower while we waited for the changelings' parents to see the tru-casts and come forward. There wasn't much in the way of beds, so we slept on the floor, the changelings piled up like puppies.

The next morning, a couple of adult jackers came to Maria with their stories. They submitted to the truth magistrate, too, which made me laugh. They must have been hiding in plain sight, like all the jackers that had avoided the camp. After a while, I stopped watching the repeats of the tru-casts, including my video tell-all at the hospital. It creeped me out seeing my face over and over.

For lunch, Maria had some pizza delivered. Thirteen-year-old changelings could eat an unbelievable amount, although twelve-year-old Xander ate more than three of them put together. I was munching on a bite of rapidly cooling pepperoni with extra cheese when pictures of the camp came up on the screen. I stopped mid-chew. I knew Maria had sent a cameraman out to the camp, but I didn't know they had pictures already.

Breaking Tru-Cast blared in red under a picture of the camp, and Maria's report scrolled along the bottom of the screen. Open-air trucks, piled with the limp bodies of prisoners, caravanned across the hard-packed desert road. The images were blurred, like they were taken from a long way away, and Maria's words talked about a new kind of person—a *jacker*—who could control people's thoughts.

The inmates weren't moving. My eyes pricked. I told myself they had to be gassed for transportation or the jacker prisoners would overwhelm the guards. And the Feds wouldn't kill them, not while they were necessary for Kestrel's research. But then Kestrel was probably still sleeping off the gas in his apartment.

The pictures made my stomach clench. I set the pizza down. After only a few images flashed by, they started to repeat. The changelings were transfixed by the screen. I didn't have to link into their minds to know those photos were giving them flashbacks.

I shuffled over to Maria's desk, where she was busy sending a scrit on her phone.

"You got pictures." My voice was just a whisper.

Maria faced me. "My photographer only transmitted a few

images before they stopped him." The distress in her voice chewed a hole in my stomach.

"Oh. Maria, I'm so sorry..." *What did they do to him?*

"He's okay," she said quickly. "He woke up in Albuquerque. Until I showed him the pictures, he didn't know why he was there. He didn't remember any of it."

Maria was surprisingly calm, given that my prediction about the mind-wipe had come true. I swallowed. "Do you think they'll come after us?" The changelings had flopped on the stubbled carpet, entranced by the tru-cast, and a few reporters worked stories at their desks.

"No. They can't wipe the minds of everyone in North America, Kira. The story is too big for the Feds to pretend it didn't happen."

"But the photographer—" I waved at the looping pictures on the screen.

"He's getting another camera and heading back out there. They're going to have to release the prisoners, Kira. You did a great thing, coming to me with this." I hoped she was right. I hoped the Feds couldn't make all of us simply disappear, that it would be too coincidental to cover up. Her phone vibrated again, and she turned away to mentally answer it. This was probably the tru-cast of her lifetime, but the pictures were making it hard for me to breathe. In all the chaos of rescuing the changelings from the hospital, I had shoved thoughts about the Camp of the Flies aside. But I hadn't forgotten.

I remembered the stifling heat. Holding hands in the truck with Simon. My feet pounding across the desert. Simon's blood on my hands. The walls of the castroom pressed in on me. I fled to the windows at the far edge of the room.

My hands pressed against the cold window panes, and I breathed clouds of moisture onto the surface. The city of Chicago blurred under my gasping breath. I closed my eyes and touched my forehead to the cool glass until my stomach started to unclench. Footsteps pattered behind me.

"You okay?" asked Laney. She put a small hand on my shoulder.

I managed a smile. "Yeah. Just, you know, hard to see it again." Some babysitter I was, leaving the changelings to fend for themselves with those images on the screen. I took a deep breath and tipped my head toward them, huddled together. "Let's go see how everyone else is doing."

Laney tucked her hand in mine and led me back to the group. The changelings were dealing with it better than I was and they quickly lost interest in favor of the pizza. As the pictures cycled again, I noticed a shock of red hair in one of the trucks. If Molloy was still alive, he was certain to be planning my murder in several painful ways.

With Maria calling for an investigation on the tru-cast, I could see why the Feds would have to shut down the camp. They could keep the dangerous jackers in jail, and I hoped Molloy would be one of them, but there was no reason to hold the jacker kids.

Later that afternoon, Maria's photographer returned to the camp, but it was empty. The Feds had moved the prisoners, but there was no word on the release of any of them. In fact, there was no word about the camp at all.

Even though Maria tru-cast the pictures of the now-empty camp ringed with barbed wire and covered in camouflage, the Feds were denying that it had been a prison camp. I didn't understand how a secret camp in the desert could be explained away, but they claimed the pictures were manufactured.

Later that afternoon, the Navy made a great show of opening the basement of the hospital, only to find a warehouse of medical supplies. The scenes they cast, opening each of the cells and showing them filled with boxes of gloves and syringes, made me so angry I had to be alone in one of the cast cubicles for a while. Of course the government would hide what they had been doing. It made me clench my fists and kick the industrial carpet.

I still had Kestrel's vials of liquid with my name on them, but I couldn't figure a way to use them to prove the experiments had actually happened. Did Kestrel take my DNA as a routine matter, genetically profiling all the kids that came through the jacker processing center at the hospital, or had he already started experimenting on me? Were the vials only my DNA or some kind of serum he already injected into me and that was why I was different?

No. I was different from other jackers, but I had my Impenetrable Mind before I ever crossed paths with Kestrel.

My video from the basement and my vials weren't sufficient proof that any experiments had actually occurred. It was only a lab room and some vials of liquid.

Without proof, the jacker kids I left behind at the camp were stuck in whatever new prison the Feds had constructed.

No one would go looking for them because no one believed they existed. I'd had my chance to free them and I hadn't. That I had saved some reader lives in Rock Point, Arizona, wasn't much consolation when I imagined the horrors the changelings were enduring.

Kestrel seemed to have disappeared as well. Despite the jacker agent's whispered accusation at the hospital, the Feds were denying that an Agent Kestrel even existed. When Maria's crew arrived at his apartment in the city, it had been scrubbed clean, as if no one had ever lived there. I didn't know if he had fled, or the Feds were covering up for him, making him officially disappear so he would be free to continue his heinous experiments.

Either way, Kestrel knew I had liberated the changelings and must have figured out who shot him full of darts and stole his passring and car. He wouldn't forgive me just because I left his car unharmed in the hospital parking lot. And if he was still doing experiments, he'd want me back for that.

I wished that I had wiped all of Kestrel's true memories about me when I had the chance.

At least my family seemed safe. I asked Maria to check on them, and she said the agents were no longer parked at my house. My family was also asking about me, wanting me to come home.

I wasn't so sure that was a good idea. Even if the Feds weren't harassing my family openly, my dad was probably upset about me revealing the family's big secret on a national tru-cast.

There certainly were a lot of people angry about it.

By the evening, the protests had started. Outraged readers,

some of them demens by the looks of them on the screen, gathered at the entrance to the Trib Tower, protesting the dangerous mind control freaks the Trib was keeping on the 10th floor.

I was having serious doubts about going public until the changelings' parents started coming forward. Most had been jacked to believe that their children had run away or been snatched and were thrilled to have them back. The changelings couldn't pretend to be zeroes or even readers, but they could go home. The Feds seemed more concerned with denying their involvement in secret camps and scandalous experiments than harassing kids.

Maria coordinated with the parents, making arrangements for them to come get their children, which went well until Xander's mom grabbed her fifteen minutes of fame by publicly stating she didn't want him back. When Xander's change came, he had accidentally jacked his abusive step-father and knocked him out. Soon after, Xander had been caught on camera jacking a mini-mart clerk to give him ice cream, and the Feds had picked him up. He was only twelve, and his mom was a worthless, raging alcoholic, if her performance on the tru-cast was any indication. Her rant fed the hate-groups protesting outside, and Xander became the poster-child for dangerous jacker kids. The protesters wanted him locked up. Because stealing ice cream definitely made him a danger to society.

I told Xander he could stay with me.

As the night wore on, the changelings got antsy from being hyped on the news all day and being cooped up in the castroom. I kept them busy practicing their jacking skills. They didn't have much control, and I had to keep a constant eye on them.

"Xander's turn," I called out, interrupting an argument that had broken out among the girls. Laney shushed them for me so I didn't have to reach into their minds to get their attention. I didn't do that unless it was necessary, trying to set a good example. The grumbles went round our jacker group in the corner, but they dutifully gave their verbal permissions for him to link in.

I brushed their soft, still-forming minds. "Remember," I said to Xander. "Only link your thoughts."

Xander linked into all seven minds and tried to gently send a thought to them. *Who wants pizza for dessert?* His words rang loudly, reverberating through all their heads at once. It was too much command, and they all echoed back, *Pizza! Pizza for dessert!*

We already had pizza for lunch and dinner, so that wasn't their free will speaking. I linked a thought to Xander. *Easy there, changeling. If they were readers, they'd be hijacking the nearest pizza delivery van.*

Xander threw me a smile.

Focus. And gently this time.

Random thoughts about pizza still skittered through their minds. *Who wants cheese curls for dessert?* Xander linked in. It was almost too soft, only a whisper, but they heard it. Choruses of *No! Gah, those are disgusting!* overlapped each other. They were getting tired of the vending machine food as well. Xander's back went rigid as he tried to process the seven different responses.

I didn't link my thoughts to him, not wanting to add to the cacophony in his mind. Instead, I strode over and put my hand on his shoulder. His eyes were unfocussed as he tried to navigate the raging mental conversation with the other changelings.

At least he didn't knock anyone out. He would slowly get it.

Xander reminded me of Simon and what he might have been like, if someone had been around to help him when he changed. The memory of Simon lying dead in the desert was seared into my mind, but my other memories of him were starting to return—the kisses and sweet promises, as well as the lies. I still wasn't sure which ones were which. I wondered if he would approve of me outing jackers to the world.

The next day the changelings' parents started braving the crowd of protesters to come pick up their kids. Maria made arrangements for them to leave by hydrocopter from the roof, so they didn't have to run the gauntlet with the changelings in tow.

I explained to the parents what had happened to their children in the hospital. At least, what I could guess. The worst part was the two changelings whose minds weren't quite the same anymore. They could jack, but they were often confused, as if the true memory part of their brain had been wasted away by whatever Kestrel injected into them. I had to explain to the parents that their children's brain tissue was damaged, and there was nothing I could do to fix it.

Afterward, I had to be alone for a while. I curled up in a corner cubicle and dreamed of a dozen ways that I could repay Kestrel for what he had done. A dart to the chest was far too good for him.

One by one, the changelings left until only Laney and Xander remained.

When it was time for Laney to leave, I shared her excited smile but I didn't really want her to go. The sunshine of her smile when she jumped into her dad's arms made me grin in spite of the small pain in my chest. Her dad shook my hand and her mom gave me a hug, then I beat a hasty retreat. I didn't need a truth magistrate to see the love they had for her.

She was back where she belonged.

chapter THIRTY-SIX

Now it was just Xander and me.

I wasn't about to turn him over to Child Protective Services, but the kid couldn't spend the rest of his life camped out in a castroom. He needed a real home, and I only had one to give. I sent a message home through Maria, to see if it was okay to come to Gurnee. My family sent back two words.

Come home.

Except I wasn't sure what waited for us there. I had spilled my family's big secret, the one they had hidden for generations. The Feds were avoiding any obvious harassment of my family, but who knew what other fallout had rained down on my dad. I didn't know if my family understood the choice that I had made. I only hoped they wouldn't hold it against Xander.

If they let him stay, Xander should be fine with my family, like the other changelings with theirs. If the Feds openly arrested any of them, it would be proof that they had been sending jackers to camps and experimenting on them all along. The Feds could pretend they hadn't been hunting down jackers, but they could no longer say that they didn't exist. Especially now that more and more jackers were coming out every day.

The Feds couldn't arrest me out in the open either, but that wasn't the only danger in going home. Tru-casts or no, if Molloy ever escaped the Feds, he would hunt me down, and my home was the first place he'd look. Kestrel might be forced to give up the changelings I'd rescued, but if I was the genetic link he wanted, he would never stop searching for me. He'd have no problem with making me disappear one night without the formality of actually arresting me.

I wasn't at all sure going home was a good idea. But I could at least drop off Xander and make sure he had a place to stay.

Maria arranged for a hydrocopter to take us to Union Station so we could avoid the protesters. I borrowed a tally card from her to pay for the train and transit fares from there to Gurnee.

The train out of the city was empty, with most commuters already at work. The bus arrived at the train transfer station shortly after we did. As soon as the bus door whooshed open, I linked into the driver's mind. *Does this route go to Gurnee? I need to get to Manor Road.*

The driver crinkled a smile on her heavily lined face. *Sure does, sweetie. There's a stop real close to Manor Road.* Her smile faltered, thinking she recognized me from somewhere. I hoped we could get through the trip before she realized my face had been all over the news for the last two days.

I gave her a smile and climbed the steps of the bus with Xander behind me. She swiped Maria's tally card across the scanner and handed it back to me. *There are a lot of stops before Manor. Make yourself comfortable, dear.* She leaned away from Xander as he passed. He must be hesitating to link into her mind, not quite sure of his skills yet. Which wasn't a bad idea, but it left the driver thinking he was a zero. She mentally commanded the door shut behind us, and we worked our way to the back of the bus.

Xander fidgeted in the bus seat next to me. He kept spinning a leather bracelet he'd managed to keep through the camp and the hospital. I wasn't sure what the significance of it was, but I didn't link in to ask. Privacy was different than secrets.

Fall had come to Illinois, and the leaves were starting to drop. There were splashes of color everywhere. As we wound through the side streets of my hometown, I spied a tree made entirely of gold, except for a single red leaf. A thousand tiny orange leaflets flew past on a gust of air.

It felt like a million years since I had been home.

The bus pulled to a stop a block from my house. I had already swept the neighborhood to make sure there were no jacker agents waiting to capture us, but there were only my normal neighbors doing their normal things. At least I guessed it was normal—I'd never kept tabs on the neighbors before.

As we approached my house, my mom flew out the door and met us halfway across the lawn. She nearly knocked me over when she hugged me.

"Hi, Mom." I tried to say more, but my throat tightened up at having her close again.

She took my cheeks in her hands. "Kira, you can link with me, sweetheart. It's okay."

I linked into her mind and was overwhelmed with the happiness I found there. *I'm so glad you're home, Kira. And I'm so proud of you.* She replayed images of me on the tru-cast, and I cringed.

I had to get them out, Mom, I explained, even though she wasn't asking. *I couldn't let the Feds take them back to the basement.*

I know, honey. I understand.

I pulled her hands from my face and peered around to the open front door. *Does Dad understand?* I had reached into the house when I made my sweep before, but I hadn't lingered in the minds there, nervous about what thoughts I would find.

I'll let him explain, she thought.

I motioned to Xander, who was watching us with undisguised longing. "Mom, this is Xander. I was hoping that, maybe, he could stay with you for a while." She, along with everyone else, had to know what had happened to Xander. His mom had made sure of that on the tru-casts.

My mom beamed a smile at him and switched to speaking aloud without missing a beat. "Of course he's welcome to stay with us." She offered her hand, and Xander awkwardly shook it.

I wanted to be up front, so there were no misunderstandings. No more secrets. "There's just one thing, Mom." I cleared my throat to get rid of the quaver. "I'm really here to drop Xander off. I'm not sure it's such a good idea for me to stay." Her face twisted up like I had gone demens right in front of her. "It's just that it's not really safe. For me, I mean. Xander will be fine. If he stays with you. If that's okay." I stopped my stuttering because my mom seemed like she was about to cry, and that nearly killed me on the spot. "I... I want to stay, it's just that..." I didn't even know where to start. She shushed me by patting my arm and blinking back the tears.

"You should talk to your father. He's waiting to see you." She looped her arms through Xander's and mine. I let her tow us toward the house. The second floor window had been broken, and two large boards crossed over it with plastic wrapping hanging from the edges.

I cleared my throat. "What happened to the window?"

"Oh, that. Um, nothing." It was a wonder my mom had kept our family secret for so long, because she was so fantastically bad at lying.

I linked gently into her head. *The truth?*

The truth is that some hateful people threw a rock through it. Your father didn't reach them before they sped off. Her lips made a tight line. *No one was hurt.*

The hole in my parent's house gaped at me. My dad was not going to be happy about this. At all.

We stepped through the darkened front doorway and climbed the stairs to the living room. Seamus hovered at the top, all gussied up in his cadet uniform. A grin broke across his face, and he swept me up in a hug.

"Aren't you supposed to be in school?" I asked while trying to pull in a breath.

"Aren't you supposed to be staying out of trouble?" he replied. My laugh came out strangled because of his hold on me. He set me down with a thump and cocked a look to Xander. "I see you have a follower."

Xander froze, scanning up Seamus's towering height.

"Just ignore him," I said to Xander. "He's oversized, but mostly harmless." Xander kept his distance.

My father was waiting at the far end of the room. I bit my lip. "Hi, Dad."

He seemed to be fighting to keep control of his features. I didn't know what he was holding back, but I didn't want to link in and find out. He unfolded his arms and strode across the room. I wasn't sure of his intentions until he hugged me harder than Seamus had.

Tears sprang into my eyes. I told myself it was because he was squeezing me so hard. "Kira, I'm so glad you're home." His voice was rough.

We didn't say anything for a while, just held each other.

Then I linked into his mind and asked the question I didn't want to say out loud, for everyone to hear. *You're not mad at me?*

Kira, I was never mad at you. Worried sick. But not mad.

I pulled back. *What about the Navy? They have to be upset that you didn't bring me in. That I went public and embarrassed them, and I thought they might take it out on you and...*

"I quit my job, Kira," he said aloud.

"What?" I asked in horror, finally noticing he was wearing civilian clothes. "They fired you? Because of what I did?"

"No. It wasn't like that," he said. "I quit. When I found out what they were doing, in that hospital. I knew it was bad, Kira, but I didn't know..." He looked pained. "I'm sorry I didn't quit sooner."

I linked back into his head. *You weren't part of Kestrel's Task Force, Dad. It's not your fault.*

No, but I didn't stop him either, he thought. *Not like a certain strong-willed daughter of mine.*

My face grew hot. I hadn't stopped Kestrel. If anything, I had probably just pushed him underground.

My dad smiled. "In any event, no one can hold my position over me anymore. And I needed a new job, anyway. It's rather difficult to be a spy with a world-famous mindjacker for a daughter."

"Dad... I'm sorry."

"Don't be. It's better this way. The government can't control jackers like they used to, not with more and more of us coming out all the time."

My shoulders sagged. "Better? I'm not so sure. What about the jackers in the camp? Do you know what happened to them?"

"No." His face turned hard. "I tried to find out more before I quit, but the Fed's aren't owning up to the camp. They must be holding the changelings somewhere new. And if they released them, it would be admitting that they held them in the first place." He took my hands in his. "You did everything you could, Kira, and I'm proud of you."

His words brought a queasiness to my stomach. "I didn't do everything I could, Dad," I whispered. His hands still held mine, but I had a hard time meeting his questioning look. "When I escaped..." I stopped. Spilling this secret would make him a lot less proud of me. I sucked in a breath. "When I escaped, I could have let them go. All of them. Everyone in the camp. But I didn't."

My dad's face clouded and water started to pool in my eyes. "So, you see," I said, "it's my fault they're trapped..."

"Kira." My dad wrapped his arms around me and I wilted into him. "It's not your fault. It's Kestrel's fault." He pulled back to look into my eyes. "*He* put them there, not you. And... and I did too."

I blinked. "What? But I thought..."

"I didn't have anything to do with sending changelings there," he said quickly. "But there were some bad guys I helped catch. They were jackers and they were dangerous. There was no other place to send them. So I *know* there were a lot of monsters in there, Kira. That's why I was so desperate to get you out." He dropped his voice. "Sometime, you're going to have to tell me exactly how you did that."

I let out a breath I hadn't known I was holding.

"I'm just glad you finally came home," he said.

I swallowed. "Right. Um, about that. I'm not sure I should stay."

My dad's face had the same disbelief as my mom. "Kira, it's safe now. The agents are gone," he said, gesturing out the broken window, "and the Feds can't come after you any more, not when you're the face of their scandal."

How I wished that were true. "It's not that simple, Dad."

His shoulders sagged. He rubbed his chin like he did when he was puzzling something out. Of course, he wouldn't remember the conversation we had about how I was Kestrel's genetic link. And he couldn't know Kestrel woke up with three darts in his chest and me to blame for it. But my dad was right—I was the face of the hidden jackers. Kestrel could make me disappear and have it look like backlash from the hate groups. And if Molloy found me first, well, it probably *would* be a hate crime.

"If you're in some kind of trouble, sis," Seamus said quietly from his spot next to Xander, "we'll help you get out of it."

I really didn't want to cry again.

"What Seamus is saying," said my dad, "is that family sticks together."

I put on a bright smile to ward off the tears and stepped over to put my arm around Xander. "Which is exactly why I brought Xander here. If it's okay with you, maybe he can stay here a while? He can have my room, if he can tolerate the pink bed."

"Xander's welcome to stay here as long as he wants," he said. "But this is your home. It's where you belong."

I strode over and threw my arms around him. "I know, Dad." Then I had to stop because my throat was closing up. I linked my thoughts to him. *I'm afraid Kestrel won't stop looking for me. And there are some other bad guys you should know about.*

"Let me help you, Kira." I could feel his shoulders tense as he held me tighter. "Bad guys are something I know a little about. And I'm not going to let anyone hurt you anymore."

My tears burned my eyes. I wished my dad could help me, more than anything. I ached to stay here, in my house, with my family, and believe that everything would work out okay. That Kestrel would forget about me. That Molloy would stay in prison forever. I didn't know if staying was a good idea, but in that moment, I couldn't force myself to leave.

I took a shaky breath. "Okay."

My dad's smile was almost as strong as the hug he wrapped around me, and I could hardly breathe when Seamus and my mom piled on. Their thoughts rang with happiness.

I just prayed my family wouldn't pay the price for my wishful thinking.

~*~

Later that afternoon, Raf came by.

I knew he was coming before he reached the door, before my mom or anyone else in all the quiet levels of the house had any idea. All day, I had been keeping a nervous watch, periodically scanning down the street, and even around the corner, to the limits of my reach. Just checking. Making sure that no one was coming.

I linked in to Raf's thoughts before he reached our house. I heard the jumble in his mind as he tried to decide what to say to me. How he was worried about the hate groups and how strange it had been seeing me on the tru-casts, telling the world secrets I had only just told him. How he was a little afraid he wouldn't have the right words when he saw me.

He rapped softly on the front door.

Hi, Mrs. Moore. Is Kira home?

She's upstairs, Rafael.

Raf's soft footfalls padded up the stairs. Partway up, I pulled out of his head, not wanting him to know I had linked in without asking. I busied myself with rearranging the few items left on my shelves, my hands shaking more than they should just for Raf.

He appeared in my doorway, a hand on each side of the frame. "Hi."

I swallowed. "Hi."

Raf gazed past me to the near-bare shelf. "You know," he said, "I could swear I won more of those for you."

I picked up the green monster that he had won for me over the summer, what felt like a zillion years ago. "You did." I examined the creature for a moment and put it back on the shelf.

He stared at me from across the room. "Where did they go? Did you not want them anymore?"

I gaped. I had thrown them away in a fit of fury of wanting to be grown up. Tough. Not pitied by the world. Now I would give anything to have them back. "I, um..."

He sauntered into the room, flashing his brilliant smile. "Relax, Kira. I'm kidding."

"Right." I tried to regain my composure. "I knew that."

He reached out and touched my hair, like Simon used to. My heart squeezed, not wanting that thought right here, right now.

"Maybe if you do your jacking trick," Raf said softly, "you'll know better what I'm thinking."

I looked into his dark brown eyes, wanting to know if he was thinking the same thing I was. That I wished I had been honest with him from the beginning. That I hoped he would still want to be with me, now that the entire world knew what I was and what I could do. I linked gently inside, and immediately the scent of his mind filled me. Soft linen and sunshine-warmed air.

I like the way your hair feels when I touch it, he thought. I swallowed as he leaned closer. *I wonder if I try to kiss you if you'll knock me out again.*

It depends. How good a kisser are you? My heart thudded erratically.

Maybe you can let me know. He pressed his lips to mine. They were soft like a summer's breeze, and his kiss reached down to my toes.

Seamus once told me that when readers touched, they shared feelings as if they were joined into one person. He said it was a very intimate experience. I would never be like the normal readers of the world.

But, for the first time, I knew exactly what he meant.

If you enjoyed *Open Minds*, please
leave a review on Amazon,
Barnes&Noble and/or Goodreads.
Or recommend it to a friend! Every
bit of word of mouth helps!

Coming in 2012

closed hearts

Book Two of the Mindjack Trilogy

Kira wonders if telling the truth and outing jackers everywhere was the right choice after all. The world has erupted
into protests and violence. A new movement is gaining ground
to identify jackers and lock them away. Kira's family has avoided
the worst of the haters by moving, and Kira hopes her famous
face won't give her away at the tiny diner where she works to
keep her family afloat. But when former jacker Clan leader
Molloy shows up at the diner and Raf slumps lifeless in her
arms, Kira realizes with chilling certainty: telling the truth has
put everyone she loves in danger.

 Join Susan's Mailing List
(for future releases)
http://bit.ly/SubscribeToSusansNewsletter

other works by

Susan Kaye Quinn

Life, Liberty, and Pursuit
a teen love story
http://bit.ly/BuyLifeLibertyandPursuit

Summer Breeze
anthology to support breast cancer research

Like My Facebook Page
(for contests and giveaways)
http://on.fb.me/LikeSusansFacebookPage

Visit My Author Website
www.susankayequinn.com

Acknowledgements

Many people, besides the author, are needed to create a novel, and *Open Minds* is no exception.

The gorgeous cover, which makes me giddy every time I look at it, is due to the artistry of D. Robert Pease. Multiple thanks go to Anne of Victory Editing for catching my typos, fixing my slang, and correcting my hideous comma abuse. Any mistakes that remain are due to things I messed up after she fixed it.

Many talented writers critiqued *Open Minds* and lent their considerable skills to making the story better. Much appreciation goes to my SCBWI writer's group for their enthusiastic support, which is an essential nutrient for any writer's soul. Thanks go to Andi Phillips, Bethany Kaczmarek, Erynn Newman, and Charity Tinnin, for reading chapter after chapter and steering me where I (and the manuscript) needed to go. Thank you to Sherrie Petersen, for feedback on kisses, technology, and endings. And for reading it *again*. And especially for loving it. Thank you to Stina Lindenblatt for liking Raf even more than Kira does and for being honest about what needed to be changed.

Double thanks are due to Rebecca Carlson, fellow science fiction traveler, for reading two completely separate drafts and for the amazing, detailed feedback that always shines up my words. A breezy aye to Adam Heine for slang tutorials and pointing out just where I cheated. A huge thank-you to Terry Lynn Johnson for reading it, loving it, and that other part, even though it didn't work out. A bucket of gratitude to Michelle Davidson Argyle for her enthusiasm and honesty, the two things I like about her most. And extra special thanks go to Kate Monson and Brandi Pease for being my teen beta readers.

And finally, apologies to my husband and three boys for all the time I spent on the computer, when you probably wished you had socks that matched and something other than macaroni and cheese for dinner. Especially since I'm going to do it again for the next book. Thanks for putting up with me!

About the Author

Susan Kaye Quinn grew up in California, where she wrote snippets of stories and passed them to her friends during class. Her teachers pretended not to notice and only confiscated her notes a couple times. She pursued a bunch of engineering degrees (Aerospace, Mechanical, and Environmental) and worked a lot of geeky jobs, including turns at GE Aircraft Engines, NASA, and NCAR. Now that she writes novels, her business card says "Author and Rocket Scientist" and she doesn't have to sneak her notes anymore.

Which is too bad.

All that engineering comes in handy when dreaming up paranormal powers in future worlds or mixing science with fantasy to conjure slightly plausible inventions. For her stories, of course. Just ignore that stuff in her basement.

Susan writes from the Chicago suburbs with her three boys, two cats, and one husband. Which, it turns out, is exactly as much as she can handle.